Dodger's Doorway

By Alessandro Reale

Thank you to all those who supported me.

Prologue

Humpty Dumpty was a fearless warrior, which was why he was made the second-in-command of the Neverland Military Arm. Right now, though, as he stood in the center of Neverland Castle's main throne chamber, he felt frightened and nervous. The fate of Neverland and possibly all of Storyworld was resting on his shoulders.

He was fairly short compared to the other citizens of the kingdom. They were all at least a head taller than Humpty, except for the children, some of whom matched his height. He may have been short in stature, but his egg-like body was wide enough to block an entire doorway. His thin white legs managed to support his heavy, rotund torso, even though they were completely absent of bones. Instead, they were made up of incredibly strong muscles, allowing him to run at an astounding pace.

Black satin shoes and a matching belt were the only articles of clothing that Humpty wore. He used to wear thick gloves as well, but discontinued the habit because they affected his fighting abilities. Humpty chose swords as his preferred method of battle, and he currently had a sleek, curved blade dangling from the side of his belt.

Humpty's lipless mouth was shut, but his egg-yolk-yellow eyes were wide-open, staring into the distance as he crossed his thin arms over the middle of his body. Thousands of thoughts were rushing through his mind, and he would not be surprised if his egg-head cracked from the stress at any moment.

"Sir Humpty?" said a voice, snapping him out of his trance.

Humpty tore his gaze from the window. A reddish hue appeared on his off-white cheeks as he murmured, "My apologies, Princess Tinkerbell."

"It is quite all right," answered the Princess of Neverland, nodding gently. She sat in one of the two adjacent thrones that stood in front of Humpty. Unlike the egg-man, Tinkerbell was tall, having inherited her height and stature from her father. From her mother, she received her majestic blonde hair, thin ears, rosy cheeks, and the baby-blue eyes, which matched her shiny flowing dress. "Do you know when the Literary is due to arrive?"

Humpty unhooked a silver watch from his belt. "Lord Rumpelstiltskin said he should arrive by the late afternoon or early evening. Unfortunately, we are unable to pinpoint his exact arrival point yet. All we can hope is that he does not appear too far from the castle."

"Sir Humpty, I am a bit worried. What if it is too late by the time he arrives? We do not have much time and there is so much work to do."

"I understand, Princess, and you need not worry. The Literaries have adapted to Storyworld at a much faster rate than their predecessors. We can train our next Literary quickly and begin his mission right away."

Tinkerbell gave a faint, reassuring smile. "I hope you are right. Neverland needs guidance soon. The kingdom is growing restless."

Humpty checked his watch again before looking back at Tinkerbell. "I shall meet with Lord Rumpelstiltskin. Perhaps he has forecasted the arrival point for the Literary by now."

The egg-man bowed and exited the throne room with a forced smile.

Chapter 1

Unpleasant Beginnings

Dodger wanted to be different. "Dodger" wasn't even his real name. His actual name was Mark Bishop, but he didn't think that was unique or exciting at all, which was one of the reasons he came up with a new title. There was no real meaning behind the word "Dodger", and Mark had no idea how or why it popped into his head, but the moment it floated into his mind one day while playing video games, he had a feeling that it suited him. He didn't have many friends to call him by this nickname, but he would be going off to college soon, so maybe he could create a new identity as Dodger in a fresh setting.

Turning to his left, Dodger caught his own gaze in the mirror hanging on his closet door. He had just gotten out of the shower ten minutes ago, so his damp, shaggy black hair was still plastered against his forehead and ears. The five o'clock shadow he had been sporting for the last week was recently shaved off except for the thin patch of black hair underneath his chin. Dodger chose to leave this faint goatee because he thought it would accentuate the piercing hanging from the left side of his lip.

Every time he saw this tiny ring or felt it as he ran his tongue across the inside of his lip, he regretted his decision more and more. He used to think it made him look cool. Now, he could only shake his head and roll his eyes at himself. The only reason he got the stupid piercing was because he had one of his feelings that told him it was a good idea, much like the same feeling that prodded him into creating his nickname.

Dodger's eyes met their own reflection in the mirror when he heard loud yelling coming from downstairs.

"You're unbelievable!" Dodger heard his father yell to his mother. Mr. and Mrs. Bishop were going at it again for whatever reasons this time. Maybe one of them looked at the other in the wrong way; maybe one of them was drinking water too loudly. Who knew when it came to the Bishop parents? All Dodger could do was fumble for the remote and raise the volume on his television as high as he could to drown out the loud obscenities and slamming doors.

When the volume was cranked to an almost unbearable level, Dodger resumed his game. As long as he kept his eyes on the screen and his hands on the controls, he wouldn't have to worry about what was going on downstairs.

Less than five minutes later, Dodger heard the front door slam, this time followed by the sounds of Mrs. Bishop and her loud sobs. Dodger couldn't take it anymore. Throwing the controller across the room, he buried his face into the pillow.

Make it stop. Please, make it all stop! he thought.

The next thing Dodger knew, it was morning. The sound of his alarm clock blared into his ears, snapping him awake. He didn't even remember falling asleep. All that Dodger could recall was that last night was like every other night for the past couple of years: a verbal battle between his parents.

Dodger got dressed slowly, as if he could delay the upcoming day. After putting on a pair of wrinkled jeans and a plain black T-shirt, he sighed heavily and shut off his television and game console. He knew the first thing his parents would say to him would be about him leaving his TV on all night. That would be their version of "Good morning!"

Once the screen went off, the shouting routine began. Dodger winced when he heard the first argument of the day coming from downstairs.

"You and Mark are so useless!" said his father.

Dodger clenched his jaw when he heard Mr. Bishop's muffled voice say these words. His parents' arguments wouldn't have affected him so much if it weren't for the fact that he was the center of most of them. The shouting usually began when Dodger said or did something that displeased his mother or father, at which point one of them would make a comment and the other would jump in until they were both arguing over something completely unrelated. It's like his very existence was the catalyst for their hostility.

This had gone on for years, and Dodger was getting tired of it. He didn't want to cause trouble for his parents. He didn't even think they were that bad. They were just miserable people who directed most of their anger and aggression toward their son as he walked in the door. That would hopefully all change in three months.

At the end of May, Dodger would be turning eighteen, meaning that he could finally move out. Over the past two years of working at a deli and tutoring after school, he had finally saved enough money to afford his own apartment. All he had to do was bear his parents' wrath for three more months.

Taking a deep breath, Dodger left his room with his backpack and went downstairs into the kitchen to see his mother leaning against the sink with her arms crossed. Dodger used to think that his mother looked good for her age. At forty-three years old, and after having a son, she had retained the attractive qualities that charmed Mr. Bishop in their college days: sleek black hair kept in a loose ponytail, olive skin, and bluish-green eyes. However, the years of fighting, shouting, and smoking had changed Mrs. Bishop's face into a gnarled portrait carrying a pair of wrinkled, nicotine-stained lips.

Mr. Bishop sat at the table with his legs crossed and the newspaper lying out in front of him, acting like nothing was out of the ordinary. Dodger had always seen his father as a villain of sorts, but not the traditional type. The antagonistic father figures shown in movies or books always came in one variety: an abusive, alcoholic, chain-smoking lowlife. Mr. Bishop was a total contradiction of this cliché. He was handsome, had a great job making a lot of money, rarely drank, and had quit smoking years ago. Aside from the verbal abuse he spouted whenever he saw his wife or son, Mr. Bishop could pass for a model citizen.

It bothered Dodger how much he resembled his father's appearance: the same thick black hair, the same wide eyes, and the same curved nose. It was common for people to joke about how they looked like brothers. Dodger couldn't think of a worse insult.

Dodger's Doorway

Once their son made an appearance, Mr. and Mrs. Bishop's attention shifted to him. Dodger paused in the doorway and stared at his parents like he did every morning. It was almost like a routine to see who would break their gaze first. Today, it was Mrs. Bishop, who huffed loudly and turned away so that she could pretend to do the dishes. Mr. Bishop crossed his arms and smirked.

"What're you looking at?"

"Nothing," mumbled Dodger, walking to the pantry to grab a bagel.

"You know, you left your video games on last night," said his father. "Hope you enjoy paying for the electric bill his month."

Dodger tried to mask the annoyance growing in his voice. "You could've walked in and shut if off yourself. It's not that hard."

Mr. Bishop's smirk vanished from his face. "Don't you get smart with me. See? *This* is why they treat you like crap at school."

"Because I get smart with people? Really? No, it's because they're all a bunch of idiots. It's not my fault."

Dodger murmured an additional insult, hoping that nobody would hear it. When he turned around from the pantry, his father was looming over him with an angry gleam in his eyes.

"What did you say?" he asked, a vein bulging in his forehead. It was a frightening sight, but nothing Dodger hadn't seen before. He tried to retort, but his father's short fuse went off and he was already yelling in his face. "Listen, Mark. As long as you're in my house, you're gonna show me a little respect!"

"And me too!" chimed in Mrs. Bishop from her spot at the sink.

"I wasn't talking to you!" retaliated her husband.

Dodger slipped away from his father, grabbed his bag, and ran out the front door. He hurried to the bottom of the driveway and stopped at the curb. He felt tears forming at the corners of his eyes, but he was able to stop them just in time.

After several minutes, Dodger felt ready to start his walk to school. During the entire trip, all he could think about was how soon he could leave home. *Three months* he kept repeating over and over in his head. *Three months.*

The apartment complex he was going to move into was a block away from his high school, making his commute much easier. Rent was cheap, and Dodger had carefully planned out his finances to afford his stay until the end of summer. Afterward, he'd be moving on to college. He was already meeting with his guidance counselor and advisors at the university to map out his future living arrangements as well as scholarship opportunities.

Dodger was going to pursue a business degree at Temple University, a college in the heart of Philadelphia. The school was roughly an hour away, far enough for Dodger to escape the reach of his old neighborhood and to leave behind unfavorable memories, but still in a somewhat familiar area. Most of Dodger's fellow graduating classmates thought the school was too close, and only two or three other students were attending Temple. The rest were planning to go to schools out west to pursue other majors and to take advantage of independent college life. This comforted Dodger, as he wanted nothing to do with most of his peers after high school.

Dodger's Doorway

Just thinking about college and his life beyond high school instantly brightened Dodger's day. Usually when he reached the illuminated sign that read "Northside High School," his spirits would sink. It wasn't that he disliked school; he just wasn't a fan of many of the other students, particularly Ryan Martin.

Dodger used to picture bullies as coming in one generic breed: brainless ogres from disheveled homes that would guffaw as they flushed their victims' heads in the toilet. Ryan was yet another anti-stereotype, much like Mr. Bishop. He was a straight-A student who lived with what sounded like two of the greatest parents ever. From what Dodger had heard, they were paying Ryan's entire full four years' tuition at the University of Pennsylvania, the same Ivy League school that had rejected Dodger months ago.

It was strange, but Ryan acted like it was his duty to torture poor Dodger. What started out as simple middle-school pranks like throwing trash at Dodger or tripping him in the hallway eventually escalated into more serious physical confrontations that left Dodger bruised on more than one occasion. Most people who knew of Dodger's rough home life just let him be, but Ryan didn't seem to care, and hardly ever relented in his bullying.

Every morning, Ryan and his friends would sit on the wall that lined the staircase leading to the main entrance to the school. Dodger called it "The Gauntlet" because he would have to trek past Ryan and his gang as they hurled insults and the occasional coffee cup at him. Today was different, as nobody was occupying the Gauntlet. *Maybe my luck's getting better*, Dodger thought, climbing the steps.

"What's up, Mark?"

Dodger sighed. *Great.* Sure enough, Ryan and three of his cronies were sitting against the wall, smoking cigarettes just out of sight of the school's windows.

"Nothing much, Ryan. Heading into school."

"Well, that's cool." Ryan sauntered over to Dodger. Even though they were the same height, Ryan was stockier and had broader shoulders. He had curly, dirty-blond hair and wide eyes that were almost always bloodshot in the morning. "How's everything at home, buddy?"

Dodger wished he had the courage to tell him off or to give him a good shove, anything that could have gotten Ryan to leave him alone. Instead, he nervously fidgeted with his lip piercing and struggled to maintain a steady voice as he muttered, "Fine."

"Oh, really? Daddy wasn't yelling at you and Mommy again, was he?" Ryan chuckled at his own comment.

Dodger was able to brush the remark off, partially because it wasn't even clever, let alone funny. At the same time, a wave of emotion flowed through the pit of his stomach.

"What's your problem, man?" He was ashamed when he heard his voice crack, but pressed on. "What did I ever do to you? Can't you leave me alone for once?"

Ryan and his friends laughed even harder when Dodger's voice cracked. "Aw, are you gonna cry? Maybe you should go back to the fifth grade. The elementary school is right across the street." With that, Ryan shoved Dodger.

"Leave me alone."

Ryan shoved him again. "What're you gonna do about it? Come on, baby."

One more push and Ryan would have sent Dodger toppling down the stairwell. Lucky for him, the school's early morning bell rang, momentarily distracting Ryan and allowing Dodger to duck away so he could sneak into the building. As he rushed into the entrance, he could hear Ryan yelling behind him, "Yeah, you better run!"

Dodger dashed into his first period class and took his seat at the back of the room. Out of all of his classes, English Literature was the one that caught his interest the most. Writing wasn't the most exciting activity, though Dodger did enjoy cracking open a book during his free time now and then. Like with video games, he enjoyed reading because it let him briefly escape his world and take part in an exciting adventure in a new realm.

None of the other students had arrived yet. The only person in the room besides Dodger was his teacher, Mr. Jenkins. He was sitting at his computer in the far corner with his eyes glued to the screen, hardly noticing the out-of-breath student who had just rushed into his presence.

"Good morning, Mark," he said in his usual monotone voice. Mr. Jenkins was relatively young, near his late twenties, but he was already balding, and the few black hairs sprouting from his head were thinning out and marked with the occasional gray sliver. He always had a tranquil expression, and there was something about his persona that demanded respect and awe from everyone who came in contact with him. Perhaps it was his soft, cool voice that he maintained at all times, even if he was frustrated with students, or maybe it was due to his mysterious vibe, as if he knew some profound secret about the meaning of life.

"Hey, Mr. Jenkins. How are you?"

"Phenomenal," replied the teacher, standing from his computer and facing the student. "Are you okay?"

"Oh," said Dodger, forcing a chuckle. "I thought I was gonna be late so I decided to hurry to class."

Mr. Jenkins stroked his chin and sat on the desk across from Dodger. "What if I said I didn't believe you?"

Dodger didn't answer.

Mr. Jenkins sighed. "I'm not stupid, Mark. I haven't been out of high school *that* long. I know what goes on. Bad things happen to good people."

Once again, Dodger didn't answer. He tried to avoid his teacher's critical gaze by fumbling with the edge of his notebook.

"Now, if you told me what was going on," continued Mr. Jenkins, "then I, as a teacher, would be expected to step in and confront whoever was causing trouble. And you want to know something? I wouldn't."

"Why not?" asked Dodger, taken aback.

"Because that's *your* job. You need to stick up for yourself."

Of course, thought Dodger. "I don't like confrontation. I don't like what it leads to."

"What's the worst that can happen?" asked Mr. Jenkins, exposing the palms of his hands. "You tell someone to back off and they either listen to you, or the situation escalates."

"That's it, though! I don't want the situation to escalate. I don't want to get into a fight. I'll get my butt kicked and I'll be in the same spot as before. Nothing changes."

"First of all, confrontations don't always escalate into physical violence, nor should they. Second, let's say that it *does* become physical. Even if you win or lose a fight, you still stood up for yourself. That's all that matters. You faced your fear. I can almost guarantee that whoever is giving you trouble will think twice the next time they pick on you. Nobody likes to get into physical confrontations, even if they think they'll win. I'm not saying you should go out and start picking fights with anyone who looks at you the wrong way; just know how to look them in the eye and tell them to back off."

Dodger looked at Mr. Jenkins like he had just transformed into a wise, all-knowing prophet.

"You probably won't get it right away," added Mr. Jenkins. "You'll understand what I mean soon."

The last comment confused Dodger. He was about to ask for clarification when the two-minute warning bell rang. A throng of students burst into the room, chatting among themselves.

Dodger's Doorway

Mr. Jenkins stood from the desk and loudly stated, "So, you don't need to worry about the test, Mark. We'll have a full review tomorrow." With that being said, Mr. Jenkins returned to his desk and prepared for the day's lesson.

When Dodger came home, nobody else was around. His parents must have still been at their offices. Dodger had the house to himself. This was a rare occurrence; he often had to work right after school and wouldn't get home until eight, long after his parents had sat and brewed in their own anger. With the day off from work, Dodger was fortunate to get home and enjoy peace and quiet for an hour or two. He figured that he could blow off steam from the school day by playing his *Spider-Man* video game and beating up virtual bad guys.

There was an hour of solitude before Mr. Bishop came home, soon followed by Mrs. Bishop. Dodger had a mental stopwatch that would tick away the seconds until his parents went off on their nightly screaming match.

"Always have to complain about something!" came Mrs. Bishop's voice.

Two minutes. Great job, guys.

The shouting went on nonstop for the next hour. It was unbelievable how two people could have so much pent-up anger and aggression to throw at each other. Dodger heard glass breaking when he finally had enough. Shutting off his television and video game, he shuffled across his room, slammed the door shut, and locked it. He then slid down to the ground with his back against the door, his knees huddled up to his chest, and his arms wrapped around his legs.

Dodger's Doorway

He wanted nothing more than to march out of his room and scream at his parents so that they could feel the pain that they had put their son through for years, but all he could do was silently rock back and forth.

Still breathing deeply, Dodger stared at his closet door across the room. As always, the door was slightly ajar, and his reflection in the hanging mirror gazed back at him. It was a pitiful sight. He fumbled with his lip ring, trying his hardest to quell his emotions before they overwhelmed him.

He kept staring at the mirror and playing with the ring until he noticed something unusual. Out of the darkness in the room, a stretch of light crept out from his closet doorway.

Dodger blinked twice. He figured he was just imagining things. All the same, he soon found himself standing and creeping up to the door. The closer he got, the more he noticed a deep humming emerging from the doorway as well. There was also warmth permeating the air around the closet. Cautiously, Dodger yanked the closet door wide open. A large expanse of blue light met him. This phenomenon occupied the entire closet; it was like the doorway led right into a warm summer's day. Dodger reached out, feeling the warmth grow stronger, and sensed a light breeze float across his palm.

It was real.

There was more yelling coming from downstairs. If he had stumbled upon this discovery at any other time, Dodger would have called someone to come see it, but now, as his parents battled it out for the thousandth time, he thought it would be best to keep it to himself.

Dodger's Doorway

Dodger gazed into the blue abyss of his closet and took one more deep breath. Closing his eyes, he raised his left foot and let himself fall forward through the doorway.

Chapter 2

Through the Doorway

"Wake up! Wake up, I say! We will be late!" shrieked a high-pitched and irritating voice that cut through the air like a knife.

"Maybe he's dead?" suggested a second voice, this one deeper and more melodic.

"Do not say that! We need him!"

"I said *maybe*. Keep your shell on, good sir. We can't afford to put you back together again."

"Do not say he is dead then. The princess said we must keep him safe!"

"Well, in that case, why couldn't the princess come get him herself?" replied the deeper voice. There was almost a giggle behind his tone.

"We are the princess's bravest subjects and the only ones she entrusts to protect him!" commented the first voice. "Do not forget that you are the one who forecasted his arrival and—"

"I get it, I get it! I was just being humorous. How can we be sure that this is truly our Literary, though? With his strange attire and that metal ring dangling from his lip, he could very well be an imposter."

"Then he needs to stop impostering! We are going to be late, and the princess said—"

"The princess said phooey! Let's stop dawdling and find out if our savior is ready to save us!"

Dodger's Doorway

A pointed foot kicked Dodger in the ribs, knocking the wind out of him. Grabbing his side, he opened his eyes to find himself facedown in the grass. "Ow! What the hell is your problem, jerk?"

"Well, that solves the mystery as to whether he is alive or not," called out the deep voice. "But he speaks strangely. Perhaps it's an evil tongue of sorts?"

"Oh, you know these Literaries, with their strange words and whatnot. They always talk in nonsensical manners. What was it that Sir Chaucer called us? 'Miserable farts' I believe?"

Dodger huffed and rolled onto his back. He was about to berate the two speakers when he suddenly yelped and leapt to his feet. The voices he heard belonged to two of the weirdest beings that Dodger had ever seen.

The creature standing on the left resembled a tiny, old, dark-skinned man who stood at half of Dodger's height. He had little pointed feet encased in brown satin shoes, making him guilty of kicking Dodger's ribs. The shoes matched his full outfit; a brown tunic draped over his torso and hanging down to his thighs, darker brown leggings covering his knobby knees, and matching sleeves protected his stubby arms. The little man's face and hands were leathery-looking, with wrinkles and scars all over. Over his scraggly black hair, he wore an oversized helmet that had horns protruding from the left and right sides. The final addition to his ensemble was a brown belt wrapped around his waist containing an assortment of vials and glass beakers filled with multicolored liquids.

Standing to Dodger's right was, in no other way describable, a living egg. Its body consisted of a large, ovular white shell with two enormous egg-yolk-yellow eyes and a thin malleable mouth. Popping out from either side of the shell were two thin white arms ending in large white hands, and coming out of the bottom of the shell were two white, branch-like legs ending in flat feet wearing black shoes. The egg-man wore a belt around the middle of his body, dividing his head from his lower torso. Strapped onto the side of his belt was a long sword with a slightly curved blade.

"What?" Dodger's heart was racing and he had to blink rapidly to make sure he wasn't hallucinating. "What's going on?"

The egg-man sighed and said, "You Literaries and your immediate questions. You never give a simple 'hello' or 'how are-'"

"What are Literaries?" Dodger interrupted, his head swimming with questions. "And what are you?" He approached the egg-man cautiously and touched his shell. It felt exactly like a chicken egg, tough and coarse, but there was a light warmth resonating from it as well. Dodger was fascinated at how the egg-man's entire body looked solid, but his mouth and eyes were able to move fluidly like a human's.

"Erm." The egg-man appeared flustered and embarrassed as Dodger continued poking and prodding his head. "My apologies for the confusion, visitor. I am Sir Humpty Dumpty, Second-in-Command of the Neverland Military Arm."

Dodger stopped. His mind exploded with amazement and curiosity. Blinking rapidly again, he felt himself getting lightheaded and had to sit back down on the ground to collect his wits. Humpty Dumpty and his companion cast concerned glances at one another.

"Did-did you just say your name was Humpty Dumpty?" asked Dodger.

"Indeed, I did."

"Like, *the* Humpty Dumpty?"

The egg-man nervously glanced at his partner again and nodded at Dodger. "That is my name, sir. Humpty Dumpty. But please, you may call me Humpty, or Sir Humpty. Whichever you prefer."

The concept was still difficult for Dodger to believe. "So, you're Humpty Dumpty. Like in the poem?"

"I'm in a poem?" Humpty bounced on his feet and clapped his hands. His frown had turned into a large smile, exposing his human-like teeth. "See? I told you, Rump! I knew he would write about me in his world. Oh, why did none of the other Literaries ever tell me I was in a poem? This is a joyous occasion! Can you please recite this poem for me, sir?"

Rump gave a loud sigh. "I thought you said we were going to be late?"

Humpty scowled at him. "There is always time to hear an amazing piece of Literary work. We can wait a few more seconds." The egg-man sat on the ground and beamed at Dodger.

Dodger's heart had finally slowed down a bit, so he recited the nursery rhyme he had learned as a child.

Humpty Dumpty sat on a wall,

Humpty Dumpty had a great fall,

Then all the king's horses,

Dodger's Doorway

And all the king's men,

Could not put Humpty

back together again

Rump fell to the ground howling with laughter and his arms clutched around his stomach. Humpty's jaw had dropped and his yellow eyes shone with rage. He huffed and stood back up, placing his hands on his non-existent hips.

"That conniving, despicable man! How dare he? I was pushed! Pushed, I tell you! I am not clumsy whatsoever! And I did just fine putting myself back together again, thank you very much! I cannot believe this!"

"I'm sorry!" said Dodger. "That's how I learned it. That's how all kids learn it."

"Are you telling me that children learn this poem?" roared Humpty. Rump was now on all-fours, trying to suppress his hilarity, but failing miserably. He was wheezing in between laughter, which only seemed to make Humpty even more outraged. The egg-man continued, "This is absolutely ridiculous; such slander being spread about me in the world of the Literaries. No wonder nobody ever told me about my reputation. Did you know that I was nearly killed when I was pushed off that wall? My near-death-experience is regarded as humorous in your world? There better be another poem describing how I courageously fought off an army of evil flying monkeys single-handed!"

"Wait. Flying monkeys?"

"Yes! Years ago, an evil witch dispatched her legion of flying monkeys to take over our allied kingdom of Oz. The Wizard-King of Oz actually requested my assistance in the battle for he had heard of my excellent swordsmanship. Surely you and your kind must know of my battle-worthy endeavors!"

Humpty's anger had slightly diminished at this point. The egg-man held his head up with an air of pride. Dodger frowned, knowing that he had to be the bearer of bad news.

"Actually, you're not even in that story."

Rump's laughter ended abruptly.

"What is that world coming to?!" exploded the egg-man. "How dare they eliminate me from my own story, especially such a heroic one at that? I fought off hundreds of those vicious beasts all by myself and nobody has even given me my proper recognition? Outrageous!"

"If it makes you feel better," Dodger said cautiously, "nobody really defeated the flying monkeys. In the story, they attack the Tin Man and Scarecrow and-"

"HA!" Humpty sneered and re-crossed his arms. "Those idiots? Local mercenaries. Swords-for-hire who couldn't tell the difference between a horse's head and its hindquarters. You mean to tell me that they had a part in the tale of the flying monkey assault and I am nowhere to be found? Does that story mention how they only offered to fight the army for a hefty price whereas I lent my services for free? And I saved their lives! The wizard-king told me- WE ARE

GOING TO BE LATE!" Humpty bellowed, pointing at the low sun as it sank past the distant mountains lining the horizon. "We need to get back to the castle now!"

Dodger was still curious. "I'm confus-"

"Curiosity boiled the egg," quoted Humpty. "We need to return to Neverland or the princess will be worried sick. There will be time for explanations later."

"No, listen, Humpty," said Dodger. "I'm not moving until one of you guys answer my questions. I have no idea what this place is or how I got here. All I know is that something freaky happened in my closet, and now I'm standing in front of a talking egg and," he looked Rump up and down, "some kind of elf."

Humpty threw his arms up as Rump chuckled.

"Sir Humpty, I think this gentleman has the right to know what's going on. Don't forget how difficult it was for his predecessors to become accustomed to our world. I'm sure the princess can wait a little longer." Rump smiled at Dodger and bowed. "I am Lord Rumpelstiltskin, Head Alchemist and Magicker of the Neverland Science Arm."

The lightheadedness came again. Dodger couldn't fathom how surreal this whole situation seemed right now. He was sitting in front of Humpty Dumpty, who commanded an army, and Rumpelstiltskin, who was an alchemist. There were more questions that needed answers.

"So, let me get this straight; this whole world is full of imaginary creatures and stuff from fairy tales?"

Rump blinked and frowned. Speaking slowly, he said, "It's hard to properly express. The people in this world aren't necessarily imaginary, although we can understand how it may seem that way. The best way to put it is that this world is parallel to your own. Throughout the ages, many of your kind have stumbled into our realm, which has been dubbed 'Storyworld' by your more recent predecessors. History tells us that whenever tragedy strikes, a Literary is transported to our world to help us through troubled times."

Dodger nodded. "You call people from my world Literaries, but why? What does that mean?"

"From our understanding, in your world, there's a type of story-telling called 'literature'. This literature often features certain aspects that are abnormal in your realm, such as Storyworld's people and creatures. Most of the tales and stories you've heard include our noblest heroes and our evilest villains. Therefore, we took it upon ourselves to call your people Literaries. Since the dawn of Storyworld, thousands of Literaries have come and gone, making huge impacts in our lives."

"So, you're saying that all these stories I hear, like nursery rhymes and fairy tales, are based on things from this world?"

"I believe so, yes."

Humpty had begun pacing back and forth with his hands curled behind his back. Every couple of seconds, he would take a silver watch from his belt, check the time, grunt audibly, and then resume pacing. Dodger ignored him and allowed Rump to continue his explanation.

"As the Head Alchemist and Magicker of Neverland, it's my responsibility to find out when Literaries will be arriving. We have no control over their appearances, but people like myself can forecast it with the help of our magic. This honor was bestowed upon me by my mentor, and unto him by his mentor, and so on and so forth. Usually, every settlement has a magicker who possesses this ability. Once the Literary arrives, a host is designated to guide them through their mission.

"Now, I have a question for you, young man."

"Go for it," said Dodger, even though he was still crackling with curiosity.

"You mentioned that Sir Humpty was in a poem, and that the mercenaries of Oz were in a story."

"Yeah."

"Am I in any of your literature as well?" Rump asked with a grin.

"Uh, yeah, you are, but I can't remember all of the details," admitted Dodger. He struggled to remember the story. "I think you're this little dwarf guy who can weave gold out of straw, and you trick this girl into giving you her baby."

Rump laughed and put his hands on his hips. "Oh, how I miss my rebellious adolescent years! That was so long ago!"

As his eyes glazed over in reminiscence, Humpty gave a loud "Hmph!" nearby. The egg-man was muttering about how ridiculous it was that he was honored in a poem about falling off a wall while the alchemist was known through a retelling of his juvenile pranks.

"Oh! And is there perhaps a story about the time I made old Rip Van Winkle fall asleep for seventy years?" asked Rump eagerly.

"That was you?" Dodger replied, laughing for the first time. "The story said that he got drunk and passed out."

"Well, let's just say that he should've kept an eye on his beverage if h-"

"IT IS GETTING DARK! WE NEED TO LEAVE RIGHT NOW!"

Dodger and Rump jumped. Humpty's shell turned slightly red underneath his eyes where his cheeks should have been. Behind him, the sun was almost gone behind the mountains. A near-opaque shadow covered the area, although the pink-purple sky still provided a little light for the trio.

"We have explained enough for now! We need to get back to the castle!" Humpty didn't wait for a response. The egg-man turned on the spot and disappeared into a nearby forest. Dodger could just see the white tip of a tower beyond the trees. Rump lowered his hand to help the Literary to his feet, and urged him to follow into the forest.

Humpty was already a long distance ahead, running at a rapid pace down a dirt path that cut straight through the forest. The trees were scattered in odd configurations; there were a few wedged together so close that their branches intertwined with one another, and there were others that were spread out, leaving wide gaps between. These gaps contained miniature dirt paths of their own that led off into other areas deeper into the brush. The treetops were covered in thick, sprawling leaves that created a natural rooftop to the forest, but they didn't completely block out the light pink sky; tiny rays of light shone enough to brighten up the path.

Dodger had trouble keeping up with Humpty as he charged through the trees. The egg-man, with his thin, feeble-looking legs, was a surprisingly fast runner, and so was Rump, who skipped a few yards behind his companion.

The whole time he was running, Dodger's mind was in several places at once. A part of him was picturing how odd this scene must look to an outsider; Humpty Dumpty dashing through the forest with a sword in his belt, followed by a wrinkly little man with pointed feet and a horned helmet, and a teenage human boy.

The other part of him was still struggling with the situation as a whole. Dodger remembered stepping through the doorway and into the blue abyss, then almost immediately waking up in the field. Everything between those two events was a complete mystery. Thinking that it was all a strange, vivid dream, he pinched his arm, feeling almost relieved that it hurt. This was all real. He was actually in this place called Storyworld.

Humpty, Rump, and Dodger ran for a long time. With each step, the light became dimmer and the forest became darker. Dodger was losing his breath, and a knife-like pain was jabbing into his side. Thankfully, he saw a light showing roughly a hundred yards away. Humpty yelled to his friends to hurry up.

As the light came closer and closer, Dodger put all of his effort into catching up with Humpty. Only a few yards from the edge of the forest, Humpty skidded to a stop and unsheathed his sword. At this action, Rump grabbed Dodger by the collar and yanked him into a clump of trees off the path.

"Hey!"

"Shh!"

Rump pressed a finger to his lips and pointed back to the path. Humpty was standing still as a statue with both of his hands grasping his sword's hilt and his eyes set straight ahead. Several silent seconds passed, and just as Dodger was about to ask what was going on, he saw three men emerge from the trees so smoothly that it was almost as if they had materialized out of thin air. They looked human-like, except much bigger than the average person.

The shortest of these men was about three feet taller than Humpty. He had on a green hood that cast most of his face in shadow except for his smirking mouth and his brown goatee. The man's outfit consisted of a dark green tunic and leggings that matched his hood and almost camouflaged him in the foliage. A bow and quiver full of arrows were strung across his back.

On the hooded man's right was another person who bore a slight resemblance to him, except he wasn't sporting a green hood or bow; instead, this cohort optioned to carry a straight sword in his belt and a dagger tucked into one of his brown boots. He had black hair long enough to reach past his shoulders, but it was swept back over his ears to reveal multiple piercings. This man was also smirking, though it wasn't concealed behind any facial hair. One of his blue eyes was swollen to the point of being almost totally shut.

The final member of this forest trio was the largest of the group, standing over six feet tall. He was hardly more than a solid block of muscle topped with a bald head. Dodger noticed that this man carried no weapons, not that he needed to because his arm muscles looked like flesh-colored boulders. The giant wore a dark green tunic with the sleeves torn off and the bottom of the leggings frayed above the knees. He didn't wear shoes, and his flat feet were covered in hair and tree-bark-looking skin.

"Traveler's toll. Pay your dues if you wish to pass," said the green-hooded man in the center.

Rump signaled to Dodger to sneak through the brush. They slowly made their way closer to the gathering, remaining as silent as possible. Dodger had his hand covering his mouth, trying to stifle his loud panting. The journey had left his heart racing and he was afraid that the thumping could be heard throughout the whole forest. He could hear Humpty speaking with a stern and confident demeanor, having dropped his original irritating and high-pitched tone.

"You are within royal grounds, thus we do not pay tolls. We also do not take kindly to having you thieves and rogues loitering around our kingdom either."

"We're not thieves, Humpty. All money we collect goes to helping the poor and the needy."

"Poor and needy indeed!" snapped Humpty, raising his sword a little higher. "You gamble and drink with all of these 'tolls' you collect. Now, clear the way, or I will clear it myself!"

Dodger's Doorway

The three forest thieves didn't move. The leader in the green hood momentarily grinned at Humpty before snapping his fingers. Dodger felt a pair of arms clamp over his chest and lift him into the air. To his right, another man seized Rump. The two captors dragged their prisoners into the clearing. Humpty didn't appear fazed by this. If he was worried, he was hiding it well.

"You were always the sneaky one, Robin," declared the egg-man in a dark tone. "Shame that you couldn't remain in the royal court with us. We would have appreciated your talents."

Robin the thief leader smiled. "Yes, yes. It was a great life, I'll admit. But it's such a bore working in that castle. No drinking, no games, no cavorting with the lovely men and women of the city. Nothing but work all the time. I think I enjoy it out here in the forest much more. I also make good coin. Speaking of which, you'll have to pay a hefty price if you want your partners unharmed. Fifty gold pieces for Stiltskin." His eyes wandered from Rump to Dodger. "And a hundred for the Literary."

"I know who you are!" exclaimed Dodger. "You're Robin Hood!"

Robin laughed. "See that? Even the distant lands have heard of me. You see how infamous I've become, Humpty?"

"Aren't you supposed to be the good guy?" asked Dodger. His captor grunted in an annoyed tone and squeezed the Literary a little tighter.

"When it comes to characters like Robin the Thief," said Humpty, his dark grin growing, "there is no good or bad. There is only cowardice!"

Robin didn't react, but the man with the long hair and piercings unsheathed his sword and charged at Humpty. Dodger closed his eyes tightly and cringed, not wanting to see the egg-man getting torn to pieces. He was surprised when he heard the sounds of metal clashing on metal. Opening his eyes, he was astounded at the sight of Humpty combatting like a master swordsman. Regardless of his awkward shape, he was agile and quick with his movements. Dodger watched him swoop and parry with his curved sword, nimbly evading strikes from his opponent and launching effective counter-attacks.

Robin's other cohort, the giant, stepped in front of Dodger and stooped down so that they were face-to-face.

"This one has a piece hanging from his lip. I bet a merchant would pay a pretty pence for it." The giant's breath reeked of bitter alcohol, and his yellow teeth were chipped and cracked. Dodger's eyes were burning from the odor and he didn't immediately grasp what he was talking about until he realized that the giant was noting his lip piercing. The Literary's face drained of color, and he desperately tried to kick free. His captor squeezed his arms and chest tighter, crushing the air out of his lungs and causing him to sputter and choke.

"Keep still!" said the captor. "Little John, would you like the honors?"

"Gladly," replied the giant. One of his massive hands wrapped around Dodger's neck. His fingers were rough and calloused and smelled bitter as well. Holding Dodger's head in place, the giant reached out for the piercing with his other hand.

"Stop!"

It sounded like Robin's voice had called out. Little John let go of Dodger's neck and swung around. As his body turned, Dodger saw past him and noticed that Humpty was kneeling on Robin's chest with his blade pressed up to his throat. The swordsman he'd been fighting before was now lying in a pool of blood on the ground with a wound in his stomach. Rump and his captor had disappeared from the area.

"I have killed Mr. Scarlett," called out Humpty. "I do not wish to do the same to your leader. Let the Literary go or I will add Robin's head to Neverland's trophy collection."

Little John scowled at Humpty, flexing and cracking his thick fingers as if he considered attacking the egg-man. Humpty responded by pressing the blade harder against Robin's neck. Little John grunted and nodded to Dodger's captor, signaling to let him go. The Literary fell to the ground and scrambled over to Humpty's side. Humpty climbed off Robin's chest and positioned himself in front of Dodger.

Robin pushed himself to his feet and brushed the dirt off his tunic. Looking around, he asked, "Where's Tuck? He vanished with the alchemist."

"He's an hour west," said Rump, entering the clearing through a puff of smoke. "I took him for a little ride."

"You will bury your dead, collect your lost, then leave this forest by tomorrow!" commanded Humpty. Sheathing his sword, he said, "And understand this: if I discover you are still out here attempting to collect tolls, I will return with the Neverland Military Arm and do a little cleansing of Neverwood Forest."

Robin and his men didn't say anything as they melted into the trees. Little John picked up Mr. Scarlett's corpse and slung it over his shoulder. The giant then went into the forest with his companions to search for their lost friend.

Rump approached Humpty and Dodger. "Sorry for not listening, Sir Humpty. You were right. Had we left earlier, we could've avoided this encounter."

"It is fine," said Humpty. "At least we got our point across that we will not be tolerating rogues in our kingdom anymore. Come and let us get to the castle at once."

"Wait a minute." Dodger had questions that were still not answered, and now he had even more that needed a response. "Okay, I can deal with the fact that we just met Robin Hood and his Merry Men."

"Is that what you people call him in your world?" asked Rump. "I guess that makes sense seeing as how he always wears that hood-"

"Shut up! Robin Hood is a bad guy in this world. I can deal with that. But he used to work with you guys?"

"He was the leader of Neverland Castle's sentries," stated Humpty. "He was not fit to work in this kingdom because he lacked discipline and willpower. It would be the norm for Robin to leave his post and visit the tavern so he could get drunk and gamble with his friends. Thus, I ordered for his replacement with someone more competent."

"Who?"

"A sheriff from the neighboring city of Himshire named John Tell. Little did I know that Robin and John have had a little feud going on that goes back many, many years. Robin was not too happy about this decision and took some of his fellow sentries into this forest where they could harass travelers. As you heard, they justify their actions by claiming that they are on the path of righteousness, saying how they were stealing from the rich to give to the poor. Such nonsense."

Sheriff of Nottingham is good, Robin Hood is bad, Dodger thought. "And what about your teleport thing?" he asked Rump. "You can travel by magic. Why couldn't you teleport us to the castle?"

"Ah, well, that's an experimental spell that I decided to test on my captor. I don't recommend using it until I have another draught of the potion ready. Robin and his gang are in for a little surprise when, or if, they find their friend."

"Any other questions?" asked the egg-man.

"As a matter of fact, I have a question for our visitor," said Rump. "What's your name, good sir?"

Through all of the chaos that had occurred in the past hour, Dodger realized he didn't get a chance to tell his hosts his name. He was a little ashamed that he didn't have an elaborate title like his newfound companions did, so he decided to get creative.

"My name is Dodger, Soldier of Philadelphia."

"That is by far one of the most interesting titles I've ever heard from you Literaries!" declared the impressed Rump. "And now, Dodger, Soldier of Philadelphia, since we're all familiarized with each other, let us finish our journey to Neverland Castle!"

Chapter 3

Neverland Castle

Neverland Castle was enormous, its tallest towers going so high that Dodger had to crane his neck to see the tops as they pierced the sky. The castle was constructed from rough gray stones haphazardly piled on top of one another in no uniform configuration. Numerous towers sprouted from various spots along the building's perimeter, with three of them standing higher than the rest. All of the spires had large holes carved into the stonework, some filled with stained-glass windows and others with simple wooden panes. The rest of the castle's exterior was plain and undecorated. It was almost as if the structure was attempting to disguise itself as a mountain.

The castle's face spanned yards in both directions. On either side of the main building, tall stone walls more than thirty feet high extended into the distance. These walls ran for what seemed like miles in either direction, eventually curving backwards and continuing down into the darkness and out of sight.

Night had fallen, but there was plenty of light at the front of Neverland Castle, allowing Dodger to take in most of its features. The only way into the kingdom was through an iron grillwork gate built right into the stone. Small wooden towers stood on both sides of this gate, and there were a dozen men and women stationed at the tops and around the bases of these outposts. Everyone was armed with a torch, spear, or longbow.

Dodger's Doorway

Humpty led Rump and Dodger up to the gate. A single man stood in their way, one arm holding a torch and the other grasped onto a spear. He had short black hair, a scruffy face, a patchy beard, and an authoritative guise on his face that demanded respect. He wore a polished metal breastplate over a suit of dark chainmail. The breastplate was branded with a coat of arms consisting of a wolf's head holding a scroll in its mouth. Strapped to the man's belt were a curved horn and a short sword.

"Welcome back, good sirs," stated the doorman to the trio emerging from the forest.

"Thank you, Captain Tell," said Humpty. "All is well, I hope?"

"Nothing new as of late. I see you found the Literary all right!"

Humpty nodded and turned to his follower. "Dodger, meet John Tell, former Sheriff of Himshire and current Captain of the Neverland Sentries. Captain Tell, please welcome our newest Literary visitor, Dodger, Soldier of Filthadelphia."

Dodger winced slightly and forced a smile as he shook hands with the sentry. John had a firm handshake and a protective aura, like a father figure. There was something trustworthy about him.

"Sorry we can't stay and chat for long," added Humpty. "We have to get Dodger to the princess to prepare him for his mission."

"Of course, of course," said John, nodding. The captain reached for the curved horn at his belt and blew three short bursts. The gate behind him retracted into the wall.

Dodger's Doorway

Humpty, Rump, and Dodger entered the gateway. As they crossed over the threshold, John's horn blasted another three times, signaling the gate to close behind them. Dodger peeked over his shoulder to watch the grillwork frame slide down to the ground. Ahead of him, Rump and Humpty entered through a pair of double doors and beckoned him to come along.

They were now walking down a long, elegant hallway filled with more torches on either side. Compared to the exterior, the walls inside the castle were more aesthetically pleasing to look at. Rectangular stones were placed on top of each other in perfect symmetry with wooden doors appearing every couple of feet. The high ceilings were supported through the use of interlocking wooden rafters and metal brackets. Each of these brackets held an elegantly forged sconce made of polished silver, and every sconce contained a bright torch, providing flickering lights to guide the trio into the heart of Neverland Castle.

Along the left wall was a series of portraits hanging underneath a golden plaque that read "Literary Heroes." Among these images, Dodger saw people that he recalled from his English and literature textbooks. Authors who had apparently made an appearance in Storyworld included J.M. Barrie, William Shakespeare, the Brothers Grimm, and many more. All of the portraits listed the name of the Literary and a brief quote.

"These are our past heroes and saviors," noted Humpty. "It has become more and more difficult to acquire portraits of our recent Literaries over the years. Through here."

Dodger's Doorway

The egg-man ushered his friends through a door at the end of the hallway. This one led into an enormous pearl-white chamber so bright and pristine that Dodger had to squint until his sight could adjust. In the very center of the ceiling hung an enormous chandelier filled with thousands of lit candles that bathed the chamber in yellow light. On the far wall opposite from where Dodger had entered, there was a long purple banner that hung from the rafters and unraveled all the way to the ground. This tapestry featured an oversized crest similar to the one on John Tell's breastplate. Imposed in front of the crest was a picture of what Dodger assumed was Neverland's royal family.

The king was a tall man with a short crop of black hair tucked under his golden crown, which was a conservative piece designed like a halo with minimal jewelry and bobbles. He wore a sharp black tunic draped over him like a short robe, leaving his wide hands and flat feet exposed. In his right hand, he gripped an antique hunting rifle propped up on the ground by its stock. The hilt of a bladed weapon could be seen sneaking out of the side of his belt.

Holding onto the king's left arm was a younger woman with long, wavy, blonde hair that fell past her shoulders. She wasn't wearing a crown and instead sported a red-hooded cape that flowed down the top half of her spotless white gown. The queen was barely taller than the king, but she possessed the same thick frame.

Standing in front of the king and queen was a much younger couple. The woman had thick lips and a small nose like the king, but had blonde hair and entrancing blue eyes like the queen. She wore a flowing blue gown, sparkling sandals, and a matching glittering headband to keep her hair out of her face.

Holding her hand was a man with a cheeky smile, bulbous hazel eyes, and thick red hair that brightened his face. This man wore a tattered light green outfit with matching tights, much like Robin Hood.

Humpty, Rump, and Dodger approached the middle of the chamber where two thrones sat next to each other. The young woman with the blue gown in the banner sat in one of the chairs while the other one remained unoccupied. Dodger was a little surprised at how different the woman looked from her portrait. She was older, and her hair was tied in a bun, but her face seemed pale and pasty, like she had just gotten over a cold. Her beauty was still ravishing, and Dodger couldn't help blushing as she smiled at him. Humpty and Rump both got down on one knee, and the Literary mimicked them, stumbling to the ground.

"Princess Tinkerbell. We have arrived with our newest Literary," declared Humpty.

Dodger was surprised his neck didn't snap from turning it so fast. Glancing at the banner, he examined the red-haired boy and felt the gears in his mind turning.

"Is Peter Pan the prince?" blurted out the Literary.

Dodger could tell by Rump and Humpty's shocked expressions that he had just said something unacceptable. The princess didn't visibly react aside from blinking a couple of times. She wiped her brow before speaking in a silky voice.

"Yes, Peter was the prince, and my husband."

Rump elbowed the Literary in the ribs once he opened his mouth again to ask what happened. Dodger grabbed his side and glared at the alchemist. Humpty cleared his throat.

"Princess, sorry for his outspokenness. This is Dodger, Soldier of Filthadel-"

"*Phil*adelphia!"

"Right. *Phil*adelphia. We would like to get him prepared for his mission right away."

Tinkerbell rose from her throne; she was much taller than Dodger expected.

"Dodger, you have been selected. Whenever a Literary comes to Storyworld, they cannot leave until they have completed a certain task. As a Literary of Neverland, it is your duty to free our kingdom from its current turmoil. That being said, you will be residing here in the castle while you complete your series of quests."

"What?" Dodger's head started spinning; he had to pause to regain his senses. The thought of returning home hadn't crossed his mind at all since he arrived; in fact, up until now, his brain still hadn't properly registered exactly what happened in the doorway.

A part of him actually thought he was still dreaming. He *had* to be dreaming. He's talking to Princess Tinkerbell, who's telling him to complete missions and stay at Neverland Castle. But if this was real, Dodger thought it must've been some big misunderstanding. There was no way he was this

"Literary" they needed. He was just a normal teenager who liked to play video games. Dodger was no hero or adventurer. He had to go back to his own world.

But what's the point of going back? he suddenly thought. All that was waiting for him was a life that made him upset. Maybe he *should* stay here in Storyworld. What if he was purposely sent here for a reason, just like Rumpelstiltskin and Princess Tinkerbell had said?

With all of these thoughts chasing through his head, it took Dodger a second to realize that Tinkerbell was still speaking to him.

"It is understandable if you are scared. The other Literaries were frightened as well. At the most dire of times, their bravery showed and helped them succeed. Like them, you will demonstrate true greatness on your journey. Do you wish to accept your mission?"

"Yeah, sure," replied Dodger, almost in a trance. He barely registered the words coming out of his mouth. It was like his instincts took over and made him accept.

"Good," said Tinkerbell, smiling and returning to her throne. Humpty and Rump stood, as did Dodger. The princess said, "Your first labor is to find the general of the Neverland Military Arm."

Dodger looked at Humpty. "I thought *you* were the general."

"Oh, no," replied the egg-man with an embarrassed chuckle. "I told you I was the second-in-command. Our leader went missing long ago."

"Correct," said Tinkerbell. "He has been missing for many years and we have had no idea where he was, until now. We have recently obtained information regarding his whereabouts."

Humpty jumped with excitement. "Oh! We've found out where he is?"

"Not yet, Sir Humpty. Our intelligence has gathered that the Forever Witch, who resides in the middle of Neverwood Forest, may know where the general is; it is possible that she may even have him as her prisoner, which is why you three will have to go into the forest and pay her a visit."

"Who exactly is the general?" asked Dodger.

Humpty stared at Dodger with his wide yellow eyes. "Why, he is one of the greatest warriors in the land: Pinocchio the Wooden Soldier."

Dodger raised his eyebrows. "Pinocchio? The puppet?"

Humpty shuddered and frowned. "Oh, I don't even want to think about the horrific stories you Literaries conjured up about him. Puppet? You mean slave!"

Rump nodded and said, "If what the princess tells us is true, then it appears that he's become a slave once again. But with our combined effort, we may be able to rescue him."

"In due time, Lord Rumpelstiltskin," said the princess. "First, we need to give Dodger his weapons." Tinkerbell reached behind her throne and revealed three items; an old-fashioned hunting rifle, a brown leather satchel, and a long dagger encased in a sheath.

Dodger's Doorway

Presenting these items to Dodger, the princess said, "Once upon a time, long before Neverland existed, there was a woman named Blanchette who enjoyed traveling through Neverwood Forest in her red hood and cape. One day, in the middle of her afternoon stroll, she encountered a ferocious wolf that almost devoured her. A young hunter stepped into the clearing, shot the wolf, and stabbed it in the heart. The hunter and Blanchette eventually wed and built the kingdom of Neverland together. These weapons I present to you are the Hunter's Rifle and the Hunter's Dagger, which once belonged to my father, Sir Gabriel, King of Neverland."

Dodger eyed the gun, taking in its dark brown wooden design and sleek metal barrel. He then looked up at the banner of the royal family and noticed how it was the same weapon held in the king's hand. The royal crest imprinted behind the family and the image of the wolf's head finally made sense. As Dodger's sight wandered to the queen's red hood, his mind began reeling again.

"Where-" he began, but Humpty interrupted him.

"- is the witch's cottage? My memory does not serve me well."

"You will take the main trail into the forest. When you reach a thick tree that forks into four branches stripped of their wood, you will leave the path and travel north into the brush. Lord Rumpelstiltskin, you should be able to detect her magic after an hour of walking. And please be careful. You two remember the tales saying how enticing her charm can be. I advise you to brief Dodger on these details prior to your adventure. Also, be wary of the rest of the forest as well, for I heard talk of Robin the Thief robbing travelers again."

"I don't think we'll need to worry about him anymore, Princess," said Rump with a giggle.

"Then be on your way. Sir Humpty, if I may, I would like to talk to you in private, please."

Rump and Dodger exited the chamber. Dodger glanced back and saw Humpty with his head bowed, listening to the princess. When the door slammed shut behind them, the Literary prodded Rump's shoulder.

"I have questions again."

"Feel free to ask, my friend."

"Where is everyone? Peter Pan's missing, and so is the Hunter, and Red Riding Hood."

"Red who?" asked Rump.

"I meant the queen. I was gonna ask Princess Tinkerbell where she was, but then Humpty jumped in and-"

"The queen passed away many years ago," Rump said with a frown.

Dodger sighed and scolded himself. *Great. Haven't been here for a day and I'm already a jerk.* "What happened?"

"It is a sad tale." Rump leaned against a pillar and fiddled with his fingers as he told the story. "Long ago, a war erupted between Neverland and the pirates of a distant island nation known as Barbaria. This was when Neverland was still a growing kingdom in its early days, yet our people were fierce and strong. King Gabriel commanded the troops in battle, with Humpty, Pinocchio, and myself right beside him. The war became so intense that we had to enlist the help of soldiers from other provinces as well, including a young man named Peter Pan and his Literary. Interestingly enough, amidst the war going on, Peter found love with Neverland's Princess Tinkerbell, We held a quiet marriage ceremony for them during a break in the fighting."

Rump smiled, but this expression quickly disappeared. When he spoke again, his voice was quivering and Dodger noticed his hands were also shaking.

"The leader of the pirates was a madman called Captain Hook. He was a vile creature whose image could strike fear into the hearts of the bravest warriors. Eight feet tall, blood-red eyes, and a voice that could strike fear into the heart of the bravest man; he was the definition of a monster.

"During one of the battles, Hook encountered Peter Pan within the very throne room you just saw. They dueled for a long time, until Hook gained the upper hand and killed the prince."

"Whoa." Dodger felt the color drain out of his face. This was nothing like the fairy tales he had heard as a child.

"It was horrible," Rump went on. "Many great soldiers were slain in those days, such as the Hatter, and my apprentice, Jack Frost."

"I'm sorry to hear that," Dodger said.

Rump nodded. "He was a powerful sorcerer, that Jack Frost. I took him under my wing after he demonstrated his unique ability to conjure ice with his bare hands, a remarkable feat that usually requires a wand or a potion of sorts. Jack was going to replace me as head of the Neverland Science Arm when I passed on. He was like a son to me. Unfortunately, he wasn't as strong as he thought and died at the hands of the pirates in one of the final battles."

An uncomfortable feeling struck Dodger. He empathized with Rump for losing such a close companion, but the pain hitting the Literary was different. It was like he was at the battle and had actually witnessed the fall of Jack Frost and other Neverland soldiers defending the kingdom. Dodger felt chills go up his spine and tried to shake this unpleasant feeling away, whatever it was. He attempted to steer the conversation away from painful memories.

"So, how did the war end?"

"It was a climactic confrontation," said Rump, wiping a tear away with his finger. "King Gabriel sent for help to our allies in Wonderland, and Queen Alice responded by supplying us with reinforcements in the form of a thousand card soldiers. And they came at the best possible time because our army was almost eradicated.

"The last battle was held in Neverland Bay, where the pirates had landed their ships. After another three days of fighting, Captain Hook ordered a retreat. His army of pirates hoisted their anchors and took off. There's been no sign of them since."

"Then you won the war! That's a good thing, right? And you all lived happily ever after?" said Dodger.

"Happily? Not entirely. Hook is still out there, biding his time and probably planning a new assault. And the war took a heavy toll on our kingdom. We lost many great people, including King Gabriel."

"What?" asked Dodger in shock.

"Yes. Our leader was gone. Queen Blanchette died from mourning soon after. Neverland was left without leadership or a standing army after the war. Princess Tinkerbell was the only semblance of authority in the kingdom; however, royal protocol dictates that a prince and princess must claim the thrones at the same time if they wish to ascend to king and queen. Therefore, Tinkerbell can only become the official queen if she finds a king to rule beside her. Unfortunately, she seems too distracted nowadays to be concerned about being wed or overseeing an entire kingdom. She spends her days pondering and daydreaming. I believe it is how she mourns...

"To this day, we Neverlanders attempt to move on with our lives, trying to recollect our society and piece together what we have left. With your help, we can move one step closer to bringing Neverland back to its former glory."

"How's that?" asked Dodger.

"Saving Pinocchio is the first step. He went missing right after Queen Blanchette passed away. We believe he went searching-"

The door to the chamber creaked open and out stepped Humpty, holding the rifle, the satchel, and the dagger. "You forgot these, Dodger. Do you happen to know how to use a firearm?"

"Not exactly," said Dodger, taking the rifle. It was awkward and heavy. "I can probably figure out how this thing works. It's not loaded yet, is it?"

Dodger's finger played near the trigger. There was an ear-shattering explosion, and a chunk of the pillar that Rump was leaning against was blown away. The area was filled with a faint gray smoke and the strong smell of gunpowder. Dodger had closed his eyes tightly and was holding the gun gingerly away from his body. Rump, who leapt out of the way just in time, was on the ground with his hands over his ears. He attempted to hold back a snicker.

"Yes, it was loaded!" said an angry Humpty, flailing his arms in the air. "Please refrain from wasting anymore ammunition!" The egg-man shook the satchel dangling from his hand. "There should be roughly twenty more shots left in here. I will reload the gun for you later and teach you how to properly use it in the morning."

"Morning?" asked Dodger. "I thought we were heading into the forest to see the Forever Witch?"

Rump's looked extremely surprised. "What? Now? I don't know about you, Dodger, but in Storyworld, we sleep at nightfall. You can't expect us to go wandering in the forest at this hour!"

"We sleep at night, too!" Dodger said defensively. "But why was Humpty rushing us this whole time? I thought we had to go right away!"

"The earlier we go to bed, the earlier we get to rise," quoted Humpty. "Once we are rested up, we can have you trained in basic combat. Then we can set off first thing in the morning. You can sleep in Pinocchio's bed in our living quarters."

"I'll make my way to my own tower," said Rump, yawning. "I shall see you both at sunrise."

Dodger's Doorway

Humpty and Pinocchio shared a room at the top of one of the tallest towers of Neverland Castle. Dodger followed Humpty up a spiral stone staircase and across a small landing, eventually coming to a tall wooden door. Humpty opened the door, revealing a wide bedroom that was apparently split right down the center, each side accommodating either inhabitant. On one side of the room was a hammock strung up between two pillars, a short brown dresser pressed against the wall, and shelves upon shelves covered in knick-knacks and odd gadgets. Discarded clothes were strewn across the floor, and there was an open window beside the hammock.

On the other side of the room, there was a long wooden table set close to the ground and two closed barrels pushed up against the wall, right underneath a second window. The wall closest to the doorway was covered in various weapons, from swords to crossbows to huge battle-axes.

Humpty unbuckled his belt, took off his shoes, and climbed into the hammock, its netting perfectly cradling his ovular body. Dodger scratched his head, gazing around the room for Pinocchio's bed, but saw nothing to accommodate him.

"Hey, Humpty?"

"Yes?" replied the egg-man, his eyes closed and his arms dangling over the sides of his hammock.

"Where's my bed?"

"Right in front of you."

Dodger blinked. "All I see is a table."

"That is your bed for the night."

A realization hit Dodger as he stared at the table. Pinocchio was made out of wood, so why would he need a regular bed with sheets and pillows like a human? "Great," he muttered.

"Be grateful!" called out Humpty. "Many Literaries never even had a bed when Pinocchio was still here. Sir Emerson had to sleep on the ground, if he ever did sleep. That poor fellow was never right in the head. He stayed awake for hours every night, talking in strange quotes and other nonsense." Humpty's voice trailed off as he immediately fell into a deep sleep and began snoring.

Dodger didn't have the same luck. It was one of the most exhausting days of his life, both physically and mentally, and he would have loved nothing more than to just pass out right away, but his body was not having it. He did all he could to get comfortable on the wooden bed, including taking off his shirt and balling it up into a makeshift pillow so that his neck and head could be cushioned. After what felt like an eternity of tossing and wincing, he fell asleep.

Somehow, Dodger found himself running through the forest again, except this time, Humpty and Rump weren't accompanying him. He was alone. The forest was dark, but he could still sense where he was going. Behind him, Dodger could hear someone yelling and jeering in a voice that sounded like his father's. When he turned his head, he saw a dark figure chasing him with the Hunter's Rifle in its hand. Dodger tripped and fell on his face. Rolling onto his back, he looked up at his pursuer, who was feet away from him, with their face covered under the shadow of a dark hood. Was it Robin Hood? The figure pointed the gun at Dodger's heart and squeezed the trigger.

"No!"

Dodger shook himself awake and sat straight up. An incredible pain went up his back, as if he had been shot. He scanned his surroundings and saw that he was still in Humpty and Pinocchio's bedroom, but the hammock was now unoccupied. The early morning sun peeked in through the two windows and lit up the room with an orange-pink light.

As Dodger motioned to get off the bed, he felt the stinging pain in his back again. It felt like knives were repeatedly jabbing him in the spine with each movement, then he remembered that he had just slept for hours on a solid wooden platform. He sat almost motionless, slowly stretching his shoulders and back to loosen his body. Humpty entered moments later, carrying a platter of fruits and vegetables. On the corner of the platter was a bottle filled with a green liquid.

"Good morning! I assume you slept terribly!" said the egg-man. Dodger glared at Humpty while attempting to work the knot out of his back. Humpty giggled nervously and continued talking. "Er, yes, my apologies. Drink this." He held up the bottle of green liquid. "You will soon feel as nimble as a cat."

Dodger winced as he reached out for the bottle. Popping the cork top off, he sipped from it; it tasted like a lemon-lime effervescent that fizzled and crackled down his throat. Almost instantly, the pain was gone, leaving Dodger staring at the bottle in amazement.

"Whoa!"

"Courtesy of Neverland's alchemy lab," said Rump, who had entered the room. "That's one of my finer potions. The Literaries love it."

"Here's a better idea, though," added Dodger, pocketing the potion and grabbing an apple off the food tray. "Why don't you guys build a guest room for your visitors instead of making them sleep on the floor or on a table? I guarantee they'll appreciate it more than this potion."

"Well, we've been working on that," admitted Rump, "but things tend to arise and we've never had the chance to actually build any spare sleeping quarters. Had I known you were uncomfortable, I would've given you one of my sleeping potions."

"Thanks for that," mumbled Dodger, biting into his apple. "Where exactly in the forest do we need to go?"

Munching on a carrot, Rump explained, "The princess said that we have to head into the middle of the forest. When we reach a tree forked into four thick branches, we take a detour north until we arrive at the cottage. I should be able to detect her magic once we're close by. Shouldn't take us more than a couple of hours."

"Hopefully it won't even take us that long," added Humpty, checking his watch. "We still have to get the Literary into weapons training before stepping foot into the Neverwood."

"Sounds like a plan," replied Dodger, finishing his meal and grabbing his equipment. "Let's go."

Chapter 4

Witches and Warriors

Humpty led Dodger to the main throne chamber and spent the whole morning instructing him on how to properly fight with his new weapons. Dodger, who had never even been in a fistfight before, found himself hesitant when it came to using the Hunter's Dagger in combat. The blade was a short, sleek piece of steel ending in a freshly sharpened point. A large metal bobble sprouted at the bottom of the hilt acting as a counterbalance, but Dodger still had trouble properly handling the dagger at first. It looked so much easier in the movies.

Humpty demonstrated how to parry and block, and how to go on the offensive. There was little time to train, so Dodger did his best to cram as much information into the session as he could. According to the egg-man, the key was to keep moving; he pressed this point over and over again until it was drilled into the Literary's brain.

Things quickly changed throughout the practice session. With each swing and swipe of the blade, Dodger felt himself getting more confident and assured in his own ability. Even Humpty noted how quickly he had developed an uncanny expertise and comfort with the dagger. He said that previous Literary wielders would often spend hours just learning how to unsheathe the blade without cutting themselves.

The Hunter's Rifle presented more of a challenge. For being such an old weapon, it felt sturdy and strong. It was heavier than Dodger expected, making it difficult to hold and aim. Humpty offered tips on the best way to leverage it into a proper position to get the best accuracy.

Dodger was also taught how to reload, aim, and anticipate the harsh recoil for when the gun was fired. Due to the low amount of ammunition, he didn't have the opportunity to practice with live rounds. He could only hope that he wouldn't have to resort to using the gun, and if he did, he prayed that it wouldn't be too much for him to handle. Humpty's constant reassurance did little to settle his anxiety.

Rump arrived in the throne chamber around noon, informing Humpty and Dodger that it was time to begin their adventure. The alchemist had donned the same thick brown belt of vials and potion bottles from the previous day, but there were now even more multicolored concoctions at his disposal. Dangling from the side of his belt was a tarnished silver mace topped with a thick, star-shaped head.

Dodger slung the Hunter's Rifle across his back and carried the ammunition satchel over his shoulder. Rump gave the Literary a magical sheath to hold the Hunter's Dagger. This sheath, which would be strapped around the inside of Dodger's shin and concealed beneath his pant leg, was enchanted by the alchemist to contain the entire length of the dagger's blade, even though the sheath itself was half its size.

Humpty directed the group out of Neverland Castle after bidding farewell to John Tell and the sentries. The egg-man didn't take any armor or additional gear for the mission except for a second, smaller sword tucked into his belt to complement his longer blade.

Dodger's Doorway

The trio entered Neverwood Forest, returning to the same dirt path that they had followed the day before. It was a rather humid day, and the thick foliage covering the trees didn't help. Rather than providing refreshing shade, the treetops seemed to trap the heat within the forest, and Dodger was sweating profusely within minutes.

Rump pointed out the tree where they were supposed to leave the path. Dodger was surprised that he didn't notice it the previous day. The trunk was so gnarled that the bark resembled thousands of intertwining and intersecting brown veins with an occasional thick root wrapping across the way. A few feet up from the ground, the tree forked off into four branches sprawling in various directions, with two of these limbs dipping over the main path. Rump steered his companions off the path.

The journey into the brush was infinitely worse. Humpty was swiping and slicing through the leaves and vines with his sword, but poor Dodger was still susceptible to the higher hanging branches and leaves that slapped him in the face and shoulders as he walked by. Each step made him more miserable as he was scratched and scraped by the vegetation. He was just about to voice his frustration when Rump spoke up.

"I feel it," murmured the alchemist. "We're really, really close. Blah, her magic leaves a bad taste in my mouth. It's like smelling a festering carcass."

Rump indicated which way to go, and Humpty resumed his carving through the forest. Minutes later, the foliage started thinning out. The branches and trees became skinnier and less invasive, until the trio arrived at the edge of a wide, circular clearing. In the center of this clearing was an old, wooden, one-story cottage. The windows that stood on either side of the decaying wooden door were boarded up by rotting planks of moldy brown lumber. The triangular roof had gaping holes here and there that looked as though they were created from heavy objects that had fallen from the sky. The house gave off an eerie vibe that made Dodger shiver.

"There it is, fellows," muttered Humpty. "The home of the Forever Witch."

"What does she do?" asked Dodger. "Like, does she fly around at night, transforming people into beavers and stuff?"

Rump snorted. "Do Literaries find that threatening? That's something I'd have done as a prank in my youth. No, the Forever Witch is a sinister being; a cannibal and a seductress with a craving for lost and wandering travelers."

Dodger shivered again. "If that's true, why can't you kick her out of the forest like you did with Robin?"

"It is a matter of politics," explained Humpty. "Robin ambushed us within yards of Neverland Castle's entrance, so he was within our jurisdiction. The Forever Witch lives right outside our borders and therefore outside our rule. Though her legendary reputation precedes her, we cannot force her from her home unless we were to witness the crime. It is all politics."

Dodger looked out at the clearing. "How do you know this lady even has Pinocchio as her prisoner?"

Rump shrugged. "It's possible that the Forever Witch may not have him at all and we wasted our time coming out here. But we have to explore all possibilities."

"How are we gonna do this, then?" queried Dodger.

"We need to be tactical about this," replied Humpty. "Rump and I shall sneak in while you provide a distraction."

"Whoa, wait a minute!" Dodger took a step back. "Where did that come from? Why do I have to be a distraction? You call that tactical?"

"She may recognize me or Rump as Neverland officials. You will have to pretend to be a traveler and let her invite you into her home."

"Are you kidding me? I'm not risking my life to save some puppet!"

"Do not call him that!" said Humpty with a scowl.

"I'll say whatever I-"

"Quit your bickering!" Rump hissed. "Here, take this, Dodger." He handed the Literary a vial of white potion from his belt. "If you think you're in danger, throw this bottle to the ground and run. It'll assist with your escape."

Dodger shook his head, suddenly feeling nauseous. He couldn't tell if his sweat was coming from the humidity or his anxiety. "No, guys, I can't do this! I'm a kid. I shouldn't even be here. I don't want to get eaten!"

"You are a Literary!" barked Humpty. "You must learn to be brave like your predecessors! They were scared as well, but they overcame their fears when they needed to!"

"I'm not like them! What part of 'I'm a kid' don't you understand? I'm not supposed to fight a witch or whatever is in there!"

Humpty sighed. Rump looked into Dodger's eyes and uttered, "Listen here, Dodger. You are armed with the arsenal of one of Neverland's greatest warriors. In addition to this, you have an expert swordsman and an alchemist accompanying you. You will be fine. You may be here to help us, but we're also here to protect you. There is little to worry about. Please, trust us."

Dodger looked at his hosts, petrified. Prior to setting off on the quest, Dodger believed that he would have a slight edge due to his fair knowledge of fairy tales and folklore, but now he felt at a disadvantage because he couldn't think of what story contained the Forever Witch and what her weakness could possibly be.

"So," said Rump after a moment of tedious silence, "will you rise to the challenge and help us with our mission?"

Dodger hesitated, biting his lip. Swallowing the ball of anxiety in his throat, he shrugged and nodded. Rump clapped his hands together excitedly as Humpty smiled.

"Excellent!" said the alchemist. "All right, Dodger, here's the plan. You'll go up and knock on the cottage door. When the witch invites you in, tell her that you were traveling through the Neverwood and got lost. Say you wandered off the path in search of water or something of the like. She hopefully won't press you with questions. It's rumored that she attempts to poison her victims before she attacks them. Therefore, and I cannot stress this enough, it's crucial that you don't eat or drink anything she offers you!"

Dodger nodded again without a word. He had begun shaking. Taking one last look at his escorts, faintly hoping that they would stop him, he sighed and slunk into the clearing.

A cool breeze entered from the opening of the treetops and swept through the area, providing a moment of refreshment for Dodger's sweating brow. Slowly, he approached the cottage, trying to delay the encounter as much as possible, but it wasn't long until he was standing in front of the decaying door and rapping his knuckles against the rotted wood. It was so decrepit and old that the Literary's knuckles left indentations in the door when he knocked. He cringed at the thought of what kind of being could possibly live in this cottage.

It took a couple of seconds for someone to answer. As the door swung open, Dodger's jaw dropped. Standing in the doorway was one of the most attractive women he'd ever seen. She was his height, with curly brunette hair, green eyes, and large pink lips curled into a deep smile. She wore a short black dress that left little to the imagination, making Dodger's heart beat faster. Was this really supposed to be the fierce and dangerous Forever Witch?

"Hello, there," she said, leaning against the doorframe and cocking her head to the side. "Are you lost?"

"Yes," was all that Dodger could say in his trance.

"How about you come in and I can help you?" she replied in a seductive tone, grabbing him by the bottom of his shirt and dragging him inside.

The mission was wiped from Dodger's mind. He stepped into the Forever Witch's cottage and heard her lock the door behind him, but he hardly registered it. He was too busy marveling at the inside of the cottage. Compared to its shoddy, disgusting exterior, the inside was immaculate. It was a quaint little residence with compact rooms and few furniture and knick-knacks.

The Forever Witch ushered Dodger into the kitchen where she made him take the rifle off his back and sit in a rickety wooden chair. "You must be parched," she said, setting a glass pitcher down on the table. "Would you like a drink?" Dodger didn't have a chance to answer, as she was already pouring a glass of yellow-orange liquid. "Fresh, ice-cold orange juice from this morning."

"I am pretty thirsty," said Dodger, which was true. The trip through the humid forest had left a dried, burning feeling in his throat, and he knew that his face was still coated in sweat. He felt slightly embarrassed.

Wiping his forehead, Dodger picked up the glass of juice and raised it to his lips, when he suddenly remembered the warning that he received from Rump about how the Forever Witch poisoned her victims. This cautionary advice struck the Literary like lightning, causing him to jerk the glass away from his mouth and spill half of the orange juice all over his pants and chair.

"Oh, my!" said the witch, not missing a beat. "That's a shame! You got it all over your clothes!"

"It's fine," Dodger said, setting the glass down. He started wiping off his jeans, but the witch smacked his hand away.

"No, no, no, you can't leave with that mess on you!"

"It's fine," repeated Dodger. "I should get going, though."

He stood up only for the witch to push him back down into his seat. She climbed on top of him, pinning him down, and began applying what looked like lip gloss from a pink vial, all while smiling at Dodger.

"You know, it gets so lonely in the woods. I haven't been with a man in ages."

"I'm not even a man, to tell you the truth," Dodger stammered. "I turn eighteen in like three months, so this can't be legal. I don't want you to get into trouble so maybe I should leave."

"No! Don't leave! I promise it'll be worth it!" The Forever Witch put a finger to Dodger's lips to silence him. Then she closed her eyes and leaned forward. Dodger panicked and reached for his belt. His fingers wrapped around the potion that Rump had given him for protection, but they also latched onto the green potion he was given that morning to heal his back pain. Dodger swung both of the vials around and smashed them across the witch's face.

A cloud of green smoke engulfed the witch. She hopped off Dodger, screaming in a high, abnormal tone. The vial of lip gloss she was holding smashed to the ground and sizzled through the floorboard like acid. Dodger was knocked onto his back, but immediately scrambled to his feet, grabbing his rifle and staring into the smoke. At that exact moment, Rump and Humpty appeared through a door across the hallway, followed by a young-looking couple.

Dodger's Doorway

The man was tall and buff, his enormous structure fitting the doorframe. He had blond hair shorn down to a buzz cut and a wide, wrinkled forehead. Covering his body was a shroud of chainmail atop a sleeveless black scale suit.

Standing by his side was a woman who also had blonde hair tied in a ponytail draped over her shoulder. She was much shorter than her male counterpart and wore a similar black scale suit, chainmail sleeves, a purple corset, and purple boots. A dagger's hilt poked out of the cleft in her boot.

Rump gazed at Dodger who was standing awkwardly with the rifle sprawled across his arms and the front of his jeans still doused with orange juice.

"Erm, did we interrupt something?" asked the alchemist, smiling.

"Whoa! No way!" said Dodger. "Listen, she came onto me!"

Rump struggled to hide his smile. "Well, we did say that the Forever Witch is a seductress but- LOOK OUT!"

Something came staggering out of the green smoke cloud. It was the witch, except she had now transformed into a stringy, fanged creature covered in sores and scars. Claws had sprouted from her fingertips and there were horns popping out in random spots all across her face and limbs. Her bare feet had transformed into bird-like talons with razor sharp edges.

"You fffffffilthy animal!" shrieked the Forever Witch, lunging at Dodger with her claws outstretched.

A cabinet came flying through the air, colliding with the witch's head and sending her body into the wall. Dodger watched as the man wearing the chainmail wrenched the kitchen door out of its frame with his bare hands and broke it into two halves as easily as if it was made of plaster. He flung the pieces at the witch, the splintering shards piercing her and pinning her against the woodwork, finally killing her.

There was brief, stunning quietness that filled the room. All that was heard was Dodger's panting and the man in the chainmail's knuckles cracking. Rump went to touch the remains of the witch, and the corpse dissolved into a pile of glittering dust.

"Well done!" exclaimed the alchemist. "Good throw, Stronghand! Mission completed!"

"Mission completed?" Dodger repeated as he rose. "What the hell just happened?"

"Dodger," said Humpty, tuning out Dodger's frustration, "meet Agent Hansel, the Stronghand, and his sister, Agent Gretel."

Dodger exploded. "Oh, that's great! So good! How did you two get here? Wait, let me guess; something ate your trail of breadcrumbs and you two got lost on your way to the house made of candy?" His anger and frustration could not be contained. He didn't care how rude he sounded. All he could think about was how close he was to becoming the Forever Witch's next victim.

Humpty placed his face in his hands and waddled into the hallway. Hansel and Gretel exchanged dubious looks.

"This is your Literary? He's acting like a child!" stated Hansel.

"No, I'm acting like someone who almost got poisoned and eaten. How about you go through that and we see how you react? And where's Pinocchio? Wasn't this whole thing about saving him?"

"He's not here," said Humpty, strolling back into view.

Dodger was beside himself. "That's just great!" He threw the rifle over his shoulder, kicked open the front door, and stormed out of the house, fuming from his ears.

"Wait!" Rump bolted out the door after him with Humpty, Hansel, and Gretel at his heels. "I'm sorry," the alchemist said in a sincere tone. "I'll admit that may have been a bit overwhelming for your first quest."

"You think? You guys used me as bait!"

"You weren't bait! I promise you! We knew you'd be able to handle the situation, and you did a great job, I might add!"

Dodger was slightly flattered by the comment. Looking past the alchemist, he saw everyone else staring at him. Gretel had a tiny grin and it seemed like there was almost a twinkle in her eye.

Rump continued. "I assure you that we'll charge into any confrontation at your side next time. No more splitting up. You have my word on this."

Dodger let himself calm down. There was still some anger coursing through his veins, but the second that he caught Gretel's eyes, he felt much more relaxed. Crossing his arms, he said, "Fine. What do we do now?"

"There we go!" said Rump, clapping his hands together. "Onward we go to our next destination: Geppetto's house!"

Instead of returning to the main path, Hansel informed the Neverlanders that they would have to head deeper into the brush in order to reach Geppetto's home. Soon enough, they were out of sight of the Forever Witch's cottage and making their way toward the heart of Neverwood Forest as the sun crawled higher into the sky.

"So, Agents, tell us how you happened upon the Forever Witch's hospitality," said Rump.

"We were on our way to meet up with you two," replied Hansel. He had a gruff tone that sounded like a dog barking every time he spoke. "Queen Alice sent us to join your escort. Word has swept across the land about how there was a Literary in your midst. On our way to Neverland, we must've taken a wrong turn and ended up at the witch's house."

"And *I* suggested," interrupted Gretel, "that we turn around and head back the way we came. My oaf of a brother thought of the brilliant idea to ask her if she had seen any Literaries lately. Don't let the Forever Witch's appearance fool you," Gretel said to Dodger, "she subdued us with little hassle."

"Did she happen to mention anything about Captain Hook of Barbaria?" asked Humpty, his eyes narrowed. "There are rumors circulating of him stirring up activity in the area once more. It has been a long time since the region was this restless."

"No," Hansel said. "The witch was most likely just another typical nuisance you find in the wild lands. I doubt she's working for anyone in particular.

But we should warn you, there're many people out there who've heard about the Literary's arrival. Wonderland caught word after one night. Rumor has it that there's a bounty on his head, so it's best if we accompany you for additional protection."

"Great," Dodger said sarcastically. "I love having people try to kill me. It's just awesome."

Rump smiled at the agents. "See? The Literary has bravery that's only surpassed by his strange attire. Quite extraordinary."

"What does that even mean?" said Dodger, not wanting to explain the concept of sarcasm. He was tired from walking and his throat was still bone-dry. Rump had stopped the Literary from going back into the Forever Witch's house to grab a drink, claiming that anything in the kitchen could be spiked with poison. "How far away is Geppetto's house? I'm exhausted."

"Will you stop complaining?" said Hansel. "Honestly, how are you a Literary? Is this a joke?" The agent swiveled his head to Humpty. "I don't feel safe with someone like him leading us on this quest."

"Shut up, Hansel," replied Dodger in an irritated tone, pushing past the agent. "I'm pretty sure we were the ones who saved your life back there. And nobody is telling you to come with us. We can probably handle ourselves just fine. What kind of agent are you if you can't even-"

Dodger's words trailed off as he heard rustling behind him. Spinning around, he found Hansel towering over him by at least two feet. Dodger's petrified gaze was locked onto Hansel's, but he could see the agent's fingers flexing out of the corner of his eye.

"Are you sure you want to finish that statement, young man?" said Hansel.

The whole group had stopped to stare. Dodger fumbled for words, taken off guard by Hansel's short temper, and he couldn't think of anything to say. The Literary maintained eye contact with the agent for as long as he could, fighting against the violent shaking building up in his knees and crawling up his body. Eventually, he lowered his head and backed up several steps.

"No," he muttered.

Hansel sneered at Dodger and continued on through the trees without a look back. Humpty and Rump frowned at each other and followed the agent. Gretel stayed behind and approached the Literary, putting her hand on his shoulder.

"I'm sorry about my brother. His temper can get out of hand sometimes."

"It's okay," mumbled Dodger. Tucking his hands into his pockets, he kept his eyes on the ground and wandered off after the rest of the group, Gretel striding beside him.

Dodger and Gretel soon caught up with the others. Hansel was strolling through the vegetation with ease, tearing vines away and snapping branches that blocked his path. Humpty and Rump were right behind him, pressing the agent for more information regarding General Pinocchio's whereabouts.

"We only glimpsed him," said Hansel. "As soon as we arrived at the Forever Witch's cottage, Geppetto came by and took him away. We watched it from the bars of our cell."

"What kind of affiliation did Geppetto and the witch have?" asked Humpty.

"They were lovers, believe it or not," said Hansel, shaking his head in disgust. "A beautiful couple, don't you agree?"

"I've seen worse," added Rump with a chuckle.

"Where exactly can we find Geppetto's house?" asked Humpty.

"He lives in another cottage at the other edge of the forest," piped up Gretel. "I heard him and the witch arguing about how they rarely get to see each other anymore because of their distance. I'm familiar with the route that Geppetto mentioned. We have a bit of a walk ahead of us."

"Let us hurry our pace then," recommended Humpty.

"I still don't see why we need to bring the child," said Hansel out of the blue. Everyone stared at him. "Geppetto is an engineer, not a beast that needs slaying. Surely us four could subdue him without having to drag the Literary along with us. He'd just get in the way."

Dodger scowled at Hansel, wondering why the agent was instigating with him. This situation reminded him of his experiences with Ryan Martin back in his own world.

"You know as well as we do, Agent," said Rump, "that Literaries only appear in Storyworld when they're needed most. Dodger is here for a reason, and he must partake in any missions along with us, no matter how dangerous or how benign."

"But he can't even fight!" Hansel pressed. "Are you planning on using him for bait again?"

"I wasn't bait!" said Dodger, growing redder by the second.

"Oh, really? And I'm assuming you were having a deadly match with the Forever Witch while she was holding you down in that chair. You showed great courage, by the way, when she lunged at you and you merely stood there. A true hero in the making, you are!" Hansel smirked.

Dodger opened his mouth to argue once more, but this time, it was Humpty who cut him off. "This is coming from the man who spent the night imprisoned in the witch's cellar," said the egg-man fiercely. "You may be one of the Stronghands, Agent Hansel, but you have no right to tell anybody off or mock them for their lack of heroism. Now leave the Literary alone!"

Hansel looked like he had just swallowed something bitter. Gretel quickly stepped in front of her brother and spoke.

"The path goes on this way."

Humpty smiled politely at Gretel, and then began cleaving through the vines and branches. The young woman shot a glare at her brother before following the egg-man.

"Come along!" Humpty yelled back to the rest of the troop.

"You don't expect us to walk the entire way to Geppetto's house, do you?" spat Hansel.

Humpty didn't answer. His ovular shape shrunk smaller and smaller as he cut into the forest with Gretel by his side.

"Apparently, he does!" Rump said loudly, pulling Dodger with him down the forest path.

Chapter 5

The Bridge

The quintet traveled for hours. Humpty and Rump had engaged in a deep conversation, reminiscing about their past adventures with previous Literaries. Hansel remained in a bad mood throughout the journey, trudging along at the back of the group with his eyes darting around at the surrounding trees as if he was expecting someone to jump out at any minute. Dodger had begun a conversation with Gretel, who showed a fascination with the world of Literaries. She asked him all about his realm, explaining how it had been so long since she and her brother had hosted their own Literary, so Dodger regaled her with details about high school, video games, reading, and his other interests. He made sure to leave out the parts concerning his parents' verbal abuse and Ryan's bullying.

"So, you hold this black wand on a rope," said Gretel in a curious tone.

"Yeah, it's called a controller," replied Dodger.

"Right, and it's called that because you control someone else's actions?"

"Well, the person you control doesn't exist. It's just a character in a video game. They're not real."

"That still baffles me about these video games. You keep mentioning how, in your world, people take on the actions of other characters and see entertainment in it?"

Dodger shrugged. "Yeah, pretty much."

"But why would anyone want to be someone else? I feel like it's a waste of your own life."

"See, the thing about videos games is that we can do things we can't normally do in our own world. Like in this one game, *Spider-Man*, you play this superhero who swings across the city, beating up villains and saving people."

"And you can't do this in your own world?" asked Gretel.

"What, swing across the city?"

"No, be a hero."

This response caught Dodger off-guard. He saw Gretel smiling at him, waiting for his response, but all he could do was shrug and keep walking while his cheeks burned a fierce red.

The group hardly spoke over the next hour. They passed by a flowing stream that Rump indicated was safe to drink from, and decided to take a short break.

After gorging on water, they kept walking. Dodger's legs were aching, yet he refused to complain for fear of Hansel's backlash. The adventurers shambled past more trees and bushes as the day drew out. The forest had cooled down and Dodger was thankful for the huge drop in the humidity. He closed his eyes to take a deep refreshing breath and bumped into Rump, who had stopped in his tracks.

"Ouch, Rump! What gives?"

"Sorry, Dodger," said the alchemist, "but we have a little problem."

Rump pointed to the path ahead, where Humpty stood with his hands on his hips and his left foot tapping impatiently. It looked like the egg-man had paused at the edge of the forest; there was nothing but a line of thin, leafless trees marking the border. Dodger walked up the hill and saw why they had stopped.

The forest hadn't ended; it was just split into two halves by an enormous canyon that sliced through the ground. Dodger and his companions were standing on the edge of one of the cliffs, next to a chasm with a seemingly endless drop into a dark abyss. About a half-mile away, on the other side of the chasm, stood the other cliff and the line of trees marking the other half of Neverwood Forest. Rump, Gretel, and Hansel approached the cliff.

Rump sighed and glanced at Humpty. "I was afraid we'd come across this. I just hoped we'd find Geppetto's house before now." The alchemist turned to Gretel. "Did you know this was here?"

"I wasn't aware of which direction we'd be coming from," said the agent. "I thought we'd miss the canyon altogether."

"What do we do from here?" asked Hansel.

"Obviously, we need to cross," said Humpty with a scoff.

"And how do you suppose we do that?" Hansel replied through gritted teeth.

"We could go around?" said Dodger.

"Don't be stupid, child," chided Hansel. "This is the Brobdingnagians' Door, a fault-line in the ground that reaches for miles. There's no telling where it will end. It'd take us ages to go around it, and Sir Humpty feels the need to remind us that we're on a tight schedule."

"I didn't know that," Dodger muttered. "Maybe there's a way we can cross?"

"Indeed there is!" said Rump. The alchemist pointed down the edge of the cliff. There was a long rope bridge, similar to the kind that Dodger had seen in countless adventure films. The tattered ropes that made the handles looked worn and frayed, and a few of the wooden planks that composed the footpath were missing or cracked down the middle. Just looking at the bridge made Dodger anxious. There was no way it could be safe. Even as he looked at it, he noticed how a light breeze made it sway and creek ominously.

"Is-is there another way across?" asked the Literary, fidgeting with his lip piercing.

"I think not," said Humpty, waddling over to the two posts that marked the bridge's entrance. These posts were roughly the egg-man's height and supported the ropes that suspended the bridge. Humpty grabbed one of the posts and pulled on it, nodding when it didn't move. He then grabbed one of the rope handles and gave it a sharp tug. With a swift nod, he stepped onto the first wooden plank of the bridge.

"Wait!" called out Dodger.

Humpty paid no attention to the Literary and took out his sword. He prodded the next board with the tip of his blade and advanced one more step.

"What is it?" asked the egg-man, poking the board in front of him with his sword.

"Shouldn't we all cross together?" asked Gretel. It was apparent that she was just as worried as Dodger about the stability of the bridge. Hansel also looked nervous as he gaped at the far cliff. Another breeze had rolled in and caused the bridge to rattle and quake.

"That is a bad idea, Agent," replied Humpty. "This bridge is very old and we can't rely on it to support all of us at once." He stepped onto another board and began hopping up and down. "We can walk across two at a time. Except for you, Stronghand." He nodded at Hansel. "You'll have to cross alone. Agent Gretel, I want you to cross with me first. Agent Hansel can come next. Rump, you will escort Dodger."

"Absolutely, my good egg," agreed the alchemist.

Gretel slowly stuck her foot out and stepped onto the bridge as the others watched. Humpty guided her across, poking and prodding each board ahead of him with his sword to ensure that it would remain intact. The agent stayed close behind, her knuckles clenched onto the rope handles. At one point, a plank splintered apart at Humpty's touch and broke off of the bridge. The pieces of wood whistled down into the dark canyon and disappeared from sight. Dodger thought he heard a distant echo of the board cracking against the ground far below. What did he get himself into?

After fifteen grueling minutes, Gretel and Humpty reached the other side of the bridge. Dodger smiled as Gretel leapt onto the grassy turf and glanced back at the swaying bridge. Humpty hopped off the last plank and gave the two wooden support beams several hard tugs. The egg-man waved his hand in a beckoning motion, indicating that it was Hansel's turn to cross. Before entering the bridge, he took off his chainmail and handed it to Rump.

"Hold this," demanded Hansel. Dodger assumed that, with his larger size, the agent was scared to walk on the bridge, so he had to drop as much weight as possible. Rump draped the armor over his shoulder and watched the Stronghand start his trip across the canyon.

Hansel walked much slower than his sister and Humpty did, pausing frequently and tapping each board with his foot. The bridge creaked and squeaked more often, but Dodger felt more relaxed seeing the structure support Hansel's immense size. The Literary's eyes wandered from Hansel to the other side of the canyon where Gretel and Humpty were standing.

When they were all in the Forever Witch's cottage, Dodger was so caught up in the hysteria that he didn't register Gretel's beauty. It was probably just his imagination, but for some reason, Dodger felt like the young woman had a thing for him. As he thought this, he noticed her peek across the canyon and catch his gaze. Gretel smiled and returned to watching her brother cross the bridge.

Dodger had never dated. He had always told himself that he would not get involved in a relationship until after college, when he thought things would be easier and when he had his life sorted out. Now that he had met Gretel, though, things may start to change.

"Hurry up before I hatch!" yelled Humpty.

"Quiet!" Hansel shouted back, three-quarters of the way over the bridge.

Rump snorted and Dodger grinned, still staring at Gretel. His gaze drifted to Humpty, who was leaning on his sword and watching Hansel with a bored expression, and then back to the bridge, where he noticed something unusual. Underneath the ledge where the bridge connected to Humpty and Gretel's side, there was an enormous hole in the rock-face, like a cave entrance. Dodger squinted and thought he saw movement within the shadows. He blinked and shook his head, assuming he'd just imagined things, though he couldn't shake the odd feeling from his thoughts.

"Finally!" said an exasperated Humpty. Hansel had reached the other side of the bridge.

"Your turn, Dodger. Are you ready to cross?" asked Rump.

"Y-yeah," said Dodger, gulping.

Rump allowed the Literary to go first. Dodger grimaced as he stepped onto the first plank. The board creaked and sagged under his weight, making his heart rate soar at a rapid speed. He took the Hunter's Rifle off his back and prodded the next board with the butt of the handle. Deeming it safe, he made the next step, mimicking Humpty's process. Rump climbed onto the bridge right behind Dodger and followed him as he led the way to the other side.

"Come on!" called out Hansel. "Three of us crossed already. I think the boards will hold your weight!"

"Don't listen to him, Dodger. Take your time and walk at your own pace," said Rump.

"Thanks," said Dodger. It was unwise for him to look down, but each time he prodded a board, he could see through the gaps and into the darkness below. More chills covered his body when he imagined falling from this height.

"Want to know why they call this the Brobdingnagians' Door?" asked Rump, drawing Dodger's attention from the drop.

"N-no."

"Well, the Brobdingnagians were one of the races of giants who inhabited Storyworld long ago. Once us little folk populated and civilized the lands, there was a war between the giants and us, and we emerged victorious. So, the giants went into hiding. Some went to live up in the clouds and others sought shelter in the middle of the world. It's speculated that this canyon we're crossing is an entrance to their new home that they never closed up all the way."

"Really?" asked Dodger. "You mean, you guys have myths and folk tales in Storyworld, too?"

"I'm not sure what you mean by 'folk tales,' but when you say 'myth,' you're implying that my story wasn't true? Because I can assure you that it's very true."

They were at the halfway point and Dodger's fear had dissolved. He was no longer tapping the boards with the rifle, and he was moving at a quicker, yet still cautious pace. Just a few more steps and it'd be all over.

He looked across the bridge and noticed something moving in the cavern in the rock-face again. Something resembling a large, gnarled foot poked out from the shadows and slammed onto the ground with a dull rumble. A little higher up from the foot was a pair of glaring white eyes.

"Oh, no," said Dodger, growing pale. Behind him, he heard a sharp intake of breath and felt Rump's tiny fingers prodding his back.

"Run, Dodger. Run to the end of the bridge. Hurry!"

Dodger didn't need telling twice. Swinging the rifle back over his shoulder, he began sprinting, ignoring the creaks and squeaks of the boards.

"Glad you hastened your pace, boy," called out Hansel. Humpty tossed a disgusted scowl at the agent and was about to snap at him when he did a double take. His eyes were transfixed on Rump and the look of horror on the alchemist's face.

"Something's wrong," muttered the egg-man.

A gray, clawed hand extended from the cave's shadows and latched onto the bottom of the bridge, followed by another hand. The bridge shook and swayed haphazardly, causing Dodger to wrap his hands around one of the rope handles and hold on for dear life. Looking back, he watched Rump grab on as well, but the alchemist kept one of his hands free to retrieve a vial from his belt. He yanked the cork out of the top of the glass with his teeth and chugged the reddish-orange liquid inside.

The bridge swayed more, but the alchemist paid no attention. He dropped the glass over the edge and held his free hand out in front of him. A jumble of red and yellow lights started dancing across Rump's hand. They swished around, forming a ball of red-orange light. In an instant, they turned into a fierce-looking fireball that resembled a miniature sun. Rump wound up his arm and threw the orb like a baseball, sending the spell down into the cave and hitting the target with a bright flash. A loud roar echoed from the shadows and the two beastly hands released their grasp on the bridge. The creature that possessed these arms emerged from the darkness and stepped into the light. Dodger's heart almost popped out of his chest.

It was a giant monster standing ten feet tall and three feet wide. Its skin was gray and tough-looking, like an elephant's hide. It was wearing an animal's pelt as a loincloth that wrapped around its waist and draped down to its lower thighs. The monster's facial features were perhaps the most terrifying aspect; its melon-shaped head had indentations in its bald scalp, like it was beaten with a hammer once or twice. The eyes were lop-sided, with one white, bloodshot marble halfway up its forehead and the other next to its crooked nose. Its mouth was clenched in a wide grimace as the creature peered out at the bridge.

"Troll!" shouted Rump, producing another fireball to hurl at the monster. The spell hit the troll in the shoulder, making it roar again even louder. It grabbed onto the two sides of the bridge and, with a low grunt, hoisted itself up with surprising agility. The entire bridge sagged under the troll's weight as it landed on the floorboards. Dodger was pleasantly surprised that the structure didn't break away, but he thought he could hear the supporting ropes and beams snapping apart.

The troll stomped down the bridge toward Dodger. He was paralyzed with fear and gazed up at the monster's hideous face as it approached him.

Suddenly, the troll stopped in its tracks and began to claw at its back, like it had an itch that it couldn't reach. It spun around on the spot, still writhing and twitching, and Dodger saw Humpty climbing up its back, stabbing it repeatedly in the spine with his sword.

"Now's your chance, Dodger!" said Rump. "Run to the end!"

Dodger did as he was told and made his escape. The troll waved its arms around wildly, attempting to grab the egg-man assaulting its shoulder blades. Its legs were spread apart just wide enough for Dodger to sneak through. The Literary bent down, ready to make a dash for this opening, when he recalled what Rump had said earlier.

You know as well as we do, Agent, that Literaries only appear in Storyworld when they're needed most.

Dodger shook his head at this random surge of bravery (or stupidity) that had suddenly overtaken him. Cursing himself, he stood up and armed the Hunter's Rifle. He took a deep breath and aimed at the troll's misshapen head. The creature was still shambling around, but its head was staying in the same spot, right in Dodger's scope.

As Dodger was about to squeeze the trigger, there was a series of snapping sounds, and the entire bridge trembled. Dodger's finger slipped and he accidentally fired the gun, sending a shot directly into the troll's shoulder. The creature's roar was deafening. It threw its arms up and screamed. Dodger could just see Humpty's rotund form hanging onto the sword, which was impaled deep into the creature's back.

Dodger's Doorway

The troll slammed its feet, triggering another several snapping sounds. Dodger felt his stomach drop, the same feeling he experienced when he was on a roller coaster. He knew at that moment that the bridge had given way and was about to fall into the dark canyon below.

The bridge ceased falling immediately and the ropes snapped taut. Dodger looked around and noticed yet another jaw-dropping sight. Just over the troll's head, he spotted Hansel standing at the very edge of the cliff, supporting the bridge with his bare hands. The ropes had broken off the posts and were now wrapped tightly around the agent's hands and forearms. Hansel's face was scarlet as he dug his heels into the ground and held the bridge and its occupants. Gretel stood beside him, calling to Rump, Dodger, and Humpty to hurry up.

"Run, Dodger!" Rump said a third time. Dodger decided to listen this time and took off. Humpty retrieved the dagger from his belt and stabbed it into the troll's back, drawing its attention away from the Literary who was trying to run through its legs. The monster screamed and returned to clawing at its shoulders and back. Dodger barely squeezed through the gap and was almost at the cliff when the bridge shook violently. Hansel had lost his grip and the ropes were sliding out of his grasp. The bridge dropped several feet, causing Dodger to lose his footing and trip. He tumbled forward, over the edge of the bridge, and landed right in the middle of the troll's cave.

Dodger quickly recovered from the fall. He suffered no injuries aside from a scratch on his arm, yet his knees felt weak when he stood. He looked around the cave and saw that he had somehow landed on top of an oriental green and gold silk carpet. At the edge of this carpet was a pile of bones with a swarm of flies buzzing around it. The sight made Dodger feel sick.

Shouting was heard outside.

They need me out there! Dodger thought. *I need to get out there to help them!*

No sooner had these thoughts crossed his mind that he felt an odd sensation underneath his feet; it was as if the ground had become liquefied and he was standing on top of calm waves of water. Glancing down, he saw that the carpet was now levitating a foot off the ground. Dodger hardly had time to react as the carpet propelled itself out of the cave, taking him for a ride. Dodger grabbed onto the carpet, struggling to keep himself from having a full-on panic attack. He gasped as he was taken into the sky, above the bridge and the canyon. His companions were far below, still combatting the frantic troll. Hansel had regained his grip on the bridge and Gretel was shouting to Rump and Humpty.

"He can't hold on much longer!" came the faint voice of Gretel.

The troll gave up pursuing Humpty and now focused on Rump. The alchemist kept launching fireballs with all his might, but even from this distance, Dodger noticed that the spells were diminishing and becoming less powerful. Dodger knew that he had to take action right away.

"Rump! Humpty! Get out of the way!" yelled the Literary.

Everyone stopped and looked up at the flying carpet. Humpty did a backflip off the troll while Rump crawled between its legs and scurried to the cliff. Dodger leveled the gun's sight up to his eyes, silently hoping that his trembling hands would hold still for even one second. The troll spun around and chased Rump, waving its arms wildly. Dodger fired the rifle, and this time the bullet hit its target on point, burrowing deep into the troll's forehead.

"Bull's eye!" Dodger shouted.

The troll swayed side-to-side and gave one last painful roar before it toppled over the edge of the bridge and fell into the canyon.

Hansel lifted the ropes, allowing Rump to exit the bridge and scramble onto the cliff. Hansel let go of the bridge, allowing it to swing down and slam across the opposite side's cliff-face.

Dodger couldn't stop smiling. The euphoria swelling inside him almost made him forget an important detail: how was he supposed to land? The magic carpet he was sitting on floated in the air over the battlements, its rippled golden edges fluttering in the wind. Dodger looked around, desperately searching for some sort of steering mechanism.

How do I get down?

The carpet rapidly dropped through the air. Dodger gripped a handful of the cloth and felt the color drain out of his face. For a moment, he thought he was about to follow the troll's corpse into the abyss. The other adventurers watched him fall through the air, until the carpet suddenly diverted its course, rocketing toward the cliff. Dodger was about to get sick when his magical vehicle slid along the grass at Hansel's feet, almost bucking the Literary off.

"That was a strange sight for all of us!" said Rump, marveling at the flying carpet.

Dodger smiled weakly and rolled off the carpet. He stood, avoiding the quaky feeling in his legs and the intense panic swimming around his head.

"Good to see that you have marksmanship comparable to King Gabriel's," added Humpty, grinning and clapping Dodger on the shoulder.

"Marksmanship?" questioned Hansel, giving a disgusted look at the Literary. "He almost killed you with that first shot! He should've made a run for it like Stiltskin told him to!"

Dodger was beside himself. "Are you kidding me? I just saved everyone!"

"You should've ran like you were told to, you nuisance," said Hansel. "Instead, you wanted to be the hero and earn some extra glory for yourself. You *would* fancy returning home and telling people how you beat a troll, wouldn't you?"

Dodger was speechless. It was a lost cause arguing with Hansel; he was just one more bully who was bent on giving him a hard time.

An awkward silence lingered over the party. Rump stepped forward and threw the chainmail at Hansel's chest. "Here's your armor, Stronghand. Put it back on if you can fit your arrogance through it."

The agent scowled at Rump and Dodger as he donned his armor. Humpty started forward, his yellow eyes narrowed and his mouth in a matching frown, but Rump grabbed his shoulder and shook his head. Dodger frowned and absentmindedly fiddled with the rifle. The magic carpet was now hovering at his feet.

"At least I found a way to get to Geppetto's house faster," said the Literary, standing on the carpet.

Rump's face lit up and he playfully punched Dodger's shoulder. "There's that Literary resourcefulness!"

"How are we going to all fi-" Hansel said, but he quickly closed his mouth. The carpet, which was originally big enough to fit only Dodger and one more passenger, had magically expanded itself to the width and length of a compact car. The Stronghand blushed and stepped onto the carpet without a word, as did his sister.

"Agent Gretel, where do we go from here?" asked Humpty.

Gretel scanned the surroundings, first peeking back at the cliff, then up at the sun, now blazing in the middle of the sky. The agent pointed into the heart of the forest and said "That way!"

The carpet soared straight up above the treetops, and zoomed through the air, following the direction of Gretel's pointing finger.

Chapter 6

Geppetto and the Prisoner

The carpet ride was surprisingly smooth and fast, like traveling in a silent car on a perfectly flat road. There must have been a magical aura or shield surrounding the carpet because, despite the rapid speed, there was no wind blowing on the riders. Dodger noticed how Hansel sat in the center of the carpet with both of his hands tightly gripping the fabric.

"My brother is a bit afraid of heights," Gretel whispered. She and Dodger chuckled to themselves. A few moments later, the agent stood and yelled, "There it is!"

Dodger, Humpty, and Rump knelt up. Gretel pointed ahead where the trees started to thin out, exposing another clearing in the midst of the forest. In the center of this tiny area was a cottage that looked almost identical to the one the Forever Witch lived in, except this building had a tall chimney sprouting from the roof with faint wisps of smoke streaming out of the opening.

Finally having mastered the art of controlling the magic carpet, Dodger willed the vehicle to slow down and descend through the trees until it landed on the edge of the clearing. Dodger wondered what to do with the carpet as everyone hopped off, but once again, it must have sensed his thoughts as it shrunk down to the size of a playing card and zipped into the Literary's back pocket.

The edge of the clearing was occupied by tree stumps, fallen branches, and more vines. Humpty crouched behind one of the taller stumps and scanned the area. The rest of the group crept up behind the egg-man and took up hiding spots behind the other stumps.

Gretel narrowed her eyes. "Rumpelstiltskin, do you have a spell-detector potion?"

"Already three-and-a-quarter steps ahead of you, Gretel," replied the alchemist, producing another vial from his belt. This one didn't contain a liquid and instead held pure white smoke. Rump lobbed the whole bottle into the clearing, where it shattered upon a stone.

An enormous cloud of white smoke filled the area like a thin fog. Dodger squinted through the smoke, hoping to see something extraordinary, but was left slightly disappointed when nothing happened. The cloud merely lingered in the clearing.

"Aha!" Rump exclaimed in a loud whisper. "Just what I thought!"

"What?" asked Dodger.

"Geppetto must not want anybody intruding."

"I still don't see it!" said the frustrated Dodger.

"The door, you fool!" said Hansel.

Dodger's pursed his lips angrily, but he avoided scowling at the agent. He was taken by surprise when he saw what Hansel was talking about: the front door of the cottage was on fire, or it at least looked that way. There was a strange, crimson flame consuming the door, but it didn't touch the frame or any other part of the house.

"What is that?"

"An Asher," said Gretel. "It's a rare yet highly dangerous spell used as a security measure for people who leave their homes. Nobody can enter an Asher-protected house except for the person who summoned the spell. Hansel and I heard the Forever Witch telling Geppetto about it when he came to retrieve Pinocchio."

"Can't we bust through the wall or a window?" suggested Dodger.

"No, that won't work," said Rump. "Anything that tries to get past an Asher, by magical or physical means, will be incinerated. The only way to deactivate the spell is if the caster re-enters the building. Clever move, Geppetto."

"He should be home, though," reasoned Gretel. "Why else would there be smoke coming from the chimney?"

"I think it's a trap," suggested Rump. "He might have wanted to lure people in so that the Asher would catch them."

"Can't you bypass it, Stiltskin?" asked Hansel.

"I don't have a potion to neutralize it or to help us cross through."

"Some alchemist…"

Rump did a good job masking his annoyance. "My apologies for not having a potion for every single situation and scenario, Agent. Asher's are forbidden in most kingdoms since they are a form of the darkest magic. I never thought I'd actually encounter one."

The group sat in silence, observing the clearing. Dodger strained to think of a way to get into the house. He was going to ask Rump if maybe he could teleport in, but the alchemist already mentioned that he was still testing the spell, and apparently Ashers protected against magical intrusions as well.

"So what do we do? Do we just wait 'till Geppetto gets home?"

"No, no, no," said Humpty. "We need to take advantage of Geppetto's absence. It's best to avoid any confrontation. We must get into that house before he returns."

"The Literary isn't too bright, is he?" remarked Hansel with a chortle. Dodger's face grew red. He glared at Hansel, ready to say something in defense until Rump piped up.

"The Literary!" the alchemist exclaimed. "That's the answer!"

"What do you mean?" asked Dodger.

"The Asher spell was created ages ago, long before the Literaries ever visited us. Since your kind arrived, alchemists and wizards have had to modify spells so that they apply to Literary biology; however, a few spells were never fully reconfigured."

"I don't know what you're get-" the Literary began, until he saw Rump looking him up and down. "Oh, no! No! Come on! Seriously?"

"You're the lone person who can pass the Asher, Dodger!"

"We're not even sure about that, though! It sounds like you're just guessing!"

"I'm not guessing. I'm positive about this. You can enter that house without being harmed. Trust me. I know magic like I know my own feet!"

Dodger glanced pleadingly at Humpty. "Please, don't make me do this. We don't know if it'll work."

The egg-man pursed his lips and furrowed his brow, as if he couldn't decide on whether to agree with Dodger or with Rump. Slowly he declared, "Rump is an accomplished alchemist and magicker. If he says it will work, then I trust his judgment."

"Of course you trust his judgment! You're not the one who'll get turned into toast if his judgment is wrong!"

"I have put my life in Rumpelstiltskin's hands more than once, Dodger," replied Humpty, his voice turning cold. "How dare you think that I would allow someone to jeopardize your life?"

"Okay, if you trust him so much, why don't *you* try to go through the Asher? You're an egg. How do we know your 'biology' won't be affected by it? Put your money where your mouth is!"

"It's much more complicated than that, Dodger," said Rump. "Nobody from Storyworld can pass through that spell besides the caster. Unless we can find another Literary, then you're the only other person with a chance. Please trust us. I wouldn't let you go through it if I knew you were in danger."

"Does nobody see how crazy this is?" asked Dodger. "Did you all forget what just happened back at that witch's house? I'm pretty sure I was in danger back there! And what happened to the whole 'no more splitting up' thing?"

Rump sighed and rubbed his temples. Hansel, Gretel, and Humpty all looked from the alchemist to the Literary, their faces expressionless. By now, the smoke in the clearing had evaporated, but the essence of the Asher could still be seen flickering upon the door.

Eventually, Rump nodded and said, "You're right, Dodger. We can't send you into such a risky situation once again. I am sorry for putting that pressure on you. We'll wait for Geppetto to return so that the Asher will disappear."

"But I thought we were avoiding confrontation," Hansel said.

"It does not matter," replied the alchemist. "It's not worth endangering any of our lives. Knowing General Pinocchio, he wouldn't want us to needlessly risk ourselves to save him."

Humpty stood by the alchemist. "Don't worry. We can formulate another strategy for the time being."

Rump and Humpty sat down next to a stump with defeated looks on their faces and began to discuss a new plan as Hansel and Gretel joined them. Dodger did not move. He still had his arms crossed, and he was trying to find satisfaction in having avoided another dangerous task, but the dismay on his companions' faces only made him feel guilty.

I don't need to risk my life for them. I don't need to risk my life for them. He kept repeating the phrase over and over in his head. It took all of his power to convince himself that he shouldn't feel bad for not wanting to go through the Asher. But the more he said it, the worse he felt. Dodger sighed angrily and threw his arms up in the air.

"Fine! Fine! I'll go! I'll go into Geppetto's house. Happy?"

The group looked up at him.

"You don't have to, Dodger," said Rump. "We understand that you're not too comfortable with this."

"I'm not comfortable with it at all. This is probably the last thing I want to do right now. But what else are we going to do? Just sit here and wait for Geppetto to get home? It could be hours."

Rump hopped to his feet and grinned. "Very good! I knew you'd have it in you! Let's get you in there and save our general!"

Dodger rolled his eyes. "How am I supposed to do this? I can't just grab Pinocchio and walk out, can I? The Asher will stop him from leaving."

"From what I recall, Ashers only work one way. They keep things out, not in. So it's safe to say that you won't have a problem leaving."

"Are you just making these rules up as you go along?" asked Dodger.

"No. It's just one of the flaws of an Asher, and we're going to exploit it for our own gain!"

Humpty stood up. "It is a small cottage, so you should have no trouble finding him, if he is in there. If Geppetto comes home prematurely, the Asher will come down and we'll be able to help you and Pinocchio escape."

Dodger hated Humpty using the word "if" so much. This sounded more daunting than his encounter the Forever Witch, especially with Rump's unconvincing explanation of the Asher's functionality. Despite all this, Dodger felt somewhat more comfortable with this mission than his first task. Beating the troll had instilled a strange sense of resilient confidence in him that wasn't easily shaken.

Dodger took a deep breath and readied himself to enter the clearing. Humpty and Rump gave him pats on the back with a wish of good luck. Gretel hugged him and pecked his cheek, making him blush deeply. Dodger armed himself with the Hunter's Rifle and started forward.

"Leave the gun," came Hansel's voice.

Dodger froze. The agent had his arms crossed and a smug frown etched on his face.

"What did you say?" asked the Literary.

"I told you to leave the gun."

"What are you talking about?" asked Rump slowly.

"How many times do I have to say it? The Literary should leave the gun! I think it's a bad idea for him to take it in with him.

Humpty looked at Hansel incredulously. "Agent, are you aware of what you are saying? You think it wise to send the young man into the house without any protection?"

"It's cumbersome," stated Hansel, refusing to uncross his arms. "If Geppetto comes home, he won't be able to hide well with the rifle. Also, if Geppetto finds the boy without a weapon, he will probably spare him. He will look less threatening."

Dodger shook his head. "There's no way I'm goin-"

"Leave the gun," declared Rump, cutting Dodger off. The Literary and Humpty glared at him. "Hansel's right," he said with a shrug.

"Lord Rumpelstiltskin, have you gone as mad as the Hatter?" asked Humpty. "We can't send Dodger in there without a weapon."

"I never said he should go in without a weapon; I just said that he should leave the rifle," replied Rump. The corners of his mouth twitched, but he maintained a neutral expression.

"What're you talking about?" asked Dodger.

"He means that your mind is the greatest weapon of all," Humpty said hurriedly, nodding at Rump. Hansel narrowed his eyes at the Neverlanders while Dodger grew red in the face.

"Will you guys stop acting weird and just tell me what the hell you're talking about?"

"No time at all," reminded Humpty, shooing Dodger to go on.

Dodger wanted to yell at him, or hit him, but the egg-man's subtle eye movement was oddly reassuring. He knew something that Dodger didn't. Whatever it was, it better be worth the sacrifice of leaving his only weapon behind. Sensing defeat, the Literary sighed and tossed the rifle to the ground. He glared at the group and ventured through the stumps into the clearing.

This is ridiculous, he thought, winding through the maze of fallen trees. Dodger felt a sense of déjà vu as he entered the clearing. After his earlier encounter with the Forever Witch, he hoped that Geppetto wouldn't come home anytime soon.

Dodger approached the door, just out of reach of the Asher's flame. He could feel the warmth emanating from the spell like it was a blazing fireplace. Closing his eyes and mustering his courage, he reached for the door handle.

Dodger's Doorway

The flames closed over his wrist and forearm, but they didn't burn him. Dodger peeked out from under his eyelids and saw his hand gripped onto the door handle and his unburned arm encased in the magical fire. It was truly an odd sensation; it felt like he had plunged his hand into warm sand. The flames were licking his forearm and lapping against his skin, but they weren't harming him. Off in the distance, Dodger thought he heard Rump clapping and cheering, probably about his correct assumption of the Asher spell.

Dodger yanked the door open. The Asher still wasn't hurting him, but he felt uncomfortable being so close to the fire. Passing through the Asher brought on another strange sensation, like he was walking under a warm shower. The door closed behind Dodger as he crossed the threshold into Geppetto's house.

The entire building was like an enormous workshop. The area was filled with numerous tables, all covered with strange, half-assembled contraptions and piles of sketches and documents. The walls were adorned with an assortment of tools including hammers, saws, axes, chisels, and what looked like a giant vice.

Dodger breathed in the thick, musty air that smelled like a mix between a fireplace and wood shavings. It was eerily quiet aside from a distant crackling sound and the creak of the floorboards. The aura made the hair on Dodger's neck stand up.

Like the tables, the ground of the workshop was littered with thousands of sheets of paper displaying drawings and sketches of strange machines. One paper had a diagram of a human with labels and notes scrawled across his limbs. Another document looked like the design for a catapult or a similar siege weapon.

What caught Dodger's attention, though, was something on the far wall of the workshop. He took a few steps forward and cringed at the chilling sight.

"Pinocchio?"

The general was hung from the ceiling by strings attached to blades piercing his body. There was one blade impaled into each of his hands and feet, and another one implanted right in the center of his head. Underneath him stood a firepit filled with embers and coals, still crackling and resonating with a light orange-red glow.

Dodger slowly approached the puppet. Pinocchio's design was simplistic; his body was cylindrical like a tree trunk and covered in a black tattered shirt featuring the Neverland crest. He wasn't wearing pants, and each of his legs consisted of two thinner cylinders connected to one another at the kneecap with a small wooden ball. His feet were rounded platforms with black soot covering the undersides. Pinocchio's arms and hands were of a similar design as his legs except that he had thick and articulate fingers.

His head was fascinating. Pinocchio's round face was a light tan color as opposed to the dark brown of the rest of his body. His eyes were closed and his mouth was hanging slightly open, like he was asleep. He was bald with two large ears and prominent wooden eyebrows. Dodger would have laughed at how cartoonish he looked if he wasn't strung up like a tortured prisoner with blades in his body. It was a horrifying sight. Remembering his mission, Dodger reached out to grab Pinocchio's leg, and the general sprang to life.

"I will never talk!" he bellowed in a thunderous voice. Dodger fell backwards over a stool and landed on the ground hard. Pinocchio swiveled to face the Literary. His wooden eyebrows spun around in circles like the hands of a clock, and his eyes kept blinking one at a time, making a soft *click* sound when the lids closed.

"Who are you? A friend of Geppetto's?" continued the general, tugging at his restraints and flailing his legs. "Let me down!"

"Or else what?" snapped Dodger. "I'm here to rescue you!"

"A likely story!" said Pinocchio. "You were hired by Geppetto, were you not? He's hoping to trick me into talking by using a Literary! I won't have it!"

Dodger was entranced by the puppet's animation. The way he moved was so fluid that it was hard to believe that he was only a few pieces of wood latched together. Pinocchio's eyebrows continued spinning as he yanked at the ropes suspending him.

"I don't think you'll get out of those by yourself," said Dodger. "You're going to need my help."

"Your help? I'd rather have a horde of termites help me! You can tell Geppetto that he can take his hammer and chisel and shove-"

"Just listen to me!" demanded Dodger. "I'm here with Humpty Dumpty and Rumpelstiltskin. We're on a rescue mission from Princess Tinkerbell of Neverland. Does any of that ring a bell?"

Pinocchio paused, but only briefly. "Lies and deception! I don't believe you!"

"Come on, man. How can I prove it to you?" *Maybe if I cut him down, he'll know I'm here to help. I just need a knife or something.*

Dodger froze. How could he have been so stupid? He rolled up his pant leg and saw the Hunter's Dagger still tucked into the sheath around his leg. He then recalled what Humpty and Rump were implying earlier with their cryptic exchange.

I never said he should go in without a weapon, Rump had said. *I just said that he should leave the rifle.*

Dodger yanked the dagger out of the sheath. Pinocchio's jaw dropped with a soft *click*.

"The Dagger of King Gabriel! How did you come across that?"

"I told you I was here to save you. Now are you going to let me help?"

The puppet blinked, then moved his arms in a motion as if he was bowing in mid-air (he did the best he could with the ropes and blades hindering him). With a voice barely above a humble whisper, he uttered, "I apologize for not believing you, foreign warrior."

"It's fine. Let's just get you down from there." Dodger dragged a stool over next to the firepit.

"Where are my fellows, Humpty Dumpty and Rumpelstiltskin? You said they accompanied you?" asked Pinocchio.

"They couldn't get in here because of this Asher thing on the door. Rump said I was the only one who could get through. They're waiting for us with these Wonderland agents we rescued from the Forever Witch." Dodger started to cut through Pinocchio's restraints with the dagger, but stopped when he heard a humming sound coming from what he thought was the puppet's body.

"Are-are you humming?" asked Dodger.

"That sound isn't coming from me," Pinocchio said slowly.

The two looked at each other. Pinocchio spun his head around to face the window directly behind him. He swung his head back and faced Dodger, his eyebrows twirling in circles again.

"Geppetto is back!"

Dodger went pale. "Let me cut you down and we'll-"

"No! There's no time! Hide under one of the tables!"

"He's an old engineer. What's the worst he can do?"

"He's more dangerous than you could ever imagine. Go hide now!"

The urgency in the general's voice was enough to convince Dodger. He jumped off the stool and ducked below the nearest table. Geppetto's humming grew louder as he walked along the side of the house. From his hiding spot, Dodger glimpsed his hunched shadow passing across the curtains.

"Don't worry," whispered the Literary, "Humpty said that once the Asher was down, they would come in and help us."

"What?" said Pinocchio. "No!"

Outside, there was a loud hissing that sounded like a fire being extinguished, followed by the turning of a door handle. Pinocchio let his head droop and his mouth fall open, allowing him to play dead. His eyes were half-closed, leaving the tiny slivers of his pupils to poke out from beneath the eyelids.

Dodger's Doorway

Geppetto entered the building and slammed the door shut. Dodger watched the engineer reach to the left of the doorframe and pull a piece of string from a spool. This string stretched across the doorway and through a metal loop on the other side. Geppetto then dragged the string up to the top of the frame and tied it to a small pin. The pin was plugged into a socket of a complex mechanism made of springs, gears, and a long lever that supported a tall metallic board covered in sharp spikes.

It was a trap.

The engineer ambled through the workshop, still humming his eerie tune. Dodger recalled how Geppetto was portrayed as a feeble old man in the story, but in person, he was absolutely ancient. His hair was made up of long, thin strands of white wires that poked out from the top of his head and around his ears. Wrinkles covered his face like hundreds of tiny streets crisscrossing each other. He wore a fluffy white shirt and straw-colored trousers that came down to his knees. He had no shoes, and his hairy, dirt-encrusted feet had overgrown toenails curling into miniature talons. His old, decrepit appearance aside, there was something about Geppetto that Dodger found absolutely terrifying.

The Literary's heart pounded so loudly that he was worried the sound might give his location away. Geppetto's knobby legs stepped past his hiding spot and stopped in front of the firepit, where he kicked the stool aside.

"Wake up!" growled Geppetto, grabbing Pinocchio's leg and shaking it. Pinocchio pretended to be startled awake and glared down at his captor.

"What do you want? I was enjoying the time you were gone."

"Watch your tongue! Are you ready to tell me what I want to hear? Or shall I rekindle the fire?" As Geppetto said this, he produced a pouch of coals from his pocket and dumped them into the firepit. A tiny shower of sparks popped out.

Dodger snuck out of his hiding spot and slowly crept up behind Geppetto, holding the dagger at the ready. He didn't know what he was going to do, but a feeling in the back of his mind was compelling him to take action. He knew he had to take out Geppetto.

Pinocchio's eyes widened, but his gaze wasn't on the Literary; his attention was focused on the front door. Dodger glanced back and saw Humpty outside the window, standing next to the door with his hand extended and three fingers out. The edge of Hansel's large outline could be seen next to him, standing in front of the doorway.

Humpty lowered a finger and mouthed the word, *Two*.

"No!" Dodger shouted. He popped out of his hiding place, causing Humpty to look at him. "It's a tra-!"

Something hard hit him in the back of the head, throwing him into a table. Blinking stars, he whipped around and saw Geppetto wielding a plank of wood like a club and advancing on him. The engineer swung the board down in a wide arc, but Dodger ducked and tumbled out of the way.

"Don't come in here!" the Literary yelled over his shoulder.

Geppetto charged at Dodger with the plank raised over his head and swung it downward again. Dodger leapt to the side, but Geppetto swatted the board to the left, smacking him in the shoulder. Dodger grimaced and grabbed his arm, stumbling to his feet. He made a break for the door where he could faintly see the string stretched across the frame.

The board came flying through the air, striking Dodger in the back of the legs and knocking him to the floor. He groaned and rolled over to see Geppetto now advancing with a large hammer in his hand. There was a creepy, excited expression in his pale eyes that made the blood rush out of Dodger's face.

"Geppetto!" yelled Pinocchio from the other side of the workshop. He had freed one of his arms from the bindings and was now tugging at the other one with all of his strength. "You are an old goat! An untalented, sad, pathetic man! Come back here and fight someone of your own creation, you mongrel!"

Geppetto ignored the puppet's cries and continued walking toward Dodger, smacking the head of the hammer onto the palm of his hand. A combination of shock and fear made it impossible for Dodger to stand. The Literary shuffled backwards, eventually finding himself up against the door. The Hunter's Dagger lay just beyond his reach and he moved to grab it. Geppetto snaked his foot out and kicked it away.

"You won't be needing that," wheezed the engineer. Dodger closed his eyes tightly and held his hands up in front of his face.

At that moment, the front door swung wide open, and Dodger fell backwards out the doorway. His head landed outside of the entrance and he opened his eyes, but he immediately wished that he had kept them closed; Hansel was pointing the Hunter's Rifle right at his face and pulling the trigger, which gave a light *click* but did not fire.

Geppetto lifted his hammer with a yell. Dodger snapped out of his shock and saw the trap's string hanging above his face. He grabbed it and tugged down with all his might.

The string yanked the bolt out of the trap mechanism, triggering a spring to release. The spike-covered board swung down and struck Geppetto in the back. He stood there for a moment, unaware of what had just happened, his eyes darting from side to side. His knees buckled and his expression darkened as the hammer fell out of his hands and his body went limp.

Dodger's arms were trembling but he had fortunately regained the ability to stand. Pushing himself up, he made sure he did not touch any part of Geppetto's corpse. He went to sit down at the closest table and buried his face in his hands, breathing heavily. Hansel and Humpty entered the workshop, sliding past Geppetto's hanging body partially blocking the doorway.

"Dodger? Are you okay?" asked Humpty, putting his arm on the Literary's shoulder.

"I-I don't kn-" Dodger vomited all over the floor.

"Apparently, he isn't."

Dodger spat a couple of times and worked on catching his breath. His heart had spent the last five minutes bouncing around his ribcage like a wild animal. The image of the trap's blades impaling Geppetto's back was branded into his mind. It was a scarring sight that he was sure would never leave him.

"Humpty!" called Pinocchio from the other side of the workshop.

"General!" replied Humpty, waddling over to the puppet and unsheathing his sword. "Fear not, sir! We'll have you down before you can say 'Mother Goose.'"

Humpty pulled up the stool and cut through the ropes that suspended Pinocchio's limbs. He gently lowered the puppet to the ground, and gently plucked the blades out of his head and hands.

"It's been a long time, my good friend," said the puppet, clasping Humpty's arm.

"Far too long, I agree. We apologize for the wait; we were holding out for the arrival of the Literary."

Dodger was still sitting down, trying to eliminate the image of Geppetto from his thoughts. There was a sound of heavy clunking on the workshop floor that made him look up. Pinocchio stood in front of him with his arm crossing his chest as if he was giving an oath.

"Stranger from the Other Side, Wielder of the Dagger of Gabriel, Visitor of Storyworld," said Pinocchio, "I, Pinocchio, Creation of Geppetto and General of the Neverland Military Arm, am forever indebted to you."

Dodger fidgeted nervously. Still breathing heavily, he wheezed, "Um, I, Dodger, Soldier of Philadelphia, Son of Eric, accept your offer?"

"Thank you," said Pinocchio, bowing. He nodded to Humpty and Hansel. "And thank you both as well for participating in my rescue."

"It's good to see you, too, General!" said Rump, shuffling past Geppetto's corpse nonchalantly. "I'd say that this mission was a success!"

Dodger's nausea suddenly disappeared. His excitement overtook his shock and he stood up. "Wait a minute! We finished the quest or whatever. Does that mean you guys can send me home now?"

Humpty and Rump looked at each other uncomfortably.

"Unfortunately, we can't," replied Rump. "Once a Literary completes his task, he is automatically transported back to his own world. We can't send you home by our own accord. Apparently, there are still more journeys that await us."

"Honestly, though," started Dodger, his legs beginning to quiver, "I don't know how much more of this I can take. I've never killed a person before, and this," He trailed off. He felt sick again and sensed that his heart would never return to its normal pace.

Rump approached the Literary. "Dodger, you've shown great courage thus far. Geppetto was vile, and he was more of a monster than a man. You slayed a beast that had no place in Storyworld, just like how you helped destroy the Forever Witch and the troll. We never could've rescued General Pinocchio without you. Please, stay with us. You're an invaluable teammate."

Obviously, I have no choice, Dodger thought. The dagger was lying on the ground where Geppetto had kicked it. He went to pick it up and re-sheathe it when he heard Hansel speak up.

"Didn't we agree that the boy should've gone in unarmed? No wonder he was attacked."

Dodger had been trying to tune out Hansel's comments, but this remark made him absolutely livid. He glared at Hansel. "You tried to kill me!"

"What?" said Hansel, bewildered.

"When you opened the door, I saw the rifle pointed at my face. And I heard you squeezing the trigger, you idiot! You tried to kill me!"

"It's not like that!" mumbled the agent. "We heard the scuffle after you yelled. I had the gun ready in case Geppetto was at the door. It was an honest mistake!"

"Yeah, right!" said Dodger. "You're either trying to kill me or you're the biggest moron in Storyworld."

Dodger had no idea where this courage came from. It even surprised Humpty and Rump, who looked at each other with wide eyes. Hansel's face went from nervousness to a mix of anger and hatred. He suddenly advanced on the Literary.

Pinocchio stepped in front of the approaching Hansel, halting him in his tracks. Dodger suddenly noticed how tall the Wooden Soldier was, but he was nowhere near the height of the agent; however, the general's demeanor and confidence easily made up for this. Rump and Humpty joined Pinocchio's side.

"Agent Hansel, Stronghand of Wonderland," declared Humpty in an official tone, "by the power in me as Second-in-Command of the Neverland Military Arm, I hereby dismiss you from this fellowship. Not only have you constantly threatened and disrespected Dodger with your poor attitude, you have put his life in danger as well. Your actions almost led to the death of a Literary, a crime punishable by execution in many provinces. I command you to return to

Wonderland immediately while we notify Queen Alice of your inappropriate actions. She will decide on the best course of action to prosecute you."

Hansel went pale. "No, no, you can't do that. Please. It was an honest mistake. Do not subject me to this. I made a mistake!"

"Nearly dropping the bridge and almost letting a Literary fall into the Brobdingnagians' Door was a mistake," uttered Humpty (Pinocchio's eyebrows spun out of control when he heard this). "But firing a weapon into the face of a Literary is just foolhardiness and idiocy. You are lucky that we do not arrest you now and bring you to justice in Neverland. We will let your own kingdom handle it instead. You may receive mercy."

Dodger crossed his arms in satisfaction and smiled. It was about time Hansel paid for his actions.

Sensing defeat, the agent sighed deeply and muttered, "Very well. I'll take my sister and leave at once."

"Wait!" said Dodger, quickly uncrossing his arms. "I think we should give him another chance."

Pinocchio, Humpty, and Rump's heads simultaneously swung to Dodger.

"Excuse me?" said the general. "Did you not just say he was trying to kill you?"

"It was a mistake. It happens. I mean, he saved us during that fight with the troll and the Forever Witch. We wouldn't have made it this far without him."

Humpty looked like he couldn't believe what he was hearing. Pinocchio stared at Dodger with a hint of disappointment.

"And you guys said that we had more quests to take care of," reasoned Dodger. "Won't we need all the help we can get?"

Pinocchio frowned, but then nodded. "So be it." He turned back to Hansel. "It looks like the Literary is kind enough to show you mercy. Just so you know, Stronghand, I'm keeping my eye on you."

Hansel nodded. His face had gone green, and he refused to look anyone in the eyes.

"I think we should return to Neverland, lest we keep Princess Tinkerbell worried," added Humpty. He was refusing to look at Hansel *or* Dodger.

"An excellent idea," replied the general.

The group filed out of the cottage after Humpty had removed Geppetto's corpse from the trap and placed it onto a table. Hansel exited first with his head down and his hands knotted behind his back, followed by Rump and Humpty. Pinocchio was about to escort Dodger outside when he stopped and ventured back into the depths of the workshop. Dodger watched the puppet reach up onto the wall of tools and pull down a long, two-handed, war hammer. The hammer's head was a flattened circle on one side and a curved, claw-like point on the other. Pinocchio slung the weapon over his shoulder and marched to the door, beckoning Dodger to exit first. The duo left the house and slammed the door shut.

Chapter 7

An Unexpected Adventure

Gretel was sitting with her back against one of the taller tree stumps when the group returned. Humpty explained what had happened inside the cottage regarding her brother's incident. Immediately, she went into a rage, scolding Hansel like he was a child.

"And you nearly kill him? What would Queen Alice say if she heard about this? Imagine what would happen to you if you were sentenced for killing a Literary? You'd be beheaded! Or tortured! If we were lucky, they'd probably throw you in the dungeon for the rest of your life, you buffoon!"

"Agent," interrupted Rump, "Dodger has indicated that he'd like to forget about this whole ordeal and proceed with our mission. Humpty has agreed not to report his crimes to the Neverland court either. Lucky for you both, Dodger is a forgiving man."

Gretel exhaled loudly and walked away, leaving Hansel to lean against the tree with his arms crossed and his eyes trained on the ground.

Dodger, who had turned away from the scolding, felt a prod in his back. Gretel was standing behind him with a sympathetic and apologetic expression.

"You're far too kind to forgive my brother. I wish I could make it up to you."

"It's fine," mumbled Dodger.

Gretel smiled and stroked his cheek tenderly. Dodger grinned and peeked over her shoulders to see Rump smiling mischievously and nodding.

"Let's go back to the castle!" Dodger said loudly, rolling his eyes at Rump. The Literary retrieved the carpet from his pocket and set it on the ground, where it magically expanded again. Pinocchio's eyebrows spun and his mouth dropped as he gazed at the flying vehicle.

Back to Neverland, Dodger thought once everyone had climbed aboard. The carpet quivered before rising above the treetops, and zoomed away into the distance where the sun was setting behind the faraway towers of Neverland Castle.

"Welcome, soldiers!" shouted John Tell, saluting the group as the carpet touched down in front of Neverland Castle. The adventurers hopped off so that it could shrink down into Dodger's pocket again. John's narrowed eyes lingered on Hansel and Gretel, and he arched one of his eyebrows inquisitively. His expression quickly lightened when he saw Pinocchio at the back of the group.

"General Pinocchio!" John crossed his arm over his chest. The other sentries standing around the gate followed suit and began mumbling to each other.

"Good evening, Captain," said Pinocchio. He nodded to the other sentries. "Soldiers. I trust that you've protected the castle well during my absence?"

"Absolutely, sir," said John. "All has been peaceful in these parts. No major happenings or troubles; although, I have noticed Robin Lox and his company lurking at the edge of the Neverwood again. I think they might be looting caravans or hunting wild game."

Humpty grunted and reached for his sword. Rump placed his hand on the egg-man's arm.

"Sir Humpty, please. It's far too late and I'm far too tired to clean the forest. Let's get our rest and we can deal with it later."

Humpty loosened the grip on his sword without another word, though Dodger could sense a twinge of bitterness in his demeanor. The captain blew into his horn and the gate behind him retracted into the walls. Pinocchio nodded to John before entering the castle, waving at the other sentries as he passed. Hansel and Gretel went in next. John attempted to introduce himself to the agents, but Hansel ignored him and shuffled past without even a glance, while Gretel happily shook the captain's hand. Rump mimicked Hansel's slouched presence and shuffled after him with an over-exaggerated scowl, making John chuckle. Dodger gave the captain a high-five when he saluted him, leaving a befuddled John staring at his hand as the gate slowly closed.

Princess Tinkerbell sat on her throne with her legs crossed and her hands on her lap as the adventurers walked into the chamber. Humpty, Rump, Dodger, Pinocchio, Gretel, and even Hansel knelt at her feet. Humpty reviewed the entire journey, detailing events like the troll under the bridge, the Forever Witch encounter, and the incident at Geppetto's cottage (he made sure to leave out the details of Hansel's mishap). After the brief recounting, the princess strolled over to Pinocchio and rested her hand on his shoulder.

"It is truly wonderful to see you, General," she said in her silken voice.

"Likewise, Princess. I am sorry for my absence."

"Do not worry. You are home safe and that is all that matters."

"Thanks to the excellent teamwork of our kingdom's top warriors," said Pinocchio, nudging his head at Humpty and Rump. "Not to mention the brave actions of their Literary."

Tinkerbell beamed at the alchemist and the egg-man. "I'm proud to have these two as part of our kingdom. Nobody represents the success of Neverland as well as they do."

"With your permission, Princess," said Pinocchio, "I'd like to extend an invitation to Dodger to possibly join the Neverland Military Arm. We could use his talents in our ranks."

Dodger's head shot up. *What did he say?*

The princess smiled. "Is that so? My, Dodger must have really impressed you with his work thus far."

Rump chimed in. "Even though he's one of the youngest Literaries to come across our world, he's proven himself quite experienced."

"Well, hold on," said Dodger. "Don't you think it's a little too soon? I don't think I'm cut out to be a warrior. I'm just a kid."

Almost everyone was smiling at Dodger, except for Hansel, whose face was expressionless, and Humpty, who was sporting a deep frown.

"He makes a good point," said the egg-man. "Dodger is a brave young man, but he has only been in this world for two days. Do you think it wise for him to join the army so soon, at such a young age?"

Dodger was thankful that someone else was seeing the absurdity in all this. Before he could further press his point, the doors to the chamber swung open with a loud groan. In walked John Tell, along with a man who was perhaps a little older than Dodger. He was wearing a short white toga and a pair of silver sandals with wired straps that wrapped up to his knees. A metal band held his thick, curly brown hair to his head, and there were two small axes with sharpened black blades strapped on either side of his waist.

"Excuse my intrusion, Princess," said John with a hint of impatience, "but this man has arrived demanding assistance. He ignored my declarations that we were busy and was rather tenacious about his request."

The princess sat back down in her throne and crossed her legs, her face shifting to a stone-cold demeanor. "State your name and purpose," she said curtly.

"I am Jack Horner, Guardian of Amrya," the man said, matching the princess's short tone. "I'm here seeking aid on a mission. I would prefer to speak to the king or queen of this land."

"The king and queen are not available. Any questions, requests, or concerns shall be addressed to me, Princess Tinkerbell."

The man hesitated. "My request is rather important. Like I said, I would prefer to speak to the king or-"

"And like *I* said," hissed Tinkerbell, "the king and queen are not available. My title should not be a reason for you to doubt my authority. Or are you always this condescending?"

The visitor took a step back. Dodger wasn't sure, but he could've sworn he heard Humpty give a satisfied "Hmph!" behind him.

The man cleared his throat loudly. "Very well. It has come to our attention that a Literary has arrived in your kingdom." He looked at Dodger.

"What is the mission, Horner?" asked Humpty, also adopting a nasty-sounding voice.

"Last night, a trio of giants living in the clouds snuck into our town and abducted my sister, Jill, who I'm afraid will either become their slave or part of their next meal."

"Some Guardian you are," snapped Hansel. "Looks like you weren't doing your job too well, were you?"

Jack sneered at Hansel. "Bite your tongue, *sir*, or I'll take care of it myself." There was a glint off of the blade of one of Jack's axes. "As I was saying, I am the town Guardian, but I was severely outmatched against the three giants. My sister should not pay for my errors, which is why I am here, humbly asking for help."

The chamber went silent. Tinkerbell's expression softened a little, although she still had a trace of annoyance when she spoke. "It is up to the Literary if he wishes to assist you with this quest."

"We'll do it!" said Dodger without hesitation. In the back of his mind, he thought that maybe *this* was the mission that had resulted in his being transported to Storyworld. *Maybe if we help Jack, I can go home before they ask me to join their army again,* wondered the Literary.

"Thank you," said Jack, standing up and bowing. "Your help will be greatly appreciated."

"So be it," commented the princess. "Jack Horner, I'm entrusting you with my most talented warriors and my kingdom's Literary. Be informed that while I sympathize and respect your need to save your sister, I expect you to return my men safely, especially the Literary."

"I will do my best, Princess Tinkerbell."

"Your best better not make me regret this decision."

It was dusk when everyone stepped out of the castle. The sun sank below the horizon, but there was a pinkish hue still settling over the region. It was a little chilly outside, but Dodger couldn't tell if he was shivering because of the weather or because of his nervousness over the next mission.

The group sat around the entrance, staring at Jack inquisitively. The visitor sighed loudly. "Do you mean to tell me that there isn't one horse in all of Neverland? Shall we all walk to Amrya? It should only take us a few months. Maybe the giants will have left us scraps to save by the time we get there."

"You came here asking for assistance and you failed to bring transportation?" countered Humpty.

"I assumed you had your own transportation. You *are* Neverland, after all. Shouldn't your stables be filled wi-"

"It's okay! It's okay!" said Dodger, standing between the two. He revealed the magic carpet from his pocket and placed it on the ground. Jack's sneer disappeared as the carpet expanded to its normal size, permitting everyone to climb onboard. Jack scoffed and crossed his arms.

"Well, I suppose that'll have to do." He jumped up, and a pair of tiny, white, bird-like wings sprouted out of the sides of his sandals and began fluttering. The man from Amrya began levitating, just like the carpet. Jack did a backflip in mid-air and sped off in the direction of the rising moon, the magic carpet close behind.

The group traveled for what felt like hours with little conversation. Jack led the way, flying in front of the carpet with his head pointed forward and his legs arched back. At one point, he spun around in mid-air and flew backwards while signaling to the carpet-riders. He pointed over his shoulder to a huge black mass sprouting from the ground and extending into the sky. Whatever this object was, its top vanished into an ominous gray cloud that lingered over a tiny city with twinkling lights. The cloud was motionless, permanently imprinted against the purple-black sky and hovering in a solitary position over a large area. As the carpet flew closer, Dodger gasped upon noticing that the solid object looked like a vine, or even a…

"Beanstalk!" shouted Jack, slowing down so that he could fly next to the carpet and speak to his followers. "After the Giant Wars, you know how our titanic enemies escaped underground?" Everyone apart from Dodger nodded. "Well, a few of them used magic to grow this beanstalk so they could hide in the sky. See that cloud? There's a whole city of them living up there."

"It's a good thing we have this carpet or else we probably would've never gotten up there," said Dodger.

"Amrya has a fleet of griffins you could use. We can stop by the stables if you wish, unless you want to take that ragged house item up into the cloud city."

"We are fine, thank you very much!" said an annoyed Humpty.

Jack grinned and shot toward the beanstalk. He slowed down and stuck his legs out in front of him. His feet touched on the plant, and he began running up its thick trunk. The carpet froze inches from the beanstalk, and then floated directly upward, sticking closely behind Jack.

"Why did you build your city so close to where giants live?" asked Humpty.

"I did not build it, so don't ask me," said Jack. "But my guess is that the soil is rich due to the enchantments that grew the stalk. Amrya was supposedly founded to open up agricultural channels." Vines and branches popped out of the stalk's trunk. Jack hopped and leapt from one branch to the next like a monkey as the carpet shifted left and right to avoid the obstacles. "Anyway, we never had problems with our airborne neighbors for years. But then we discovered Amrya's founders weren't correct about our crops thriving under the stalk. Our economy spiraled out of control and we were almost out of food and money. Amrya was

dying. Luckily, a Literary arrived and accompanied me up into the cloud-city to

retrieve-"

"A chicken that lays golden eggs," finished Dodger, remembering the

fairy tale.

"It was a simple mission, and I'll admit I was a little surprised that the

giants didn't retaliate right away. The city council assumes that the recent

kidnappings might be attributed to the theft, possibly retribution against me."

"After all these years? They know how to hold a grudge, don't they?"

"It's what giants are known for," interjected Rump. "Grudges, greed, and

trickery."

"And appetites for blood," added Jack.

The beanstalk rose higher and higher. There were less branches and

vines, so Jack resumed his running up the trunk. Dodger peeked over the edge of

the carpet and marveled as the tiny city and the forest disappeared into tiny specks.

Jack zipped up through a small gap where the stalk poked through the cloud, and

the carpet followed him.

The moment the carpet passed through the gap, the group was greeted by

a blinding whiteness. They were floating in a bright valley made entirely of

clouds. There was no sun visible, but the area was lit up like the late morning, and

there were additional smaller clouds coasting across the sky. Dodger was amazed

at how the cloud floating over Amrya appeared to span roughly a mile, but the

cloud-valley stretched a great distance, far enough to cover the horizon.

Jack whistled for the carpet to keep up. He flew toward a hut standing not too far from the beanstalk. Looking back, Dodger saw that the plant ended in a sprawling treetop with thousands of branches and millions of dark green leaves.

The hut was a solitary tan building amidst endless clouds with no other structures in sight. Dodger wondered how many giants actually populated this cloud-valley. He was also curious regarding the size of the hut; it was about five stories tall with one enormous door in the side

"I thought you said the Brobdingnagians were huge," Dodger said to Rump.

"They are," answered Jack. "Brobdingnagians are enormous, but they went underground. Those that live in the clouds are a smaller race called Lillis. Few remain, so hopefully we won't be seeing too many during our trip up here."

Dodger sighed in relief. Jack directed the carpet through a big knothole in the hut's wooden door. The interior of the building was plain, tidy, and had an eerie presence reminiscent of the Forever Witch's cottage. The walls were lined with shelves full of pottery and glasses, and an enormous table and chair set occupied the center of the room. There were two more doors that were shut and locked with large metal deadbolts.

"Horner!" said Humpty when the carpet passed through the door. "You didn't tell us that we would be going into a house! It is not safe to enter without clearance! This is not safe protocol."

"Calm down!" snapped Jack, hovering next to the carpet. "This will just take a few minutes. Lillis don't pose much of a threat anyway. We seven could easily handle ourselves in battle."

"You are going to get us killed," hissed Humpty. "I am honestly baffled that Amrya designated you as its Guardian. This is poor leadership coupled with rash decisions. We are going about this whole mission wrong!"

"Will you both quiet down?" said Pinocchio, his deep voice slicing across Humpty and Jack's bickering. "Let us just look for the prisoners and get this over with!"

Gretel called out when she spotted something in the middle of the table. Jack and the carpet touched down on the wooden slab and gazed at an enormous golden cage with rusted bars as thick as telephone poles. The group peeked in through one of the gaps and saw the inside of the cage lined with straw and dirt, like the interior of a birdcage. Chills crawled up Dodger's spine when he spotted bones and torn clothes scattered on the ground. Jack whimpered softly.

"Jill! Are you in there?"

"Quiet!" Humpty whispered.

"She's not here! She can't be dead!"

"I see someone!" said Gretel, who was poking her head in through a gap on the opposite side of the cage. Hansel, Dodger, and Jack ran over while Rump, Humpty, and Pinocchio kept watch on the surroundings.

A young woman in a black robe slept in a pile of straw with a tattered cloth as a makeshift blanket. There was no doubt that this was Jill. She had long, brown, bushy hair and the same thin lips and curved nose as her brother.

"Horner," whispered Humpty, "exactly how many people from Amrya were kidnapped prior to your sister?"

Jack wouldn't take his eyes off his sister. "Why does that matter? She is the one we're rescuing right now!"

"It matters because it makes me question your guardianship!" barked Humpty.

Jack turned to him. "What are you going on about, egg-man?"

"You told us the giants kidnapped your sister for retribution. I want to know how many people before her were kidnapped and how many perished! Judging by these bones lining her prison, it seems to be a lot! Why is it only now that you asked for help in rescuing her?"

Jack's cheeks flushed. The group stared at him. He didn't answer.

"Show us your seal that proves you are a Guardian," demanded Humpty.

"What? Why do you need to see my seal now? I told you I forgot it in Amrya. We have more pressing matters!"

Humpty grabbed Jack's shoulders and pinned him up against a bar. "You lying rat!"

Rump and Dodger had to pull the egg-man off of him. Pinocchio walked over and stared at the scuffle.

"What is going on? Are we saving the woman or not?"

"This man is a liar! I knew we couldn't trust him!" roared Humpty, fighting against Rump and Dodger's restraints. Hansel and Gretel were looking on in confusion as well.

"Humpty, calm down!" said Dodger. "What's going on? What's he lying about?"

"Jack Horner is no Guardian of Amrya," breathed Humpty. "Any high-ranking official such as a Guardian must carry a certified seal when requesting assistance from another kingdom. If Horner is really who he says he is, then he should have no qualms about showing us the document!"

Dodger was still confused. Pinocchio looked from the egg-man to the Amryan. Jack was leaning against the bars of the cage, his arms up defensively.

"Mr. Horner, do you have your seal?"

"He doesn't!" said Humpty! "He is not a Guardian! He is probably just some peasant who wanted our assistance to do his dirty work."

"I needed my sister back!" said Jack, his eyes starting to tear up. "We are too poor to have a Guardian in our city. We cannot do anything to defend ourselves."

"You liar!" said Humpty. He was no longer fighting against Rump and Dodger's hold, but his eyes were still menacingly wide.

"Hold on, Humpty," said Dodger. He was annoyed at Jack as well, but he was not as livid as the egg-man. "Jack just wanted to save his sister. We can't blame him for this."

"And what about all those other men and women who were taken before his sister? He did not want to risk his life to save them! And he dares disrespect the title of Guardian for his city?"

"I'm sorry!" pleaded Jack. "My sister is the only person left in my life. You have to understand my reasons."

Jack began to sob. Dodger could feel Humpty's body still shaking, but his expression had softened.

"I am sorry," repeated Jack in between sobs.

Dodger sighed. This entire ordeal was too much to take in. It was bad enough that they had no way of rescuing Jill, but now they had this drama. Pinocchio and Rump both looked clueless as to what to do, and Hansel and Gretel stood by with the same confused faces.

"Listen, Jack," Dodger finally said. "We'll help you get your sister out of here. We can deal with you lying and everything else later. The giants could be back at any minute, so let's work on breaking into that cage."

This proposal seemed to satisfy everyone. Jack stopped crying almost immediately and went back to peeking in between the bars at his sister. Rump let go of Humpty. The egg-man glared at the Amryan, but he didn't try to attack him again.

"How do we get her out?" asked Jack.

"Maybe we can find the key to the cage?" suggested Dodger.

Hansel scoffed. "Do you know how long that would take? We've wasted enough time as it is, you dull-witted, lit-"

"Watch it, Stronghand!" said Pinocchio.

"You're a Stronghand?" asked Jack, suddenly excited. "Are you able to break through the bars?"

Hansel glanced at the cage. "I might be, as long as the cage isn't enchanted." He grabbed onto two of the bars, grunting and straining as he pulled with all his might. The bars didn't move an inch. Hansel took a breath and tried once again, tugging as hard as he could, until he heard the tiniest creak of metal bending. Jack smiled and cheered him on, but he was quickly silenced by a distant rumble outside.

Everyone's attention shifted to the door. The sounds of grumbling, laughter came closer and closer, accompanied by the noise of stomping boots and clapping hands. Dodger knew that whoever or whatever was coming through the door wasn't going to be alone.

"We need to hide!" said Dodger.

"We're not hiding!" said Jack angrily. The Amryan unsheathed the axes from his belt and twirled them in his hands. "Those giants killed my townsfolk; I won't let them lay another finger on my sister! We're staying here and we're going to fight!"

"Arm yourselves," ordered Pinocchio with no hesitation. The Wooden Soldier grabbed the war hammer from his back while Humpty unsheathed his sword and dagger and Rump unhooked the mace from his belt. Hansel cracked his knuckles and Gretel drew the dagger out of her boot. Dodger took the Hunter's Dagger in his hand; he regretted leaving the rifle back at the castle.

Dodger's Doorway

The front door swung open and three giants stomped in. They looked almost exactly like regular men with black hair and shiny dimpled cheeks, only they were standing over three stories high. Silence fell on them when they discovered the miniscule intruders on the table. The giant in the center, the tallest one by a head, stepped forward. "What brings you here, pests?"

"I came here for my sister!" blurted out Jack.

"You came here to join us for dinner," said the giant on the left, guffawing to his companions. The breath that came with the giant's laughter was like a smelly, hot wind that blew on Dodger and his friends.

"Now, now," said the tallest giant, holding up his hand, "we shouldn't be rude to our guests. I admire their fearlessness, or recklessness, or whatever you call it. Let's make this entertaining, shall we?" He sat in one of the gigantic chairs and placed both of his hands on the table. "You know, since the war, we've been stuck in here with little to do. Sure, we like to venture down into the world of the little folk and pick up some snacks, but it's incredibly boring down there, too. You can provide us with some entertainment by competing in our trials."

"We refuse to play your games," called out Pinocchio.

"I do not think you are in much of a position to negotiate, twig-man," replied the tall giant.

Jack kept his eyes on the seated giant. "What kind of trials?"

"Trials that will test your might, your will, and your personalities. If you pass, say, three out of five of our trials, we'll let you leave with the young maiden."

"And if we don't pass them?"

The giant smiled. "We can worry about that later."

Jack huffed at the giant and looked back at his companions, giving them a brief nod. Everyone froze. Humpty continued glaring at Jack, but eventually gave a deep nod, and everyone else followed, except for Dodger, who spoke up to the giant.

"How about two trials?"

"Five trials!" roared all three giants in unison.

"Five trials. Gotcha," said Dodger, his voice cracking. The color had drained out of his face and he had dropped the dagger.

"So it begins!" said the leader giant. "Sheathe your weapons and the first trial will be underway!"

Chapter 8

The Trial of the Giants

The tallest giant introduced himself as Phemus, and his friends as Paul and Loki. He extended his hands onto the table, permitting the adventurers to climb aboard, and then lowered them down to the floor of the hut where he dropped them off. The giants slid the chairs and table against the wall to clear a space in the middle of the room. The cage holding Jill shook and rattled about, but the prisoner remained in her deep sleep.

"Our first trial will be a test of strength and physical force," announced Phemus. "Who's the strongest of your troop?"

"I am," stated Hansel, stepping forward. "I'm one of the Stronghands."

"Are you now? Well, then you're the perfect candidate for this trial. I'll have you fight my brother, Paul."

Paul was the shortest of the giants, but compared to Hansel, he still had a major size advantage. He wore baggy brown overalls and a checkered red and black shirt that was halfway unbuttoned, exposing a bulbous belly that sagged over his belt. A thick brown beard covered most of his windswept face, and whatever flesh was showing looked like it had endured years of brutal weather and exposure.

"That's not a fair fight!" Dodger said to the others.

Jack stared at the Literary. "Not a fair fight? Don't you know about the Stronghands?"

"He does not," called out Hansel, not looking back, "but he's about to find out."

Paul and Hansel met at the center of the room. Paul smirked down at Hansel, who responded with an aggressive glare and his arms out in a wrestler's stance.

"First one to take his opponent to the ground is the winner!" said Phemus. "Let the trial begin!"

Dodger was taken aback at the trial's sudden start. Paul brought his foot in the air and slammed it down onto Hansel. Dodger covered his ears and turned away, anticipating a sickening crunch of the agent being squashed. He then noticed his companions cheering and shouting encouraging words at Hansel. Cautiously turning back around, the Literary was aghast at the sight of Hansel holding up Paul's foot with both of his arms. The agent huffed and threw the foot off with all his might, making Paul stumble backwards. Paul grumbled and tried to kick Hansel, but he retaliated by swatting the foot away with both of his hands. It was an unusual sight to behold; like an ant fighting a horse.

"So, what's with this whole 'Stronghand' thing?" Dodger asked Rump, not taking his eyes off the fight.

Rump's gaze was also glued to the battle, but he explained to the Literary. "The Stronghands are a race of men descended from the Giant Wars. Back during those battles, the giants had a severe advantage over us little folks. The only way we stood a chance was to even the odds through a combination of magic and science. Alchemists and sorcerers from all over Storyworld

experimented with the blood and biology of giants to create a strength potion."

Paul launched another kick. Hansel grabbed onto the giant's swinging

boot and started climbing up his leg. The giant swatted at him, but the agent was

too quick and avoided the attacks like a nimble spider.

"The potion was administered to hundreds of soldiers, thus creating the

original Stronghands," continued the alchemist.

Paul grunted and kept reaching for Hansel to no avail. The agent jumped

from the pant leg and latched onto the giant's thick index finger.

"The tide of the wars changed in our favor," said Rump. "But after we

won, we were faced with a new problem; there was a hormone in the giants' blood

that spawned an increased level of aggression in the hosts. It was decided that we

discontinue the practice from there on out."

Paul brought the hand close to his face and scowled at Hansel dangling

from his finger. "You're more annoying than a bad itch!"

"I can be even more irritating," said Hansel. He wrapped his arms around

Paul's finger like he was giving it a tight hug. The giant went from annoyed to

panicked as he was dragged hand-first down to the ground, slamming his chin onto

the wooden floor. There was a loud smash that shook the hut's foundation and

kicked up a light cloud of dust. When the commotion settled down, Hansel was

standing on top of the defeated giant's outstretched hand, rotating his shoulders

and grimacing. "I think I passed the trial of strength," announced the Stronghand.

The adventurers cheered as Gretel went to hug and congratulate her brother.

Rump finished explaining to Dodger, "Unfortunately, the potion effects were irreversible, so we couldn't change the Stronghands back to their original forms. They went on with their lives, breeding with regular folk and fathering descendants. As more generations were born, the giant-blood potion diluted more into their biology, and that's how we have arrived at Agent Hansel."

Jack patted Hansel on the shoulder with a grin. The Stronghand's face went sour at the sight of Dodger and the Neverlanders. He pursed his lips and turned his back on them.

Paul rose, brushing himself off with a scowl. Loki chuckled and gave him a playful shove. Phemus also laughed and beamed down at the guests.

"It seems that we're in for a challenge! Good show! You win the first trial, little ones. Let's see how you fare in the trial of speed."

Phemus lowered his hands, inviting the adventurers to climb on again. This time, he took them outside the hut and set them on the ground. The cloud terrain had a firm surface with a soft cover; Dodger compared it to walking on soft grass as it sagged under his feet. A layer of thin white smoke covered the ground and reached up to Dodger's shins.

Several hundred yards away was the beanstalk. Dodger wondered how easy it would be for him and his companions to escape if he could just get the carpet out of his pocket, but he remembered that they still had to rescue Jill from her cage.

"Whomever is the fastest of your company, step forward," demanded Phemus.

Jack bounded forward, as did Loki. This giant had a much different visage than his brethren. He possessed the same shiny cheeks and slick black hair as they, but he was skinnier and had striking blue eyes. Loki also had a hint of stubble under his chin that matched his extra long sideburns. Dangling from his left earlobe was a pair of silver hoops.

"You'll race my fellow, Loki, who I hope will give you more of a challenge than Paul did. You see, we giants have a reputation to maintain, so we don't take too kindly to losing any competition."

"First person to touch the top of that peak and return will win," said Loki, pointing at a mountaintop poking through the clouds about a mile away. "On my mark, we shall go."

Dodger frowned at yet another display of unfairness in the trial. Jack did not seem bothered by this and took up a running stance with his hands placed on the ground, his feet cocked back, and his eyes locked on the mountain peak. The small wings popped out of the sides of his sandals and began flapping.

"Go!" said Loki without warning. The giant and Jack took off down the valley. Jack's winged sandals propelled him across the clouds, leaving Loki stomping along behind him.

"Whoa!" said Dodger, impressed.

"That makes *two* trials that we've won, giant," said Hansel with a grin.

"I wouldn't be so sure of that," replied Phemus, nodding at the racers.

They watched as Jack reached the mountain and began bounding up its slope toward the peak. Loki caught up with him and merely reached his arm out, tapped the tip with his finger, and retreated to the hut. Jack paused, staring dumbfounded at the giant. He leapt into the air and soared to the mountaintop. He then kicked off the peak and raced after Loki, but it was too late. The giant crossed the finish line just seconds ahead of Jack.

"You failed the trial of speed, and I hope that teaches you a lesson on arrogance," said Phemus.

Jack skidded to a stop at the finish line with a crestfallen look on his face. "I did my best. I'm sorry, Jill…"

"Your best was obviously not good enough," said Loki, chuckling. Jack scowled and balled his fists.

"Well, you've faced off against us, so I think it's time we focus the trials solely on you people," commented Phemus.

"Wait a minute. Are you making these trials up as you go along?" asked Dodger.

"Of course! We never expect company. Now that we have guests, it would do us well to have fun!"

The giants let out hearty laughs. Humpty leaned over to Rump and whispered, "They're mad."

"You!" shouted Phemus, pointing at Rump. The alchemist looked to his left and right, and then pointed at his chest while staring back at the giant. "Yes, you will participate in the next challenge! This won't be any physical challenge, though. This will instead be a trial of the mind."

"Easy!" said Humpty. "You think you can stump one of the greatest brains in Neverland?"

Phemus frowned and furrowed his brow. "What did I just tell you about arrogance? You never learn, do you? This won't be your average test of intelligence, and I won't be asking about history or common world knowledge. This will be a riddle; a hard one at that." Humpty went silent. Phemus resumed his calm demeanor and peered down at Rump as he explained the riddle. "A stranger walks into a new town where he's never been before and meets a street performer. The performer tells the man, 'If I can write down your exact weight on this piece of paper, you must give me all the money in your pockets.' The stranger agrees to the bet. In the end, he actually has to give all of his money to the performer. How could this have happened?"

Dodger could tell that Rump was clueless. The riddle even stumped the Literary, who thought as hard as he could for the answer. His concentration must have shown in his face because Phemus pointed an accusing finger at him.

"This challenge is for the alchemist and the alchemist only! Nobody else better answer, including you, boy!"

Rump sat down, crossed his legs, and pondered with his fingers steepled. The giants watched him in silence, occasionally whispering to each other. Dodger grew worried and anxious; if they lost another challenge, they would be in real trouble.

"The performer gave the stranger a truth potion and asked him what his exact weight was," answered Rump, shrugging.

The giants collectively shouted, "NO!"

"Arrogance, arrogance," repeated Phemus, shaking his head. "I knew you alchemists weren't that clever. Guess your magical education didn't serve you well this time. The answer to the riddle was given to you! The performer said he would write down 'your exact weight', and that is exactly what he did! He wrote down the words 'your exact weight' on the slip of paper!" The giants boomed with laughter.

Dodger scowled at them. "You know, jokes aren't funny if you have to explain them."

Phemus's laughter stopped abruptly. Lowering his face to Dodger's level, he grumbled, "You're lucky that I'm in a good mood, boy. But if you retort like that again, I'll hang you over my fire pit by that ring in your lip."

Dodger gulped and stepped back a few feet. *I need to keep my mouth shut.*

"Maybe we should make him partake in the next challenge," suggested Paul.

"No!" said Humpty. "I'll be the next participant. What's the challenge?"

Phemus's gaze wandered to the egg-man. "Well, not everything has to be so serious. We can make the next challenge a trial of joy."

"What do you mean?"

Phemus pulled an enormous animal-skin bag from his belt and placed it on the ground in front of Humpty, where it swished and sloshed around. "Tell me, egg-man, are you a fan of Maple Ale?"

Dodger's eyes widened. "Is that alcohol in there? How much is Humpty supposed to drink of that?"

"Until I say that he's had his fill," said Phemus. "That should teach you about arrogance and smart mouths. Are you ready for a drink, egg-man?" The giant popped the cap off the bag's nozzle. A pungent, bitter smell like sour apple juice filled the vicinity. Dodger was extremely thankful that he wouldn't have to do this challenge. There was no way he could drink that enormous amount, but how was Humpty going to do it?

Humpty raised his hand. "I *am* pretty parched, now that you mention it." He took one of his swords and stabbed it into the pouch, poking a thin hole through the canvas. Yanking the sword out, he unleashed a stream of golden liquid, which further permeated the air with the smell of alcohol. Humpty bowed to his companions, then to the giants, and placed his mouth against the opening.

Dodger stared as Humpty drank the ale, wondering how the anatomy of a talking egg worked and how someone of Humpty's physique could possibly ingest food or drink. As he wondered this, he noticed the pouch slowly deflating. The giants were also aware of this and exchanged concerned glances. Rump opened his mouth, but Dodger elbowed him to prevent him from talking lest he incite any more penalties on arrogance. Humpty continued to drink, draining the bag more and more.

Just as the container was three-quarters of the way empty, Phemus spoke up. "All right, all right! You passed! Save the rest for me!" The giant snatched the pouch and emptied the remaining contents into his mouth.

The adventurers cheered. Humpty threw his arms up in celebration and toppled over on his side. Pinocchio and Rump pulled him to his feet. Dodger saw that the egg-man's eyes were no longer their original orange-yellow hue and were now coated in a pink glaze; Humpty Dumpty was drunk.

"Let that be a lesson" he slurred. "It's not the size of the egg that matters, but the amount of yolk that counts!"

"Alcohol hits him pretty fast," remarked Dodger.

"He'll be drunk for a while," observed the grinning Rump.

"You won this round by sheer luck, little ones. Let us go inside for the final trial." For the third time, Phemus lowered his hand for everyone to climb on (it took Rump and Pinocchio a minute to drag Humpty over their shoulders and onto the hand).

"This final test will decide whether you all go free or not," said Phemus, depositing the group on the floor.

"And what if we lose?" hiccupped Humpty.

"Let's just say that we intend to get our ale back," said Paul.

The giants laughed in unison and the adventurers shared worried looks, except for Humpty, who kept staring up at Phemus.

"I don't get it?" he said.

"The last trial," announced Phemus, ignoring Humpty, "is a test of bravery, courage, and heart. And this time, the young boy will complete it alone."

Even though he knew it was coming, Dodger still panicked. Pinocchio stepped forward.

"I will take the challenge in his place."

"No, you will not!" said Loki. "The egg already took over the last trial for the boy, so he's competing in this one alone. No substitutions!"

Pinocchio glared at the giants. Dodger gave him a look of gratitude and put his hand on his shoulder.

"It's fine, Pinocchio. I'll handle it." Dodger looked up at Phemus. "What's the challenge?"

Phemus put his fingers to his mouth and let out a shrill whistle. Seconds later, a distant roar was heard.

"Here's a fun fact," chimed in Paul, nudging his head at the little prison holding Jill. "See that cage? It actually belongs to our pet."

Dodger gulped. He could only imagine what kind of beast required a cage with such thick, strong bars that Hansel couldn't easily break. As if in response to his curiosity, another loud roar sounded, this time much closer to the hut. Something flew in through a window. The beast landed in front of Phemus's feet and roared so loudly that Dodger had to take a step back.

"Behold the Jabberwocky!" said the leader giant.

Compared to the giants, the Jabberwocky was the size of a dog. It towered over Dodger and his companions, with feet large enough to squash

Hansel. It had blue and gray scales covering its body, enormous gray claws protruding from its hands and feet, two fleshy wings sticking out at odd angles from its back, and a long scaly tail that rose up and slammed down onto the ground. The head was the most frightening aspect of the beast; it didn't have a snout, but a flat face with bulbous black eyes similar to glassy cannonballs, and pointed teeth bigger than its claws.

"Whoa," said Dodger quietly. The Jabberwocky's head turned sideways, displaying pointed ears that twitched lightly when it heard the Literary speak.

"Oh, he's not so big!" said the drunken Humpty. "I could take him!" The egg-man drew out his sword and swung it above his head. Pinocchio grabbed his wrist and forced him to drop the sword.

Phemus stated, "The last trial is a fight to the end. If you win, then you all get to leave. If you lose, well, the Jabberwocky will be the first of us to feed."

Dodger gulped again. He wasn't sure what scared him more, the Jabberwocky or the giants' threats. He attempted to shake off the uneasy feeling, summoning optimism and courage to replace the sense of dread.

"Good luck, Dodger," said a voice behind him. The Literary turned to thank Pinocchio, but it wasn't he who spoke; it was Hansel. The Stronghand gave a nod of encouragement, as did his other companions. This tiny act instantly boosted Dodger's confidence, and suddenly, he didn't feel as scared anymore.

The Jabberwocky roared and took flight, kicking up clouds of dust as its wide wings propelled it into the air. Dodger squinted up at the beast circling over the area.

"What the h-" Dodger ducked and threw his hands over his head. The Jabberwocky dove at the ground and glided across the floor. Its feet snatched at the open air above Dodger and nicked his arm with one of its sharpened claws. It flew back up into the sky.

"Dammit," said Dodger through gritted teeth. The claw left a thin gash across his forearm, but it wasn't bleeding too heavily. "This isn't fair! I can't fly!"

"Then you're at a disadvantage!" said Loki, prompting all the giants to laugh.

Dodger was extremely annoyed with the giants' sense of humor, and he was furious at them for having the nerve to criticize the adventurers for their arrogance. He should have known they would rig the game so they could win. Dodger stood no chance with the Jabberwocky. This beast proved to be a bigger challenge than the troll, which Dodger never could have defeated if he hadn't found…

"The carpet!" Dodger reached into his back pocket. The Jabberwocky swooped to the ground again, sticking its feet out and opening its claws wide. Dodger moved out of the path of the oncoming creature and threw the playing-card-sized piece of cloth in front of him. The carpet instantly expanded, and Dodger hopped on. It took him all the way up to the ceiling, out of the Jabberwocky's reach.

Everyone down below cheered, except for the giants, and Humpty, who was tenderly stroking Rump's arm with a grin. Dodger clung to the carpet, which was now flying almost completely vertical. When it leveled off, he peeked down and saw the Jabberwocky resuming its circling pattern near the ground.

"What's going on?" Dodger said aloud. The Jabberwocky's head twitched and it zoomed up at the carpet. Dodger steered out of its path and commanded the carpet to rise until it was inches from the ceiling. Once again, the Jabberwocky didn't chase him; it simply glided around the lower area. Dodger looked at its unblinking black eyes and its tall twitching ears.

"You're blind!" exclaimed the Literary. The Jabberwocky flashed upward, opening its mouth wide and closing down on thin air, missing the carpet by inches. Dodger maneuvered himself to a corner of the hut's ceiling. Meanwhile, the Jabberwocky continued circling.

You can still hear me, thought Dodger. He smacked his dagger on the woodwork of the house, making a loud clanging sound, but the Jabberwocky didn't react. He hit it again, harder this time, and there was still no reaction.

"Hey!" he shouted. The Jabberwocky darted at him and he flew out of the way.

You know my voice, Dodger thought. Now he understood the monster's ears twitching at the beginning of the trial.

"Row, row, row your boat, gently down the stream," Dodger sang loudly; he was yelling the first thing he could think of to get the beast's attention.

The Jabberwocky followed his every move, coming close to catching him in its jaws on multiple occasions. Luckily, the carpet was faster and more agile. "Merrily, merrily, merrily, merrily, life is but a dream!" There was a wall coming up and Dodger had an idea. Down below, he thought he heard one of the giants whistling at him, but he chose to ignore it.

Still singing, Dodger urged the carpet to fly quickly toward the wall. At the last minute, he swerved to the left, coming within inches of the paneling. Dodger spun around, expecting to see the Jabberwocky crash, but he was shocked that the beast was nowhere to be found.

A loud noise caught the Literary's attention. Looking down, Dodger saw the giants stomping along the floor of the hut while jeering. The Jabberwocky had flown to the table and had snatched up the cage holding Jill. Phemus pried open the hut's door, letting his pet fly outside.

Balls of red light were being thrown at the giants' legs from an ant-sized attacker whom Dodger assumed was Rump. Another figure, presumably Jack, flew out the door after the Jabberwocky, only for Loki to step in front of him and block his way. Dodger steered the carpet out the door, zipping under the giant's outstretched arm, and pursued the Jabberwocky through the cloud valley.

"Hey!" Dodger shouted. The creature's ears twitched and it slowed down, craning its neck backwards. The magic carpet accelerated and soon caught up with the beast.

They both flew faster, heading farther and farther away from the hut. Dodger didn't know what it was, but he had another one of those strange feelings; a sort of confidence and reassuring notion that willed him to take a risk. Flipping the dagger upside-down into a stabbing position, he gritted his teeth and leapt off the carpet.

Dodger landed on top of the beast's back, sinking the dagger between two scales, and hung on for dear life. The creature's body felt like tree bark with the toughness of stone and a thin slimy coating. The Jabberwocky roared at the blade impaled in its body and let go of the cage. Dodger briefly panicked, but focused on the task at hand. He latched his free hand onto the edge of one of the wings, and used his dagger to stab every part of the beast he could reach.

After five or six hits, the Jabberwocky issued one final roar and fell through the air. Dodger yanked the blood-covered dagger out from its back and held onto the wing for dear life. He looked around for his carpet, but it was nowhere in sight. Trusting his instincts, as they had helped him so far, he jumped off the Jabberwocky's back.

Falling into the valley was as frightening as when Dodger was on the bridge. He saw the cloudy terrain drawing closer and closer until an ornamental design swept underneath him and broke his fall. It was the carpet, now the size of a parking lot and carrying Jill's cage.

Jill was awake and pressed up to the bars of her cell. "Where am I? Who are you?" she demanded.

"I'll explain in a second," said Dodger between breaths and with his hand on his chest, attempting to slow down his heart rate. "We have to go back and get your brother first!"

The carpet swung around and retreated back to the hut. They hadn't gone too far. The door was still ajar, but there was no sign or sound of activity coming from within. Dodger hoped that his friends were okay.

As if on cue, Jack flew out the door carrying Gretel in his arms. Hansel came out after him, with Rump and Pinocchio close behind carrying Humpty on their shoulders.

Dodger's heart leapt. The carpet hovered near them and he beckoned them to hop on. When the last person climbed aboard, the carpet zoomed to the beanstalk.

"Jack!" said Jill.

Jack dropped Gretel onto the carpet and ran up to the bars of the cage, smiling widely with tears in his eyes.

"Jill! I'm so sorry the giants took you! I went to Neverland for help." Jill stared at Dodger suspiciously. Jack chuckled nervously and said, "He's a Literary. I know he looks strange, but we can trust him."

Dodger gave a weak smile and shrugged. Jill was about to say something when she screamed and pointed over the Literary's shoulder. The Jabberwocky was flying at them, roaring and dripping splotches of blue blood from the gaping wound on its back. Rump conjured a blazing fireball in the palm of his hand and hurled the spell with a loud shout. The beast swallowed the ball whole and continued charging without faltering, although it did cough a puff of smoke out. Rump prepared to throw another fireball, but Hansel yelled.

"Watch out!"

Hansel pulled Rump and Gretel off to one side of the carpet, and Pinocchio and Jack pulled Humpty and Dodger off to the other. The Jabberwocky flew straight down the center of the carpet and clamped its jaws on the cage bars.

The bite was so strong that it bent the bars apart, leaving a wide gap for Jill to crawl through. She escaped her cell and dove forward to embrace her brother. The stunned Jabberwocky roared and shrieked as it struggled to free its stuck teeth from the cage bars. Rump unhooked the mace from his belt and Pinocchio retrieved his hammer, and the two pummeled the beast's skull over and over. Hansel joined in with his fists.

"We need to get you two back to Amrya," Dodger said to Jack and Jill over the crunching sounds of Pinocchio, Rump, and Hansel's attack. Humpty watched the scene while giggling.

Just before the carpet reached the beanstalk, Dodger looked at the hut, expecting the giants to be in pursuit. Rump briefly stopped the pummeling and waved his blue-blood-soaked hand.

"Don't worry, Dodger! We took care of those oafs. Their fighting abilities matched their intelligence, or lack thereof. Amrya will no longer have to worry about giants."

Jack and Jill smiled at each other. Even Dodger sensed relief washing over him. As the carpet entered the gap between the beanstalk and the clouds, Hansel shoved the cage and the Jabberwocky's corpse (or what was left of it) off the side. The carpet shrunk down to its car-sized length and squeezed back below the clouds. Dodger and his friends emerged into the sky above Amrya, where they could see the morning sun coming over the horizon.

"Hold on a moment!" said Rump. The alchemist lifted his hands above his head. He used the last of his magic to shoot a stream of fire from his fingertips at the beanstalk. Two flaming ropes coiled around the plant, encasing it and snaking their way up its length all the way above the clouds. Another two streams of fire followed the beanstalk down to the base, just above Amrya. Rump motioned his hands as if he was pulling two coils of rope apart, and the beanstalk instantly disappeared in a flash of red and yellow, temporarily blinding Dodger. The Literary's eyesight came back in time for him to witness a light dust falling from the sky, similar to snow. Dodger looked at the flakes landing on the carpet and discovered that they were actually pieces of ash.

"That should keep any more Lillis from coming to Amrya ever again," said Rump, dusting his hands.

Chapter 9

A Place to Rest

A strong wave of exhaustion struck Dodger, forcing him to yawn widely. He hadn't had a wink of sleep since he first arrived in Storyworld and he was shocked at how long the group had stayed in the cloud-city. It would take at least another hour or two for the carpet to return to Neverland.

"Is there anywhere we can go to sleep? I feel like I'm going to pass out," said the Literary.

Everyone shared this sentiment. There were shadows under Rump's eyes, and Hansel kept stretching and yawning nonstop. Even Pinocchio was in a daze, his eyelids half-closed and his eyebrows twitching slightly. Humpty was the sole member of the group who showed any signs of energy as he laughed quietly to himself. Rump agreed that bed-rest would do the egg-man good and that he might be able to sleep off the drunkenness.

"There are plenty of inns across Amrya that you're more than welcome to stay at," indicated Jack. "After helping save my sister, the least I could do is pay for your lodgings."

"Actually," said Hansel," the Fallen Timber Inn isn't too far from here, and it's owned by a good friend of mine. I'm sure we could get a free room, as well as some food and drink."

Dodger's Doorway

The carpet's riders shared a nod of agreement. The Stronghand instructed Dodger where to direct the carpet so that they could get to the inn. By his directions, it was less than a mile south of Amrya.

The carpet sailed smoothly above the treetops. It was early morning, and the cool air accompanying the dawn was refreshing. A light breeze rippled through the forest and flowed upward, fluttering the edges of the carpet. Dodger let his hand fall over the edge so that it dangled carelessly in the wind. The scratch from the Jabberwocky had stopped bleeding thanks to Rump's healing potion, but his arm was still sore, and the breeze soothed the pain. Dodger's entire body ached and he could hardly stay awake. His exhaustion prevented him from enjoying the colorful and awe-inspiring sight of the sun swimming above the horizon. He twitched when he felt a hand on his back. It was Gretel.

"Hey, you," she whispered. Dodger cast a worried glance in Hansel's direction. He was sitting near the edge of the carpet, clenching the fabric and occasionally glancing down at the trees while talking to Rump. Gretel laughed and said, "Don't worry. I think my brother is starting to like you. He respects your courage and sees what a fool he's been."

"Well, I'm glad he doesn't hate me anymore. It was getting kinda hard to talk to you." Dodger smiled and brushed a lock of hair over Gretel's ear.

"Was there something in particular you wanted to say to me?" she said.

Dodger smiled again. A burst of energy flowed through his body. He closed his eyes and leaned in, meeting Gretel's lips with his own. His heart skipped a beat and he no longer felt exhausted. For the first time in what seemed like forever, Dodger was truly happy. The kiss drove away all of his negative thoughts; his neglectful parents, Ryan Martin, the countless near-death experiences, and even the nagging curiosity as to why he was still stuck in Storyworld even after he had finished his quests. Dodger didn't care because, at this point, he was in no rush to get home.

"Down there," said Hansel, pointing at an upcoming two-story building poking out of the trees.

There were several windows at the top of a derelict shack and only one visible entrance in the form of a pair of black double-doors. Tethered to a post outside the door were four horses, which were grazing at a patch of grass at the steps. A giant wooden sign hung on the upper story of the building and featured the words "Fallen Timber Inn" above a woodcut of two crossed axes.

"Do they happen to serve drinks here?" sputtered Humpty.

Rump patted the egg-man's arm. "Sir Humpty, the only drink you'll be having is a tall pitcher of water to flush that alcohol out of your system."

Dodger commanded the carpet to descend in front of the inn. Pinocchio and Rump attempted to haul Humpty into the building, but he shook them off, insisting he could do it himself. By the time everyone had left the carpet and gone into the inn, the sun was finally a good distance over the horizon.

Hansel nodded to the bartender, a brutish man with an eye-patch wedging a nozzle into a barrel behind the bar. Dodger's immediate reaction upon stepping into the building was a mixture of slight disgust and unease. There were dozens of patrons populating the bar and tables, all of whom were glaring at the guests. The musty smell of warm alcohol mixed with sweat saturated the air and made Dodger's eyes water.

"Minos, old friend," Hansel said to the bartender. "Would you be so kind as to allow me and my fellows to rest here for a while? We've had an exhausting night."

Minos scrutinized each person with his solitary eye, his gaze stopping on Dodger. He nodded to Hansel.

"Fine. I just hafta warn you that there be a rowdy crowd here this mornin'. Then again, what'd you expect from people who drink at sunrise?"

"I think we'll be fine, Minos. And I also think it's perfectly acceptable to drink in the morning, depending on the situation. After defeating a group of giants at their own game, who wouldn't want to enjoy a nice beverage, eh?" Hansel cheered and patted Rump heavily on the shoulder. His companions replied to his strangely positive mood with confused stares. Several bar patrons snickered. One in particular, a rugged and lanky man wearing a tunic made of sewn-together rags, downed his drink and belched loudly.

The adventurers sat at a long table in the middle of the inn. Minos filled two glass pitchers with a dark brown liquid as Hansel continued to make small talk with him.

"I am exhausted," said Pinocchio, yawning widely and spinning his head in a full circle. "After the drinks, I'm going right to bed."

"Same here," agreed Dodger. "Actually, I can skip the drinks and just go up to bed now."

"Absolutely not!" said Hansel, carrying the pitchers over. "You'll celebrate with all of us. You've earned it."

"I'm impressed with your generous mood, Agent Hansel," said Rump. "It's nice to see you've had a change of heart."

Hansel smiled as he filled the glasses and passed them around the table to everyone, including Humpty. The agent raised his own glass.

"To a successful mission!"

Dodger examined the amber liquid and told Hansel, "I'm not twenty-one."

The Literary was met with curious stares and was about to explain, but then thought of how ridiculous he would sound if he attempted to make his companions understand the concept of a legal drinking age. Dodger shrugged and took a sip along with everyone else. The pungent smell filled his nostrils and made him cringe, but he took a deep drink the moment he felt the refreshingly cool and smooth liquid pass his lips. It tasted like sweet tea with a slight tang.

Humpty emptied his cup almost immediately and dropped it to the ground. "Oh, that was perhaps not a good idea." The egg-man rolled on his seat. Everyone scooted out of the way as he pursed his lips and let out a tremendous belch that rattled the empty glass pitcher.

Jack and Jill's jaws dropped, as did Hansel and Gretel's. Dodger stared unbelievingly at Rump and Pinocchio before he began laughing hysterically. Soon, the whole table joined in, even the stoic Wooden Soldier. Humpty, unabashed, merely wiped his enormous mouth on the back of his arm.

"Dotcher," slurred the egg-man, slamming a fist onto the table and pointing slightly to the left of the Literary, "will you walk and talk with me?"

"What?"

"You," the egg-man pointed at Dodger, "me," he pointed at himself, "walk." He hopped off his seat and traipsed around in a circle.

"Um, yeah, sure. Where?"

"Outdoors! Fresh air!" Humpty unsheathed his sword and waved it around. Rump, sitting next to him, ducked down with his hands wrapped over his head. The egg-man charged out the door, his blade leading the way. Minos threw his hands up in exasperation, and Hansel shrugged apologetically. Dodger exited the building right after Humpty, hoping that he wouldn't hurt himself.

For a moment, Dodger panicked because Humpty was nowhere in sight. That was when he heard hiccupping mixed with coughing and sobbing. He traced the sounds around the corner of the inn and found Humpty sitting on the ground crying with his sword sprawled across his lap.

It was odd watching him cry. Humpty blinked yellow tears, and his hiccups were so powerful that his entire body hopped off the ground. The sound of his sobs was human-like, though, and Dodger couldn't help but empathize with him.

"Humpty, what's wrong?" asked Dodger, kneeling next to him.

Humpty blinked out another large yellow tear. "What can I do? I'm an egg?"

Dodger chuckled nervously. "I, uh, I thought you knew this already."

"How will she ever love me?"

"Who?"

Humpty sniffled. "Princess Tinkerbell."

It took a moment for it to click in Dodger's mind. "Whoa, what? You have a thing for Tinkerbell?"

"I love her! I really love her a lot! I want to be her prince and I'm just an egg!"

Dodger rubbed Humpty's round back. He wasn't sure how to give relationship advice to someone, especially an egg in love with a human princess. "Why don't you just tell her how you feel?"

"I c-c-can't. She'll never love me. Peter Pan died and she has to find a prince. Why would she want me?" Humpty slurred.

Dodger pondered for a moment. "Listen to me, Humpty. You can't be afraid to tell a girl you like her. That's no way to live. I mean, I'm probably not the best person to give advice on this stuff, bu-"

"You're so brave!" slurred the egg-man. "Y-you're not afraid to tell a woman how you feel. You're not afraid of anything! You're a fearless soldier!"

"I'm afraid of my own shadow," explained Dodger. "I'm just a kid. I'm a loser. I'm such a loser that I had to make up a new name for myself to sound cooler. Did you know my real name isn't even Dodger? It's actually Mark; plain and boring, like me. Am I really someone who should be your role model?"

"I've seen nothing but courage from you while you've been here," Humpty said. Another two hiccups. "I've seen you fight trolls and witches and all.

I'm a leader for the Neverland's armies and I'm afraid to tell Tinkerbell that I l-love her."

"Like I told you, Humpty, you can't be afraid to tell somebody that you love them. You deserve to have someone care about you. Don't hold back how you feel about Tinkerbell. You're just torturing yourself by thinking about it. That's not a way to live your life."

"B-but what will others say? What will she say? You don't know how difficult it is for me, an egg, to live like this. I just want to be happy, and I want her to be happy! Life is so hard." Another hiccup.

Dodger had to pause and think about what he was about to say. The next words he spoke were almost directed at himself as much as Humpty.

"Life is tough. I'm a miserable kid who could change his life if he wasn't so afraid. Don't let that happen to you. Don't get hung up over something, especially when you can easily solve it. If you like someone, tell them. And if things don't work out, it's not the end of the world. That simple."

Humpty blinked and squinted at the Literary. "For a young man, you have a lot of knowledge of these matters." The egg-man suddenly stood up, wiping the tears away. "Come, let us go back to our friends."

Humpty waddled into the inn, leaving Dodger sitting on the ground caught up in his own thoughts. His mind replayed the conversation over and over again.

Don't get hung up over something, especially when you can easily solve it.

Dodger suddenly felt lightheaded. Assuming it was from exhaustion, he took a deep breath, and entered the inn. A couple more minutes and he could finally pass out in a warm, comfortable bed.

Hansel and Minos were conversing at the bar, now joined by Humpty, who was loudly demanding another drink. Rump and Pinocchio were locked in an arm-wrestling match at the table, with the Wooden Soldier effortlessly beating the alchemist, and Jack and Jill were missing, possibly having gone up to bed.

Gretel was standing at a neighboring table. It appeared that she was trying to return to her friends, but the man who had belched before Hansel's toast was blocking her way. He was loudly slurring pickup lines at the agent and waving his arms about.

Anger suddenly replaced Dodger's exhaustion. He approached the man and called out, "Hey, is there a problem?"

The man spun around, swaying heavily on his feet. He wore a ragged cap that matched his dirty green outfit, and there was a thick stench emanating from his body. A pointy gray beard covered the lower half of his face, and the top half was totally hairless except for his razor-thin eyebrows. The man peered down his bulbous nose at Dodger.

"There won' be a problem if you walk away."

Despite the man's low, croaking voice, his statement carried throughout the entire inn, silencing all other conversations. The patrons shifted in their seats, watching the confrontation with apprehension.

Minos broke away from his conversation with Hansel, filled a glass, and slammed it onto the bar. "Have another drink on me, Don. I'm not in the mood to clean up this place again."

"There won' be any fightin' long as this kid learns to keep his mouth shut!" said Don.

"He's more of a man than you'll ever be," said Gretel disgustedly. She tried to push past Don, but he stuck his arm out to block her again. Dodger heard chairs scuffling behind him as Rump, Pinocchio, and Hansel got up.

"Hang on," said Dodger, holding his hand up to stop his friends. *Where's this coming from?* He ignored his thoughts and stared up at Don, not breaking his gaze. "Get out."

Don laughed, his putrid breath making Dodger's eyelids quiver. "You think I'm 'fraid of a pest like you? I don't care if you're a Literary. I can pick you up and toss you across this room without breakin' a sweat."

"I don't want any trouble," said Dodger. "Just leave her alone and get out of here before-"

Don drunkenly shoved the Literary. Gretel stepped forward and slapped Don in the face. He didn't take this lightly and shoved her to the ground.

Hansel roared and charged at Don, his face ablaze with anger. Dodger balled up his fist and threw a punch that caught Don right under the chin. The drunk stumbled away, holding his mouth and howling. Dodger grabbed the back of Don's shirt, and with a loud yell, he steered the drunken man into the nearest wall and pitched him into the wooden fixture. There was a crunching sound as Don's head left a tiny crack in the wall and his body slumped to the ground.

All the guests in the inn watched in stunned silence. Dodger stood in a trance, hardly believing what just happened. Gretel looked at him in awe as he lowered his hand to her.

"Are you okay?" asked Dodger.

"I'm-I'm fine. That was impressive."

"I think I got a bit carried away," said Dodger, turning to Minos. "Sorry about the wall. He wa-"

"Don' worry 'bout it," said the bartender, waving his hand. "Don's been known to do that a lot. Nasty drunk, he is. If he's not pickin' fights in here, he's probably out attackin' windmills and whatnot. Don't know how he ever hosted a Literary."

"Some peoples just can't control their drinks," said Humpty. Finishing his glass, he passed out and fell off the chair.

Rump and Pinocchio scrambled over to help. The bar patrons all laughed, breaking the tension. The commotion resumed almost instantly. Two of Don's friends came to pick up his body and ushered him out of the inn. Hansel helped his sister back to her chair and examined her face closely, grimacing at the red mark that Don's slap had left.

"Does it hurt?" he asked his sister.

"Don't worry about me. I'm fine."

Hansel nodded to Dodger. "Thank you for defending her."

Dodger gave a half-shrug and, before he had a chance to say anything, a loud thump came from the bar. Rump had passed out next to Humpty and slumped over the egg-man's body. Pinocchio's eyebrows spun in circles.

"Rump!" yelled the general. As he struggled to shake the alchemist awake, he fell over as well. Dodger hurried over to his friends.

"Guys! Wake up!" All three of them were unconscious. "Cold water!" Dodger yelled. "We need cold water or something to wake them up!" Dodger felt lightheaded again. This time, he sensed himself losing balance. The room was spinning. When he called out for help, his voice sounded distant and echoed. His eyelids became heavy. The last thing he remembered was Minos staring at him before everything went black.

Chapter 10

Hostile Encounters

"Wake up!"

The mysterious voice echoed across the room. Dodger's eyes flashed open and he blinked a couple of times to make sure that he wasn't blind and that he was actually just in a pitch-black room. He could tell that he was lying on his back with thick, coarse ropes tying down his wrists and ankles.

"Where am I?" yelled the Literary.

"You mean 'Where are *we*?'" corrected a groan to Dodger's left. The voice sounded like Rumpelstiltskin.

"Rump? You're here?"

"I am too!" called out Humpty on Dodger's right.

"As am I," responded Pinocchio farther down the line.

"Us, too!" Jack and Jill said in unison. Jill continued, "Can't I go one day without being taken prisoner?"

"Quiet!" said the first voice that had awoken them.

A torch ignited high above them, filling the room with a dim, flickering light. Dodger squinted from the sudden glare and studied his surroundings. The adventurers were restrained in a circular room with stone walls extending so high up that the ceiling was obscured in darkness. Dodger was in the center of his friends, who were all lined up side-by-side and tied down to a metal bracket jutting from the grimy stone floor. Hansel and Gretel weren't present among the group.

"This will be a little experiment," said the ominous voice.

Dodger saw the speaker up on a stone balcony emerging from the wall above his feet. A gaunt man with waxy features and greasy black hair slicked back over his small head beamed down at them. The eerie smile carved onto his face stretched from ear to ear, and he had crossed eyes that were staring down at the prisoners. The jet-black suit he was wearing blended in so well with the darkness behind him that he almost looked like a floating face.

"Pain is an interesting concept, is it not?" continued the man. "The living body can suffer intense pain and still survive. My question is, how long can one last until pain destroys the mind?"

That doesn't sound good, thought Dodger. As he struggled with his bindings, the suited man yanked a lever on the wall next to him. A metallic chime rang out in the area, accompanied by a noise that sounded like a large piece of metal scraping over stone. A giant metal pendulum popped out from a dark crevice in the wall and swung across the room, then swung back. At the bottom of the pendulum was a semi-circle-shaped blade that soared just a couple of feet above the prisoners. The contraption kept swinging back and forth through the room, lowering itself several inches with each passing.

Everybody tugged and pulled at their ropes. Humpty appeared to be struggling the hardest due to his round body being closer to the blade than anybody else's. Rump eyed the pendulum blade in morbid curiosity.

"Dodger," croaked the alchemist, "have you ever heard of anything like this in your world?"

A story popped into Dodger's head. "Actually, yeah, now that I think about it. There's a story. I think it's called *The Pit and the Pendulum* by Edgar Allan Poe."

"I remember that name," said the man in the suit. "He was a funny little person. I first tested this mechanism on him."

"Tell me whoever was in that story escaped," said Rump, watching the pendulum swing closer and closer.

"Yeah, I'm pretty sure he did," said Dodger, struggling to remember the story that he had read in English class. The pendulum was inches from striking Humpty. "At the end, the guy gets out because... because... someone helped him out."

"Who helped him escape? Maybe they'll rescue us?"

Dodger grimaced. "I'm pretty sure the French army won't be here anytime soon. At least, that's how the story ended. But that guy in the suit said he tested this thing out on Poe, and he made it back to my world okay. I wonder how he got out?"

"I helped him!" cried another voice. Dodger and the suited man looked up. A jet-black raven the size of a vulture materialized out of the dark ceiling and landed on the ground between the captives.

"No, no!" uttered the man. "I thought you were long gone from here!"

"I came back to put an end to your heartless experiments, Roderick!" said the raven with a woman's voice. She began to peck and nip at the ropes restraining Dodger's arms. Her strong beak managed to tear through the toughened coils, but she wasn't moving fast enough. The pendulum had dropped another foot and scraped across Humpty's shell, leaving a shallow cut that oozed yellow blood. Humpty clenched his teeth and eyes.

"Save Humpty first!" commanded Dodger.

The raven abandoned the Literary's ropes and now picked at the egg-man's bindings. Roderick retreated into the shadows, and there was a muffled sound of a metal door clanging shut.

One of Humpty's arms came free and he helped undo the other ties. Every time the pendulum swung down, he would lie on his back, allowing the blade to slice through the cut it had already made. More yellow blood seeped out with each swipe.

After several agonizing minutes, everyone was freed. As the last person was released, the pendulum fell another foot and scraped across the now empty ground, eventually grinding to a halt. Humpty sat off to the side, nursing his wound. A trail of thick yellow blood left a path from his bindings to where he was now resting. Rump knelt next to him.

"I may have a potion for that," said the alchemist. He reached for his belt and a look of horror crossed his face. "My potions are gone! And so is my mace!"

The prisoners discovered that they were all stripped of their weapons, and Jack was missing his flying sandals.

"Roderick may know where your weapons are hidden," said the raven, flying up to the balcony.

"Wha-how are we supposed to get up there?" yelled Dodger.

Without an answer, the raven ventured into the darkness behind the balcony where Roderick had disappeared. Minutes passed, during which Dodger and his companions discussed how they were going to escape, when the raven returned carrying a length of rope in her mouth. She dropped the end of the rope over the edge of the balcony, allowing it to uncoil all the way down to the ground at the prisoners' feet.

"Climb up. The other end is tied around a pillar in the lab."

They shared looks of concern, but Dodger knew that they didn't have time to spare, not with Humpty slowly bleeding out. One by one, they ascended the rope. They reached the balcony and followed the raven through a doorway leading into a darker room.

Chills rushed up Dodger's neck when he entered the lab. It looked like a decrepit hospital emergency room, and there was an unbearable odor lingering in the air. There were rows of tables covered in various surgical instruments. It was eerily similar to Geppetto's workshop except it had the added terror of multi-colored blood splatters all over the walls and floor. In the corner was a makeshift shower leaking drops of dirty water down a blood-covered drain. Dodger could hear a faint weeping coming from the other side of a locked metal door at the far side of the lab.

"Roderick is in there with your weapons," said the raven. She flew to the balcony where the rope had been draped over the railing. Dodger watched as she took the rope in her beak, pulled it back into the lab, and looped it through the metal door's handle.

"Tie a thick knot in this rope and get ready to pull as hard as you can," ordered the raven.

"How will that work?" asked Dodger. "We'll just be tearing the handle off and the door will still be locked."

Rump, however, sprung forward and swiftly tied the rope into a thick knot over the handle. Giving it a hard tug, he nodded to Pinocchio, who undid the other end of the rope from the stone pillar, and tied it around his body. The Wooden Soldier commanded everyone (besides Humpty) to grab the rope and pull as hard as they could. Dodger noticed the egg-man's shell becoming paler and paler as more yellow blood poured from his wound. The Literary took hold of the rope and looped it several times around his fist.

On Pinocchio's command, they pulled. They easily broke the handle apart as Dodger predicted, scattering metal shards all over the ground. The Literary looked at the raven curiously, wondering how she planned to get into the room now. She perched on top of a table next to the door and wedged her beak into the gap where the handle once stood. There was a click, and the sound of a heavy metal object hitting the ground in Roderick's room. When the raven moved out of the way, she revealed a large gap in the door, through which they could hear Roderick's terrified screams.

"No! No!"

"A simple solution," the raven declared.

Pinocchio untied the rope and charged at the door, battering it open with his shoulder. Dodger and his companions followed as Rump stayed behind to tend to Humpty.

Roderick stood at the opposite end of what appeared to be a storage locker filled with sealed burlap sacks covered in green and blue bloodstains. The stench was worse in here. Jack, Jill, and Dodger covered their noses and mouths, but Pinocchio stood strong, his wooden hands balled up into fists. Roderick clutched the Wooden Soldier's war hammer protectively against his chest as the rest of the weapons sat in a pile at his feet.

"If you answer our questions, we might let you live," said Pinocchio. "How did we get here?"

"My friend," said Roderick, his suave demeanor gone, "he is always bringing me new test subjects. He said you were perfect."

"Who's your friend?"

Roderick laughed maniacally. "A good man. He told me to simply watch over you and to make sure you all stayed nice and quiet. 'No experiments this time!' he said. What a fool."

"Tell us his name!"

Roderick choked up another eerie, shrieking laugh, then charged at the group while swinging the war hammer. Pinocchio ducked his swing and punched him hard, sinking his wooden knuckles so deep into his stomach that Roderick doubled over. Wheezing and gasping for air, he dropped the hammer and fell to his knees. Pinocchio cocked his leg back and kicked him into a metal locker, knocking him out cold.

"So much for finding out how we got here," said Jack, approaching the weapons and distributing them to everyone else. As the Amryan tied his sandals on, Dodger noticed he was missing something.

"The carpet's gone!" Dodger patted all of his pockets but there was no sign it. The carpet was nowhere in the storage locker or in Roderick's pockets either. Turning to the raven crouched by the doorway, he asked, "Did you see him take a flying carpet when he captured us?"

The raven shook her head. "Whatever you see is what he took."

"Are my potions in there?" shouted Rump from the other room.

Dodger suddenly remembered Humpty's fatal wound. He grabbed the belt of bottles and exited the locker. Humpty's eyes were closed and his mouth hung open. Rump was pale and leaning over the egg-man.

"The green potion, give it to me," demanded the alchemist. Dodger passed him the vial and Rump poured half of it onto Humpty's injury. The potion sizzled over the wound, turning into a white bond that matched the rest of the shell. The yellow blood stopped flowing and the wound closed up completely, but Humpty's eyes remained closed. Rump dumped whatever was left of the potion into the egg-man's open mouth.

"Come on," whispered the alchemist.

For several seconds, there was no movement from anyone. Dodger held his breath, hoping against hope that Humpty would be fine. Rump didn't move an inch, but kept his eyes transfixed on Humpty.

There was a cough and a sputter, and Humpty's eyes popped open. With unexpected agility and energy, he shot up and flipped onto his feet, leaving a stunned yet smiling Rump kneeling on the ground. Dodger noticed how his pink eyes had reverted to their original yellow hue.

"That was a close one!" said the egg-man. "I haven't been that near death since I fell off that wall!"

"I thought you said you were pushed," replied Rump, clapping his friend on the shoulder.

Pinocchio presented Humpty his weapons. "Not sure if you heard what went on in there, but we retrieved our weapons and handled our captor. Unfortunately, we still need to get out of this wretched place."

"There is a way," called the raven. "Come with me."

"Hold on there," said Humpty. "Before we do anymore following, you need to tell us who you are and why you are helping us. We do not need to be lured into another trap."

The raven tucked her wings and spoke slowly. "My name is Lenore. I was once married to Roderick Usher, the man who took you prisoner here. As you can see, he was a scientist mad with power, with a love for experiments and science that surpassed even his love for me.

"One day, a man named Edgar wandered into the area. Roderick abducted him, intending to make him a new test subject. I was ordered to watch over the prisoner, but after many weeks, I fell in love with Edgar and helped him escape. The incident must have driven Roderick mad, for he made me his new test subject and transformed me into this creature you see before you.

"He has kept me imprisoned in this dungeon for years, and I have been unable to get out. I will lead you to the exit, but you must first promise me that you'll hold the door open so I can leave with you."

Pinocchio nodded. Lenore took off, leading the adventurers out of the laboratory. They went down winding stone passageways, twice taking the left path at a fork, and once taking the right path. At the end of a sloping tunnel, they saw a thin wooden door. Lenore told them it was the exit, and that it was too strong for her to open. Pinocchio charged to the front of the group, hammer first, and rammed the door so forcefully that it was blasted right off its hinges.

The group spilled outside into a wooded area that surrounded the building. It was still light out, but a glimpse at the horizon revealed that sunset was imminent.

"Hold on," said Dodger, breathing heavily, "what about Hansel and Gretel? What if they're still in there?"

"There were no other prisoners," said Lenore, fluttering out the doorway. "You were the only ones brought in this morning."

Jack was the last person to exit Roderick's house. Everyone gathered in a huddle, catching their breath and studying their surroundings. It appeared that they were in the backyard of a wooden cottage, which was erected over the dungeon where they were imprisoned. The yard was filled with several dead trees and a scattering of fallen branches. Dodger peeked past the side of the building and saw a road leading into the distance. He went to ask Lenore where they were, only to discover that she had disappeared.

"Where'd she go?"

Rump pointed at a black form disappearing into the sky and shouted, "There!"

"Where are you going?" called out Humpty.

"I must find Edgar!" responded Lenore, her body fading into the distance. "I've waited a long time to escape from the House of Usher, and I must be reunited with my true love."

"But he's not in this world anymore!" said Dodger. *He's not even alive!*

Lenore couldn't hear him (or simply chose not to listen) and kept flying into the horizon. Her tiny black form soon disappeared. Humpty growled and kicked a tree stump.

"This is just wonderful! We have no idea where we are, how we got here, or where to go!"

"It's not like we could've gone too far from the inn," said Dodger, attempting to keep a level head. "And Hansel said that it was on the way back to Neverland, so we might be around the corner for all we know."

"Hansel?" said Jack. "Hansel was probably the one who brought us to that place," he nodded back at the cottage. "How do we know we can trust that oaf? He bought those drinks *and* he seemed to be close friends with that one-eyed bartender. It was easy for him to slip something into the drinks that would have made us fall asleep. Why wasn't he in the dungeon with us? I knew that ogre couldn't be trusted; him and his little wench of a sister…"

"Shut up!" called out Dodger, fighting to keep the anger out of his voice. Turning scarlet, he said, "I don't think they could've done this to us. There's no way. We have to trust them."

"And why is that?" questioned Jill with her arms crossed.

"I can just tell. It's like a gut feeling."

The Amryan siblings exchanged doubtful looks but said nothing. This only made Dodger angrier.

"Look, if you want to talk about trust issues, then we should start with you, Jack."

Jill glanced at her brother curiously. Jack's cheeks flushed but he avoided her gaze.

"Why are you so adamantly defending them?" he retorted.

"I'm giving them the benefit of the doubt!" said Dodger.

Jack and Jill glared at the Literary. Humpty, Rump, and Pinocchio stood behind Dodger, although their faces indicated that they were also doubtful of his theory. Pinocchio stepped forward.

"I owe my salvation to Dodger," said the Wooden Soldier, "and he was brought to Storyworld to direct us on our quests. He has yet to lead us astray, so I'm inclined to believe him."

"Literaries have a wisdom far superior to our own, and I'll invest my trust in it. This isn't an argument!" added Humpty when Jack opened his mouth. "For now, we simply have to find a way to get back to Neverland or Amrya. Horner, can you fly up and see if you can spot any nearby landmarks?"

Jack sighed and flew himself above the treetops. Dodger turned to Jill and asked, "If he can fly, why can't he carry us out of here?"

"Neither he nor his sandals are strong enough," snapped Jill. "Our grandfather built them to accommodate Jack and roughly the weight of one other person. Trust me, I would ask him to fly me home right now if I didn't feel guilty about leaving you here in the middle of nowhere. My brother is right, you know. Those agents aren't to be trusted. But then again, you did help him save me. The least we can do is make sure you get back to Neverland."

Dodger was taken aback at Jill's snappy response, but still appreciated her and her brother's honor for staying with the group. Jack soon glided back down and landed in the yard.

"I do not recognize the area at all."

Dodger's heart sank. "You don't know where we are?"

"I can tell you that we're nowhere near Amrya. I know every tree, every stone, and every path around my city, but I can't figure out my bearings here. The only thing I did recognize was the Tower of Oz in the west."

"Then that's where we shall go," said Humpty, leading the group out of the yard. "The Wizard-King owes me a debt of gratitude and can surely help us home."

Dodger's Doorway

The group unanimously agreed to go west under Humpty's command, pursuing the setting sun. A pinkish, purple light covered the clouds as dusk crept over the horizon. The uncomfortable feeling that bothered Dodger in the dungeon had returned, even now that he had the Hunter's Dagger back in his hands. The incoming darkness combined with the strangeness and unfamiliarity of their surroundings was unsettling.

They were in a town that appeared to be abandoned. All of the signs hanging above the decrepit buildings were worn away or encrusted with so much dirt that only one or two letters were visible. The windows were boarded up with rotting wood and a couple of the doors had been busted in or torn apart. The cottage from where they escaped was just as bleak and decaying as the rest of the town. Who knows what other horrors were lurking in the other buildings' cellars?

Humpty led them around a bend that curved gently to the north, but still heading in the general direction of the tower. Every now and then, strange noises would emanate from the darkness; creaks, whistles, croaks, and hissing that sounded like whispers.

Another twist in the road directed the group back west, and they were faced with a surprising sight: a man on a horse. Dodger almost jumped at the sight of this figure that illuminated the area with a pale, ghostly light. The man was pale, or possibly just looked pale due to his aura, and had silver hair, a thin face, and wide eyes that peered off into the distance. He wore an all-white suit, white buckled boots, a white cape, and a little gray cap.

The man immediately noticed the group approaching down the path and rode his horse out to meet them. "Hello, wanderers! What brings you to this part of the land?"

Dodger didn't want to let his guard down, no matter how friendly this man seemed. There was an aspect of his presence more unsettling than the noises reverberating from the ghost town. Maybe it was his neon white aura, or maybe the fact that his horse left no footprints on the path as it clopped down the road. All Dodger knew was that he wasn't going to sheathe his dagger.

"We were traveling and must have taken a wrong turn," said Pinocchio. "We happened upon this town hoping for directions, but it appears abandoned except for you. Could you possibly direct us to Oz?"

"Absolutely!" said the man enthusiastically while his horse neighed loudly. "It's not far from 'ere. My name's Ichabod Crane, by the way."

A red flag shot up in Dodger's mind. That name was familiar, and he was sure he'd heard it somewhere, but he couldn't pinpoint its exact origin.

The travelers introduced themselves to Ichabod and allowed him to steer them down the left side of a forked path. Jack and Jill strode next to the horse and started a conversation with the man. Rump and Humpty came up right behind them, once again discussing old adventures. Meanwhile, Pinocchio stuck close to Dodger, keeping watch over the surrounding area.

Dodger whispered to Pinocchio, "I've definitely heard of this guy in my world. I just can't think of where."

"Was he a villain?" asked Pinocchio.

"I don't remember. It's driving me nuts, though. He doesn't look too threatening. It's probably not a big deal."

Dusk was gone, replaced with darkness. Ichabod's aura provided ample lighting, his pale glow acting like a lantern for the travelers. The horseman directed them around another curve that straightened out into a wide path extending toward the horizon. About a half-mile down the road was a thin stone bridge stretching over a calm river.

"That bridge marks the town limits," indicated Ichabod. "Once you cross over, you simply have to go straight and you'll soon end up right outside the walls of one of Oz's outermost cities."

"Thank you for your assistance, Mr. Crane," said Humpty.

"No problem at all, good sirs and fair lady," replied Ichabod, tipping his hat.

The group waved goodbye and walked toward the bridge. They had exited the town and were now venturing through the woods. Dead trees and fallen logs lined the sides of the dirt path. It was like a bleaker version of Neverwood Forest.

On the left side of the road was a sign facing away from the town. As they passed it, Dodger craned his neck to see the name.

`Welcome to Sleepy Hollow`

Dodger stumbled on a stone in the path.

"Are you all right?" asked Rump.

"Yeah, I'm fine," said Dodger, regaining his composure. Behind them, Ichabod was still waiting, smiling widely and gently stroking his horse's mane. The hair on the back of Dodger's neck stood up. "We need to get out of here. We gotta go."

"That's what we are trying to do," snapped Jack.

"No," replied Dodger, hurrying down the road. "Like, we gotta get as far from here as we can. This isn't good." He made it a few yards down the road and turned back to scowl at everybody continuing at their slow pace. Throwing his hands up, he said, "Come on! Hurry up!"

Dusk had passed a while ago. The only thing that provided light in the starless night was the aura from Ichabod and a white glow permeating the thick clouds. The full moon decided to come out from behind its cloud-cover and bathed the entire area in its pale essence. Dodger watched as Ichabod's body vanished and his aura blended into the moon's glow. The Literary knew what was happening, and he felt the color rush from his face.

Ichabod and his horse reappeared in the moonlight, this time under a new appearance. Ichabod's head had disappeared and his entire outfit looked like it had been dipped in black ink. The horse, which was originally a tame, docile pony, was now an enormous black stallion with bright red eyes and black smoke rising out of its nose and mouth. The Headless Horseman drew a thin sword from his belt and dug his boots into the horse's sides, urging it to throw its front feet into the air and roar.

"Run!"

Dodger took off down the road. The other adventurers traded confused glances until they saw the Horseman galloping at them at full speed.

"For the love of Merlin," whispered Rump. Humpty grabbed the alchemist by his collar and dragged him down the road with Pinocchio. Jack picked up Jill in his arms and used his magic sandals to fly toward the bridge.

"I wonder," panted Rump as he and his companions caught up with Dodger, "how is he so coordinated without a head?"

"Now is not the time, Stiltskin!" said Pinocchio, whose eyebrows spun in circles.

Tenth grade English, thought Dodger. *Headless Horseman. Of course we would end up in Sleepy Hollow. How did that story end?*

The Horseman closed in fast. Dodger put all of his strength into his legs, but knew that he couldn't outrun a horse. Ichabod held up his blade when two small objects shot through the air and struck him in the chest.

Dodger looked back at the Horseman to see Jack's axes embedded deep in his chest, forcing him and his horse to stop in their tracks. Dodger skidded to a halt as Jack landed next to him.

"Nice shot," remarked the Literary.

The Horseman plucked the axes out of his body and crushed them in his hand with no effort. The remnants of the weapons crumbled in a puff of black smoke, causing the grin to vanish off Jack's face.

"Make a run for it," said the Amryan, taking flight. "I'll distract him!"

Dodger's Doorway

Ichabod charged his horse down the road with sword held high. Jack flew above him and used a combination of aerial twists, turns, and acrobatics to distract the Horseman as Dodger caught up with the rest of the group and urged them to keep going.

The Horseman swiped his sword in wide arcs, failing to strike the flying man. Jack was swooping down near the horse's tail when the rider swung his sword backwards, snipping the Amryan's leg and breaking one of the magical sandals. Jack grunted and fell to the ground. He rolled out of the way to avoid being crushed underneath one of the stallion's hooves.

"Come on!" yelled Dodger. Jack pushed himself to his feet and made off down the road, limping heavily from the gaping wound in his leg. The Horseman spun his stallion around, trying to see where Jack went. Dodger watched as the black horse puffed more smoke out of its nostrils and the Horseman turned to face him. Even though he had no head, it almost felt like Ichabod was staring right at the Literary with an evil, hungry expression. The Horseman dug his spurs into his horse's sides.

Dodger waited for Jack to pass him before he ran for the bridge. On the other side, he could see his friends near the outskirts of a walled city. The Horseman charged up the dirt path and closed in fast. Just as Dodger and Jack crossed over the bridge, Dodger tripped and landed face-first on the ground, scraping the bottom of his chin and bruising his knees. He groaned and rolled onto his back to see the Horseman gaining momentum and drawing closer to the bridge. Help was nowhere in sight for Dodger. He called out for Pinocchio, or Humpty, or anybody to come save him, but they probably couldn't hear him. Dodger wanted to close his eyes, but he couldn't resist watching as his fate drew closer.

The horse galloped over the bridge and instantly vanished in a pillar of black smoke, taking the rider along with it. The smoke lingered briefly over the bridge, then dissolved into thin air, melting away in the moonlight. There was nothing but dead silence now as the moon illuminated the abandoned path. Dodger examined his surroundings, expecting the Horseman to reappear and attack, but nothing happened.

"Dodger!" said a gruff voice that made the Literary jump up with his dagger. It was Pinocchio, accompanied by Rump. The two Neverlanders helped him to his feet.

"That was rather anticlimactic," said Rump, dusting Dodger off.

"We made it to Oz," said Pinocchio. "It's right down the road, protected by that white wall."

Dodger couldn't stop shaking. There was a mysterious, lingering presence in the area that didn't sit right with him. All he knew was that he wanted to get away from the bridge as soon as possible.

"Are you all right?" asked Rump, staring at Dodger worriedly.

"I'm fine. I just want to get away from here." Looking at the distant wall, he asked, "What's the plan? How can Oz help us get back to Neverland?"

The trio followed the path to where Humpty, Jack, and Jill were waiting while Rump explained.

"The Wizard-King has a legion of griffins at his disposal. Seeing as we no longer have the magic carpet, they're our best chance at getting home."

"How do you know they'll even help us?"

"They owe Neverland a debt of gratitude."

"Why's that?"

"Did you already forget the tale of Sir Humpty defeating the army of flying monkeys?"

"I heard a different version of that story, remember?" Dodger told the alchemist.

"You heard blasphemy!" interjected Humpty once the group had reformed. "Here is the full tale: the Witch of the Winds commanded an army of flying monkeys that she was going to use to take over Oz. Even with the help of their Literary, Oz's armies stood no chance against the flying monkey soldiers. Soon enough, the kingdom found itself on the brink of defeat."

The adventurers approached the small white wall surrounding Oz. The path they were on ended at an opening underneath an archway large enough for a truck to drive through. Right behind this archway was a gray tower with an enormous bronze bell housed under a blue roof. A hunchbacked man with a horribly scarred face and a ragged green tunic sat atop this bell tower with a spear in one hand and a torch in the other. He stared at the group approaching the archway.

"Who goes there?" he called down through a heavy speech impediment.

"Pinocchio the Wooden Soldier and General of the Neverland Military Arm. With me are my second-in-command, Sir Humpty Dumpty, and Lord Rumpelstiltskin, Head Alchemist and Magicker of the Neverland Science Arm."

"I see more of ye," said the hunchback.

"Jack and Jill Horner, lead blacksmith and armorer of Amrya," said Jack.

"Is that a Literary among your number as well?" asked the hunchback, waving his torch. "Either that, or Neverlanders are dressing a bit strange nowadays."

"His name is Dodger of Philadelphia," said Pinocchio impatiently. "Now, we've had a very rough day and are in dire need of assistance."

"What is it about Oz that's attracting all these foreigners?" asked the hunchback.

"What do you mean?"

"Earlier today, two Wonderlanders arrived; said they got lost."

"Was one of them a Stronghand?"

"Aye. The other was a woman. A fine-looking one at that." The hunchback chuckled.

"Where are they?" asked Dodger, masking the irritation in his voice.

"Well, it's been a couple of hours, so I'm not entirely sure. They asked where the marketplace might be and where they could stay the night. I pointed them to the Lazy Shield right down the road."

"May we enter?"

The hunchback nodded and waved his torch at the archway. The group passed over the threshold and entered the city. Immediately upon stepping past the bell tower, they were bathed in the light of thousands of torches hanging from nearly every building in view. The city was so brightly lit that it looked like it was midday.

A yellow brick road cut through the city and wound off out of sight. Lining the road were rows of houses and other assorted buildings, each sporting torches hanging from ornamental sconces and brackets. Farther down the path, the yellow brick road split into numerous additional routes, sinking deeper into Oz. Dodger discovered that they were in just one smaller city that branched off from an enormous kingdom located down a gentle valley occupied with thousands of buildings. At the very center of this valley stood a solitary green tower that rose higher than the rest of the surrounding buildings. There was a glowing emerald gem perched at the top of this tower, acting as a beacon that shone brighter than all the other torches. This must have been the Tower of Oz, thought Dodger.

"Here is the plan," said Humpty. "We regroup with the agents and head to the tower where the Wizard-King resides."

"This actually further proves what I said earlier," said Jack. "Hansel and Gretel arrived here already, and apparently, they were more concerned with loitering in the marketplace than wondering about our safety."

Humpty rolled his eyes. "Horner, we've discussed this already. Your paranoia is starting to annoy me. And frankly, we have a difficult time trusting you as it is, so bite your tongue."

Jack balled his hand into a fist. For a moment, Dodger wondered if he was going to punch the egg-man, but Jill rubbed his arm and shook her head. Dodger actually agreed with Humpty, mainly because he was getting irritated with Jack's shifting moods and overall accusatory attitude. Rather than get into another argument, the Literary changed the subject.

"You never finished the flying monkey story, Humpty."

"Ah yes," Humpty said, his mood instantly uplifted. "Well, like I said, Oz's soldiers were no match for the mass of flying monkeys besieging the town. Having heard of the astonishing swordsman of Neverland," Humpty straightened his posture in a boisterous manner, "the Wizard-King formally requested my services from King Gabriel. In a matter of hours, I came charging into town by myself with nothing at my side except my sword and dagger. I alone vanquished the army!"

"You forgot the part where we assisted you," said a voice.

Dodger and his friends turned around and found themselves face-to-face with a strange band of characters. Humpty groaned loudly.

"Dodger," spat the egg-man, "meet the Royal Guard of Oz."

Chapter 11

The Bounty Hunters

On the far right of this new group was a man made of hay and straw, wearing a burlap sack as a shirt, a green cape reaching the ground, tattered brown leather gloves, and a brown fedora that dipped down to cover part of his face, almost making him look like a mysterious comic book villain. His face was made of stitched pieces of burlap with a roughly cut hole acting as his mouth and another two smaller holes as his eyes. A long sword with a two-handed bronze hilt was strapped across his back.

The next person in line had a human body and a jack-o'-lantern for a head; however, it wasn't like the pumpkins that Dodger had seen in his own world. This one possessed human-like eyes with orange pupils and an adjustable mouth similar to Humpty's that could distort and move freely. This person wore a jet-black suit with an orange bowtie and no shoes. His abnormal feet resembled thick green pumpkin stumps. Like the man made of straw, he also had a long, two-handed sword hanging off his back.

In the center of the group stood a man completely made out of tin; his boots, legs, torso, arms, and hands were all composed of the metal, and his head was covered by a tarnished tin helmet with a thin horizontal slit across where the eyes should be. This tin-man had a similar body structure to Pinocchio except he was much taller and wider, and he had an enormous, butterfly-bladed axe slung over his shoulder.

After the tin-man was a large lion standing on two feet and wearing torn black pants. They had two muscular arms comparable to Hansel's and curled fists the size of bowling balls. Covering his head was a thick mane of golden-brown hair that matched the short beard under his chin.

The last member of the group looked like an ordinary, middle-aged man. Dodger thought that he could pass for a Literary with an eccentric sense of style. He wore a patched brown suit on his thin frame and a matching brown wool top hat on his choppy blond hair. Around his waist he wore a clashing black leather belt with a green gem as a buckle, which matched his emerald eyes.

"Why all the bitterness, Sir Humpty?" asked the straw-man sarcastically. "The Literary may get the wrong impression and think we're enemies."

The band of warriors lined up and presented themselves to Dodger.

"I am Maxis the Courageous Lion," announced the lion-man.

"Ugu the Maker," said the man with the green gem in his belt, tipping his top hat.

"Nick Chopper, at your service," said the tin-man, whose voice sounded hollow and echoed within the helmet.

"Pumpkinhead," uttered the man with the appropriate physique.

"And I am Scarecrow," said the straw-man.

After Dodger and his companions introduced themselves to the guardsmen, Humpty launched into a tirade.

"You helped me as much as water helps start a fire! Nothing but trouble, you all are!"

"Those monkeys would've torn you apart had we not stepped in," retorted Scarecrow with his arms crossed.

"You were fighting for profit! Mercenaries like yourselves have no sense of loyalty or honor!"

"Well, that was before. Obviously we had a change of heart afterwards. Didn't we become part of the Wizard-King's personal guard after the battle?"

"Some guard you are!" Humpty looked up and down the road. "Wandering around again? Shouldn't you be watching over your king?"

Pumpkinhead leaned over to Scarecrow and loudly whispered, "I think he's jealous that we were asked to join the guard instead of him."

Humpty's jaw dropped. "How dare you? My loyalty is with Neverland and it will remain that way! None of this animosity has to do with jealousy! I cannot believe you have the audacity to say such a thing."

Scarecrow and Humpty continued arguing back and forth. Dodger backed away, feeling the heat between them escalating. As he backed up, he bumped into someone.

"Sorry," he muttered, assuming he'd bumped into a random citizen.

"Great to see you, boy!" It was Hansel. The Stronghand gave Dodger a tough pat on the back and went to greet everyone else (except for the bickering Humpty and Scarecrow). Gretel appeared from behind her brother and leapt forward to give the Literary a big hug and kiss on the cheek.

"Where were you guys?" asked an ecstatic Dodger.

"Hansel and I woke up in a strange warehouse outside of the city. Luckily, we escaped and came here seeking food and shelter. We were going to come look for you at first light. We were so worried!"

"We had a long day, too. We were stuck in this place in Sleepy Hollow and some psycho wanted to kill us. Humpty nearly died," Dodger said, nodding at the arguing egg-man

"Oh, no," said Gretel in horror.

"Don't worry. He got better," said Rump, watching the argument with a grin.

Hansel beamed at Dodger. "We're glad you all made it out alive. I'm sorry this had to happen to us. Apparently, that bartender was no real friend of mine. I'll be sure to pay him a visit soon. Must've slipped a sleeping potion into our drinks; what's this world coming to?"

The argument carried on. Pinocchio attempted to mediate the hot-tempered warriors' feud, but every time he stuck his arm out to hold Humpty back, the egg-man would slip beneath and go on provoking Scarecrow. Jack and Jill paid no attention and quietly talked among themselves. They were both huddled over Jack's broken sandals. The straps were sliced apart and a chunk of the left sandal's sole had been cut off. The man called Ugu the Maker approached the siblings.

"Pardon me, but I noticed you're in need of a repair?"

Jack nodded. "Yes. Unfortunately these are magic flying sandals created by our grandfather, Hermes, who was a magicsmith. I don't think it's possible to repair them so they'll fly again. I need a special craftsman for the job."

Ugu laughed. "You're in luck. Prior to my joining this group of vigilantes, I was a magicsmith and shoemaker for this city. If you like, I can easily repair your sandals in seconds."

Jack's face lit up. "Please do!"

The Maker held the sandals close to his face, inspecting them carefully. Muttering to himself, he pulled a handful of leather straps from the pouch in his belt and began weaving. At first, his hands neatly folded the straps over each other, magically connecting them to the shoes. His speed picked up and his fingers danced across the laces, binding them together and fastening them to the soles. In an instant, his hands stopped moving, and the sandals looked as good as new. Mouth agape, Jack took the sandals back and stammered his thanks. Jill and Ugu watched Jack don his repaired footwear and demonstrate their powers, performing several mid-air flips and twists.

"And all you did was wander through the forests!" Humpty shouted at Scarecrow.

"We were mercenaries," Scarecrow said slowly, enunciating each word as if to emphasize the point to Humpty. "Soldiers of fortune. Heroes-for-hire. We did not just 'wander through the forests'! How else were we supposed to get employment? We offered our services to the highest bidder. Is that a crime now?"

"Your kind have no sense of loyalty or honor!" replied Humpty.

"How many times must we remind you that we are no longer in that service? Sir Humpty, your stubbornness is getting-"

The ring of a bell suddenly resounded throughout the city. Everyone turned to the bell tower near the archway to see the hunchbacked guardsman furiously tugging the rope, forcing the enormous brass bell to chime.

"Enemy!" yelled the hunchback, abandoning the rope and tossing his spear beyond the wall. There was a brief pause, and then a shadowy figure jumped out from the darkness, grabbed the guardsman, and plucked him out of the bell tower. The hunchback's screams echoed in the distance, eventually fading away along with the last chimes of the bell. An eerie silence followed.

The shadowy figure returned, this time jumping so high that it cleared the wall surrounding Oz and landed right inside the city. When the torches' light illuminated the intruder's features, Dodger unsheathed his dagger.

"Hello, Oz!" said the creature in a shrill voice. It was similar to a regular human, only larger and with more balloon-like features. Its eyes were a haunting shade of orange and sunken into a maniacal face with an enormous chin. Covering the creature's head was a black iron helmet that protected its ears, but left its disproportionately large face exposed. It was wearing tight black pants and a red shirt branded with a picture of a skull and crossbones. The shoes were the most peculiar features of the intruder's outfit; they were black buckled boots like Ichabod Crane's, except they had oversized silver springs popping out of the heels.

"Humpty, what the hell is that thing?" asked Dodger, slightly repulsed.

"It's one of Hook's bounty hunters. He bears the sign of the Jolly Roger!" said Humpty, noting the emblem on the creature's shirt.

"Correct you are, my fine egg," said the intruder. "Allow me to introduce myself, Spring-Heeled Mack."

"Appropriate," remarked Rump. Humpty scowled at him.

"And I've been enlisted to capture the Literary!" Spring-Heeled Mack spotted Dodger and smiled widely, exposing his razor-sharp teeth. He bent his knees and propelled himself forward with uncanny power, shooting toward the Literary like a cannonball.

Maxis roared and leapt in front of Dodger, swinging one of his mighty fists and catching Spring-Heeled Mack across the face. The punch sent him careening into an adjacent building. The bounty hunter groaned and pushed himself out of the crater his body left in the wall. Quickly recovering, he bent his knees again and sprung into the air. Ugu's belt started shining with a green light, as did the palms of his hands. The Maker extended his arms and shot a series of emerald-colored orbs at Spring-Heeled Mack, unfortunately missing with every one.

The intruder landed right in front of Dodger, beaming and stretching out his arms. Nick Chopper dove forward and implanted his massive axe blade into Spring-Heeled Mack's back. The smile vanished from his grayish-brown face as he sunk to his knees. Nick ripped the axe out of his back and kicked the hunter over. He raised his weapon when Spring-Heeled Mack began laughing.

"You may have defeated me, but when I do not return, more shall come!"

Nick swung the axe down into the creature's chest.

Dodger started to breathe heavily. "What did he mean by 'more shall come'?" he asked slowly.

"He's a scout," said Nick, slinging the axe over his shoulder. "It means that we should prepare for battle."

An order was issued across the city instructing all civilians to barricade themselves in their homes until the attack was over. Dodger and his companions agreed to join forces with the Royal Guard of Oz to ward off the bounty hunters. Even Humpty put aside his bitterness and rivalry in the face of impending danger, grumpily shaking Scarecrow's hand with a suppressed frown. Humpty demanded that Jill and Gretel be taken into a villager's home for protection (despite Jill expressing her desire to stay and fight alongside her brother). Jack was almost forbidden from the battle as well seeing as how his axes were destroyed in Sleepy Hollow, but he refused to leave, so he was presented with a new sword from the armory.

"Where's your standing army?" Pinocchio asked the Royal Guard. "We'll need reinforcements."

"The Oz Military Arm is on a siege campaign in Camelot," replied Scarecrow.

"You sent your entire army on a siege? How do you expect to defend your city?"

"We already sent an envoy to the Tower of Oz requesting assistance, General. No need to worry."

An hour later, as Humpty was teaching Dodger additional defensive maneuvers with the dagger, the soldiers were joined by the promised reinforcements. The Wizard-King had sent twenty of his griffins to assist in the upcoming attack. Even though he had never seen them in person, Dodger immediately recognized these majestic beasts from the pictures he'd seen in fantasy and mythology books. Regardless, he was still awestruck by their incredible beauty; bodies of lions with golden pelts so shiny that they reflected the sun like glass, enormous wings covered in sparkling blue and white feathers, and eagle-like heads with curved yellow beaks, daring eyes, and stoic composure. Dodger cautiously approached the nearest griffin and was pleasantly surprised at how friendly it was, nuzzling its head against his chest and permitting him to stroke its soft neck.

"Why isn't the king coming down here to help us, too?" asked Dodger. "If he's the great and powerful wizard that I heard about in my world, can't he just wave his wand and end this whole thing in a minute?"

"The rumors of my power have been greatly exaggerated in the world of the Literaries," came a loud, intimidating voice. Dodger and his friends looked into the sky and saw a short, bald man arrive on the largest griffin in the entire herd. The creature landed right by the entrance to the city and knelt down, allowing its rider to descend.

The man couldn't have been more than three feet tall, barely coming up to Dodger's chest. His bald head and wrinkled face were tinged a light green that complemented his eccentric outfit. He wore green moccasin slippers, a green button-down pinstriped shirt, green dress pants, and a dark green hooded cape with a tall collar. The only feature of this man's persona that wasn't green was the long wooden staff he wielded; however, it was topped with a green gem. Everyone immediately bowed down.

"While I *am* capable of remarkable feats," said the little man, passing Humpty and placing a tiny hand on his shoulder, "I believe it will take our combined effort to defeat the incoming foe. I am Oscar, Wizard-King of Oz, and I am here to defend my kingdom."

Within the hour, everyone had taken their places in the defensive position around the city's entrance. Oscar led Rump and Ugu to the top of the unmanned bell tower where they sat concealed behind the dormant bell. Humpty, Jack, and Pinocchio joined Pumpkinhead and Scarecrow in a hiding spot tucked away in a narrow alleyway to the left of the archway, also out of sight. Nick and Hansel waited at the foot of the bell tower, their eyes locked on the entrance. Dodger and Maxis sat on a staircase of a nearby abandoned building. The griffins patrolled the wall around the city, ensuring that there were no surprise attacks from other vantage points.

By sunrise, the defenders were getting restless. The city torches continued burning brightly, now joined by the rising yellow light from the east. Maxis yawned, exposing a mouthful of pointy teeth. Dodger leaned against the wall, avoiding looking at the archway. He was feeling apprehensive and absentmindedly tugging at his lip ring.

"You're afraid," said Maxis, breaking the silence for the first time in hours.

"How'd you guess?" said Dodger. The lion-man smirked and arched his thick eyebrows. Dodger quickly stopped fidgeting with his lip ring. "Sorry. It's a bad habit. I guess I'm afraid because I'm not really sure what's about to happen in the next couple of hours. I've felt this way all night."

"That's no way to live, young Literary. You cannot go through life being scared of what will happen next. You end up tiptoeing between the cracks, avoiding possibilities."

"It's not like I'm afraid all the time. I just meant now that there're bounty hunters coming after me."

Maxis stroked his chin. "Didn't you encounter the Forever Witch several days ago? And you fended off a troll, from what I heard."

Dodger sighed. "It's different. Those were just random situations we ended up in. It's not like they were coming specifically for me. I was at the wrong place at the wrong time. Now, these bounty hunters are actually after me. If it wasn't for you and the rest of the guardsmen, that Spring-Heeled guy probably would've killed me!"

"If you're so afraid, why didn't you seek shelter with the villagers? You had the option to hide along with Gretel and Jill."

"Oh, trust me, I would've if I had the chance, but Humpty told me how I was here for a reason; something about me being summoned to finish a quest. Who knows? Maybe this is part of the quest. And like you said, I already fought trolls and witches and stuff. I haven't run away from anything else in this world yet, so why should I start now?"

"You speak as if you normally run away from your problems, young one."

Dodger wrapped his arms around his knees and said, "Back in my world, there's this guy, Ryan, who always picks on me. He treats me like crap. And my parents are hardly better. They act like I'm not even their son, the way they speak to me. But I never confront any of them. They get in my face and I just run away. I'm a wimp."

"Let me get this straight," Maxis said, rubbing his chin again. "You're willing to fight monsters and sorcerers and other murderous characters this world has to offer, yet you cannot stand up to your own kind? Please don't take this the wrong way, but from what I remember of the Literaries, you folks aren't that intimidating or threatening."

"It's complicated," Dodger trailed off, shrugging.

Maxis let out a deep sigh. "You Literaries are so peculiar. I've always been curious about your kind. You have strange customs, stories, terminology, and clothing. Now, you go ahead and tell me of this strange paradox." The lion-man glanced at the archway, which still showed no signs of activity.

"Did you know that I used to be called Maxis the Cowardly Lion? That was back when I was afraid of everything and anything. One day, I was chosen to host a Literary named Lyman. He was quite the brave man and loved the quests he was chosen to fulfill. During most of the adventures, I retreated with my tail between my legs.

"There was one frightening encounter with the Witch of the Winds where we were both almost killed until we were rescued by the likes of Nick Chopper,

Scarecrow, Pumpkinhead, and Ugu. Though they were simple mercenaries who cared solely about making coin and getting drunk, they were kind enough to join us on our quests.

"You heard about the Witch's flying monkey siege on Oz, correct? Lyman and I were tasked with defending the city. The mercenaries wanted payment for their assistance and were promptly denied by the Wizard-King. That was when King Oscar requested the help of Sir Humpty, who I'm sure must have regaled you with this tale numerous times by now."

Dodger took this moment to gaze at the rotund body of the egg-man poking out from his hiding place. Maxis went on with his story.

"The fight was one-sided for the most part. Although Humpty is indeed a magnificent fighter, the monkeys soon overtook him and Lyman. I was hiding in this very building, cowering like a frightened cub." Maxis thumped his large hand on the building on whose staircase they were hiding. "Finally, I had an epiphany: being afraid is being selfish. I was afraid to fight alongside someone who was risking his life to defend my home. Also, I was being selfish by preventing myself from conquering my own fears. Do you see the conundrum? What I was doing wasn't fair to Lyman, to Humpty, to King Oscar, to all of Oz, and to myself. It was time to stop being selfish and stop being afraid. I wanted to live my life with nothing stopping me. Fear would no longer have control over my actions.

"And with that, I charged out of the building and into battle. At that same moment, the mercenaries decided to return and ran into battle by my side. Our combined effort resulted in the defeat of the flying monkey army, and it was me personally who stabbed the Witch of the Winds through the heart with a broken spear shaft." Maxis puffed out his chest and smiled.

"I was a new lion that day. I became a symbol of courage across the land, and people who had heard of my exceptional bravery began to revere me. When we sent Lyman back, he told me he would recount my courageous acts to the children of your world, hoping that I would inspire them to grow up without fear in their hearts."

Dodger thought back to when he read the stories of Oz and wondered whether he should tell Maxis the truth of how he was portrayed. But before he could do so, a thought struck him.

"Wait a minute. What do you mean, 'when we sent Lyman back'?"

Before Maxis had a chance to respond, the distant bell tower started to ring. From his hiding place, Dodger could see Rump vigorously bashing the side of the bell with his mace. The last resounding gongs rang across the city, and the alchemist drank a vial from his belt. Instead of fire, he now shot blue orbs of cackling energy over the wall. Ugu joined him and shot green beams of light from his hand; Oscar mimicked him, only he used his magical staff to cast the spells.

There was no telling what was happening on the other side of the wall. All Dodger could see were flashes of green and blue. Eventually, something made it past the defenses and hopped over the wall, clearing the bell tower and landing in the city. It was another bounty hunter wearing the same spring mechanism on his heel. This second spring-heel didn't wear a helmet, allowing his bright red hair to flow like a mane. He was also larger and bulkier than his predecessor. Even from this distance, Dodger could see the craters the spring-heel's feet left in the brick road.

The hunter sniffed the air and scanned the area. Hansel charged out of his hiding spot and tackled the creature, lifting him off his feet and steering him into the stone wall, where he began to pummel it. Another spring-heel leapt into the city and landed right behind Hansel, where he was met with a heavy blow to the chest by Nick's axe.

More spring-heels cleared the wall and swarmed into the city. They all wore red shirts with the emblem of the Jolly Roger, and a select number wore random pieces of armor like large iron helmets or black breastplates. Pumpkinhead led the next charge with Scarecrow, Humpty, and Pinocchio at his heels. Jack used his freshly repaired sandals and sword to provide an aerial attack.

There was utter chaos at the entrance to the city. Numerous griffins had flown over at the first signs of battle and swooped down here and there, scratching at the spring-heels with their talons or nipping at them with their beaks. One of the bounty hunters broke free from the crowd and grabbed onto a griffin's wings. The animal gave an ear-piercing screech and made an attempt to buck off the enemy, but the spring-heel grinned widely and tore one of the animal's wings from its back, causing it to plummet to the ground.

Dodger felt sick and sensed his hand growing sweaty on the dagger's handle. Maxis descended two steps and peeked around the corner.

"Prepare yourself," he said in a low growl. "Stay close behind me. They won't get to you if I have anything to do with it."

Dodger's Doorway

Another spring-heel appeared out of the skirmish and reached for Jack's leg. The Amryan warrior, learning from his incident with the Headless Horseman, raised his feet and swooped down to slice at the bounty hunter's hand. The spring-heel snarled as it landed, glaring up at Jack. He buckled his knees, preparing to leap, but then lifted his nose in the air. A few sniffs and he suddenly shifted his face to where Dodger and Maxis were hiding.

"I found you, boy!" The bounty hunter changed his stance and propelled himself at the building with rapid speed. Maxis grabbed Dodger by the back of his shirt and pushed him over the railing. The Literary landed on the street below and glanced up at the spring-heel as he rocketed through the air and crashed into the wall where Dodger was just standing. The bounty hunter's head was stuck in the splintered wood and he couldn't pull himself out. Maxis roared and punched it in the ribs over and over.

"That was a bad idea," said Dodger, wincing from the ten-foot drop. He cringed as he stood up and found himself face-to-face with yet another spring-heel.

"Hello!" he said, bearing his spiked gray teeth at the Literary.

Dodger screamed and instinctively stabbed his dagger up into the creature's chin. The spring-heel's expression froze. He grunted and keeled over on his side. Dodger, his mouth open in shock and his hands shaking, bent down to yank out the dagger. The blade was covered in dark blue blood.

Maxis vaulted over the railing and landed on the corpse of the spring-heel. "Are you all right? I heard you scream."

"I'm fine," said Dodger, wiping the dagger on his shirt.

Dodger's Doorway

The duo ran to the entrance of the city where it was an all-out battle between the bounty hunters and the defenders. Rump, Oscar, and Ugu had descended the bell tower and were right in the middle of the frenzy with the rest of their companions. Dark blue blood splattered all over the place, mixed in with bright green and blue lights. Dodger stood right behind Maxis, letting the lion-man plow through the dozens of bounty hunter corpses that littered the ground.

Dodger briefly panicked when he felt a hand grasp onto his elbow. Maxis spun around and delivered an uppercut that sent the spring-heel into the air where Oscar struck him with a concussive blast. Dodger saw another enemy with his back turned to him as it faced off with Pinocchio. The Literary sunk the dagger into his back to score another kill. Hansel stood near the archway and had taken to picking spring-heels up and throwing them back over the wall.

One of the spring-heels with blue hair latched onto Jack's legs and dragged him out of the air. The Amryan desperately tried to fly out of reach, but his enemy's grip was like a vice. The spring-heel's feet landed on the ground and he slowly reeled Jack into his embrace.

"I'm going to pluck your arms off like a bird's wings!" growled the spring-heel.

Dodger left the lion-man's side and dove forward to sink the dagger into the bounty hunter's knee. He roared and let go of Jack, who flew out of harm's way. The spring-heel's sneer returned when it spotted Dodger.

"Ah! Captain Hook has placed a heavy sum of gold on your head. Fortunately, he didn't specify if it still had to be attached to your body." The spring-heel grabbed Dodger in a bear hug so tight that it crushed the air out of his lungs.

"H-help!" sputtered Dodger. He lashed his foot out in desperation, harmlessly pounding his captor's chest. His foot came down and connected with the hilt of the dagger still implanted deep in the spring-heel's knee. The kick drove the dagger deeper into its flesh until it poked out the other side. The spring-heel dropped Dodger and grabbed at his leg, shrieking in pain. Maxis rushed forward and elbowed the bounty hunter in the face, knocking him aside. The lion-man grabbed Dodger by the shoulders.

"Are you okay?"

"I'm fine, I'm fine," said Dodger, retrieving the dagger.

The battle raged on for at least another hour. The bounty hunters had the numerical advantage, and it seemed like more and more kept flowing over the walls and through the archway; however, they weren't the most effective fighters, and the Royal Guard of Oz and Dodger's companions proved to be a match for them. The battle ended when Scarecrow decapitated the last spring-heel and kicked the corpse out of the archway. The defenders had few casualties. Aside from three dead griffins, a gash across Hansel's chest, and a deep dent in Nick Chopper's armor, the most anyone suffered from was a scratch or a bruise. Thanks to the protection of Maxis, Dodger only had to worry about a shallow cut on his arm and a sore mouth from where a spring-heel backhanded him.

"I think that is the last time we will see any bounty hunters near Oz," said Oscar, slamming the end of his staff onto the ground.

Jill and Gretel emerged from their safe haven once the coast was clear. Rump distributed health potions to the adventurers, while Humpty conversed with Oscar and requested a ride to Neverland. The grateful Wizard-King happily obliged and provided the service of ten of his griffins.

"Also, I'll have my Royal Guard accompany you home, just in case there are more perils along the way," added Oscar.

"I'm sure we'll be fine with the griffins," said Hansel. "There shouldn't be anymore danger. You probably need the guardsman here in case more bounty hunters come along."

"Better safe than sorry. It is the least I can do. We need to keep the Literary safe, and I think he needs more protection than I do right now."

"My sister and I will accompany you as well," declared Jack.

"It's really not necessary," said Hansel.

"Dodger saved my life. I owe him my services."

"Is this going to be a recurring thing?" asked Dodger. "I know I helped you out, but you don't have to be indebted to me or anything."

"Is honor and gratitude a foreign concept to you?" asked Jack coldly.

"No, it's just…" Dodger couldn't think of a way to explain so he shrugged and said, "You know what? I'm gonna shut up until we get back to Neverland. How about that?"

Everyone exchanged their goodbyes with Oscar and departed on the fleet of griffins. There were no dangerous encounters or issues on the way home, just as Hansel had said. It was an incredibly pleasant journey, though Dodger couldn't fully relax. He was now feeling the soreness and tiredness from his past adventures. His instincts were also nagging at him, making him feel unsettled and uncomfortable. It was almost impossible for him to enjoy the beautiful, overcast late-morning.

"Are you okay?" asked Gretel, who was sitting behind Dodger on the griffin with her arms clutching his waist.

"Yeah, I'm fine," lied Dodger. "I'm exhausted. It's been a long day; a *really* long day."

"Once we arrive in Neverland, I'll make sure you get a good night's rest and relaxation," Gretel whispered.

Chapter 12

Return to Neverland

It was noon by the time the griffins touched down in front of Neverland. For the first time, John Tell wasn't present at his guard station. Instead, a younger man with a shaved head and a scar on his neck greeted the adventurers. This sentry wasn't as courteous or as friendly as John.

"Greetings," said the guard curtly, his eyes wandering to the non-Neverlanders.

Humpty nodded. "We picked up companions in Wonderland, Oz, and Amrya."

"I heard of your mission in Amrya, but I had no idea that you traveled all the way to Oz." said the guard.

"It is a long story, Roger. We want to get to Princess Tinkerbell for our debriefing."

Roger didn't say another word and blew into his horn. The gate creaked open, allowing the group to enter the castle. Dodger dragged his feet along, barely keeping his eyelids open. It was hard to believe that he had only been in Storyworld for a few days. It felt like he'd spent more than a week in the magical realm. A long, sleepless week.

After trekking through the seemingly endless entrance hallway, the group entered the main chamber (Scarecrow had stopped to glance at the splintered wooden beam that Dodger had destroyed the other day). They all approached the throne and bowed in front of the princess, who was now dressed in a flowing

white gown and wore her hair in a loose ponytail across her shoulder.

"I've been worried about you," said Tinkerbell.

"We had numerous situations to deal with on the way back from the land

of the giants," explained Humpty. "Nothing we couldn't handle, and we actually

made new friends in Oz," he added, nodding to the guardsmen.

"We can discuss it all at dinner tonight, where we will have a celebratory

feast," said the princess. "For now, I want all of you to wash up, relax, and return

here by sunset."

"Excuse us, Princess," said Ugu as he and the guardsmen stood, "but my

fellows and I have a long journey back to Oz. We'll be on our way."

Humpty leapt to his feet. "Absolutely not! You have been a major asset

and escorted us home. We want you to stay for dinner. I think that would be most

appropriate."

Pinocchio and Rump shared befuddled expressions. Dodger joined them,

confused at the egg-man's sudden newfound appreciation for his rivals from Oz.

The Oz soldiers seemed to be just as perplexed. In the end, they agreed to stay for

the feast, thanking Humpty for his generosity. The egg-man cheered and clapped

his hands loudly.

The only person who matched Humpty's enthusiasm was Hansel, who

beamed at the thought of a feast. Dodger was glad that the Stronghand's

relationship with the rest of the group had lightened up considerably over the past

few hours. Pinocchio, however, was still not fond of the agent.

"I still don't trust anything with giants' blood in it," stated the Wooden Soldier silently so that only Dodger could hear him.

Humpty and Pinocchio proceeded to their shared room up in their tower while Rump retreated to his own on the other side of the castle. John Tell arrived in the chamber soon after to tend to the guests. He led them through a back doorway behind the thrones that connected to a thin, dark hallway. At the end of this hallway was a tall set of wooden doors that, when opened, revealed a magnificent private park in the rear of Neverland Castle.

A high wall of grayish-white stones enclosed the area, and lining the park were hundreds of spreading pine trees providing ample shade from the sun. In the center of the park was an enormous man-made lake the size of an Olympic-sized swimming pool. The crystal-clear water had a steady current with a series of light waves, giving it the sensation of a calm beach setting. At the far end of the lake lay a thick clump of rocks stacked on top of each other. Beyond these rocks were smaller wading pools lined with colorful flowerbeds.

"You'll enjoy washing up, as many of our guests do," said John. "Most people stay in the royal lake for hours on end. Just make sure to come back inside for the feast later!"

The captain smiled, bowed, and returned to the castle. Immediately, Ugu, Maxis, Jack, Jill, Hansel, and Pumpkinhead stripped out of their clothing and dove into the lake. Nick and Scarecrow decided to sit under the shade of one of the trees seeing as how their bodies weren't necessarily suited for swimming.

Dodger took off everything except his boxers and stood nervously on the edge of the water. Gretel had removed her armor and was now wearing a long wool shirt and thin leggings. She walked past Dodger and dipped into the lake, turning back to the Literary and smiling at him. Dodger crossed his arms over his chest and lowered his head, keeping his eyes on his feet. Gretel giggled and beckoned him to join her in the lake.

Just go in, Dodger silently told himself. He shuffled into the water, keeping his arms crossed firmly over his chest. Chills went up his spine as he dipped into the lake, even though the water wasn't cold at all; it was the perfect temperature, making Dodger feel like he was wading through warm air. The scent of lilac wafted up from the water, enhancing the tranquility and easing the Literary's stress and nervousness.

Dodger dunked his head into the depths. Instead of hearing the roaring sound of water rushing into his ears, he heard clear, soothing music. Dodger opened his eyes and found it easy to see through the water as if it were a newly cleaned window. He swam to the base of the rocks directly ahead. As he propelled himself through the water, he noticed how the tired, achy feeling in his limbs had disappeared, which could possibly be attributed to the powers of the royal lake.

He poked out of the water and observed how the massive boulders were stacked on top of each other in a manner that would let him climb to the top. It took a bit of effort, but Dodger eventually reached the highest point of the rocks, standing more than ten feet above the rest of the courtyard. Turning his back on the lake and his companions, Dodger faced outward and gazed beyond the perimeter of Neverland Castle. What the Literary discovered beyond this area made his jaw drop.

The kingdom of Neverland stretched as far as the eye could see. Rump had mentioned how Neverland was still a growing kingdom, though Dodger couldn't imagine it getting any larger.

Neverland Castle stood on a little hilltop like a small beacon on the edge of a massive lighthouse. Beyond the castle's walls, there was a long stretch of rolling green hills and lush plains with tall grass. Miles away, past this untouched land, were hundreds of thousands of houses, all clumped together in neat little rows just like in Oz, except there was no tower at the center of the city. Dodger shielded his eyes and spotted a wide patch of land at the complete opposite side of Neverland, where more homes were being built. The kingdom truly was growing.

To the left of where Dodger stood, about two or three miles down a small incline, was an enormous bay situated within a crescent-shaped coastline. There were multiple ports, harbors, and shipyards filling this area, and even more boats drifting around in the water.

It was still early in the afternoon with the sun hanging high in the sky. Dodger let the cool Storyworld air fill his tired lungs. Not too long ago, he would have given anything to be asleep in a soft, warm bed. Once he touched the water of Neverland Castle's lake, not only did his soreness and tiredness go away, but he also felt invigorated like he'd just slept for an entire day. He smiled as he peered off into the ocean. On the horizon, he thought he could see a ship. Squinting and shielding his eyes again, he saw that there were actually multiple ships far off in the distance, listing lazily on the water.

"What are you looking at, Dodger?" Gretel had swam up to the rocks and gazed at Dodger.

"I think I see ships out in the ocean, but I'm not sure," said the Literary.

"They're probably trade ships. There are many lands across the sea, like Sartha Tenore and Glubbdubdrib. Neverland often trades with such kingdoms, so it's not unusual to see the waters filled with ships every once in a while. Now, stop worrying about the ocean and come down here with us!"

Dodger turned away from the ships and watched as Gretel swam past the rocks and into a smaller pool away from the other members of their party. She waded into a sectioned-off area where nobody could see her except for Dodger from his vantage point. The Literary hopped into the water and joined her.

"We've had quite the adventures," commented Gretel, smiling at Dodger as he approached her.

"I know, right?" replied Dodger. "It's still hard to believe that this isn't some big dream. These past few days have been amazing. I mean, it was terrifying going through everything, but I'm still glad it all happened."

Gretel cocked her head. "What do you mean?"

Dodger stared into the water as he spoke. "As weird as it sounds, coming here was probably the best thing that's ever happened to me. Look at what I did! I fought a witch, a dragon, giants, bounty hunters, and did all sorts of other crazy things. It's like a dream come true. I did things I never thought I'd do."

"Don't forget the greatest thing you did," whispered Gretel.

"What's that?"

The agent put her hand under the Literary's chin and lifted his face up to meet hers. Dodger was so close he could see his own reflection in her eyes. The aroma from the perfumed water wafted into the air, and the moment it passed his nose, his heartbeat quickened.

"You met me," Gretel said in a barely audible voice. She then kissed him passionately. Dodger put his hands on her waist and held her close, and she wrapped her arms around his neck.

The two weren't in Neverland anymore. They were far away, in a distant sea in the depths of Dodger's mind. There was nothing else in this little world: no rocks, no trees, no towns, and no people. It was just him and Gretel, in the water together, their bodies embraced and their lips sharing a kiss.

It was a long time before Dodger and Gretel left the secluded pool. Everyone else had gone inside by the time they emerged from behind the rocks. The sun had crept into the early evening position right above the horizon. It would be another hour or two before it finally set. Even now, there was a slight chill in the air as Dodger stepped out of the water.

Dodger and the agent climbed out of the pool, both smiling but not saying a word to each other. They donned their clothes in silence (there must have been more magic at work because the moment they exited the water, their skin and hair were dry).

They re-entered the castle and walked to the main chamber, holding hands and still smiling at each other. Dodger's heart was doing backflips, and he couldn't quell his happy mood. Judging by the expression on Gretel's face, she must have been feeling the same way.

The main chamber had been tidied up to prepare for the feast. The royal thrones were pushed up against the wall, and the oversized banner of the royal family had been hoisted up to the ceiling and tucked away into a corner. The candles occupying the chandelier were all lit, bathing the chamber in a bright light and casting dancing shadows upon the pearly white walls.

A long wooden table was placed in the center of the chamber and covered with an ornate white tablecloth and a wide assortment of food. Dodger marveled at the collection: platters of fruit and vegetables intricately laid out in spiraling patterns, thick biscuits and other bite-sized treats occupying little dishes, a wide bowl of amber liquid cooled with large chunks of ice, and an enormous roasted animal taking up the center of the table.

Tinkerbell sat at the head of the table with Humpty and Pinocchio sitting to her left and right respectively. Down the left half of the table sat the Royal Guard of Oz, and on the right side were Jack and Jill with four empty seats after them.

Dodger didn't fathom how hungry he was until now. He hadn't eaten or drank anything for a while. Just seeing the food-covered table and smelling the scent wafting from the roasted centerpiece made his stomach rumble loudly. The Literary rushed to the seat next to Jack and grabbed the first thing he could reach, one of the roasted animal's legs, and enjoyed a satisfying, savory bite. Jack and Jill gave the Literary a disgusted look, but he didn't care. He devoured the morsel before addressing Humpty.

"Where are Hansel and Rump?"

"Hansel said he wasn't feeling well. Rump took him to his tower to get him a potion for his stomach. They should be back with us shortly."

Jack surveyed a piece of meat before biting into it. "I have to say, this food is excellent. Would it be possible for the cooks to conjure up a small meal for my sister and I to take back to Amrya? We do not have such fine cuisines in our homeland."

"Rump can whip up something for you before you leave," said Humpty.

"Alchemist *and* cook?" asked an impressed Jill.

"It is all the same," replied Humpty, shrugging. "He likes to make concoctions and mixtures. He says 'what difference is it if you're cooking up spells or cooking up meals?' I assume it is also much easier to prepare food when you have magic at your disposal," the egg-man added with a grin.

The guests continued to dine in silence until Gretel piped up.

"Oh, no!" said the agent, grabbing the side of her corset. "One of the clasps just snapped on my armor!"

"Mind if I take a look at it?" asked Jill. "I'm the head armorer of Amrya. Maybe I can fix it." She pulled her chair up to Gretel and inspected the straps. "It looks like it's been broken for a while. The straps are worn down and there is evidence of wear on the corset. Are you sure this strap just broke?"

"I only just noticed it. It must've happened in Oz."

Jill looked at the princess. "Do you have a workshop in the castle? It doesn't look too hard to fix."

"I believe there might be tools up in Sir Humpty and General Pinocchio's room, am I correct?" Tinkerbell asked her soldiers.

"Yes, we should have something to repair it up in our room," said Humpty, nodding. "I will take you up after the feast."

"It will only take a minute, Sir Humpty. I can go with her," said Jill.

Dodger dropped his half-eaten pear and bounded to his feet. "It's fine. I can take her up there."

"Please, Dodger, I insist. You can stay here and eat. Not meaning to offend you, but I don't think you or Gretel know your way around armor."

"I'd actually prefer it if Dodger accompanied me," added Gretel with a smile.

Jill looked slightly off-put by the response, but silently dragged her chair back to her spot.

"Very well," said Humpty. "Go up to our room and check next to my bed. There should be a chest with a kit full of tools and supplies I often use to fix my own accessories. I'm sure we'll have something for Agent Gretel's armor."

Dodger nodded. Humpty raised his goblet in response and drank from it. He made a disgusted face and gagged as Pinocchio chuckled.

"Perhaps I should stay away from the ale. I think I'll just have water," said the egg-man.

Dodger's Doorway

Dodger and Gretel ascended the stairs to Humpty and Pinocchio's room. At first, Dodger wasn't sure if he remembered how to get to the tower, but the castle's layout was fairly simple, and he faintly recalled which direction to go. Gretel stuck close behind him, occasionally tickling the Literary as they climbed the stairs.

Entering the room, Dodger passed Pinocchio's bed and checked next to Humpty's hammock where he found a toolbox, just like the egg-man indicated. He scoured the contents of the chest, digging through mysterious tools and knick-knacks. Out of the corner of his eye, he saw Gretel strolling past the wall of weapons.

"An impressive arsenal," said the agent, rubbing her hand across the hilt of a sword.

"Yeah, sure," Dodger replied distractedly. He soon realized that he had no idea what tools would be needed for the job. When he turned to ask Gretel for her advice, he saw her holding a loaded crossbow with an arrow aimed at his chest.

"Whoa," said Dodger, grinning and holding his hands up. "That's not funny, Gretel. Put that down before someone gets hurt."

Gretel ignored the order and approached the Literary slowly. There was a smile on her face, though it wasn't the refreshing expression that Dodger had become accustomed to over the past few days. This grin was eerie and unsettling.

"Put it down," repeated the Literary. His own grin had vanished and his voice became firmer, yet with a tiny tremble. "What's your problem?"

"There's no problem here, boy," said the agent. "In fact, everything's finally going according to plan."

"What plan?" Dodger's heart punched against his ribcage and his entire body began to shake.

Gretel smirked. "The plan consisting of Captain Hook's return to Neverland.

Chapter 13

Interruptions

The room was completely silent except for the beating of Dodger's heart, which he could hear thumping against his chest. Much like the first time he arrived in Storyworld, his mind exploded with questions. Except this time, he wasn't sure if he wanted to hear the answers.

"What's going on?" he asked in a hoarse voice.

Gretel walked over to the window, keeping her crossbow trained on Dodger's heart. She quickly peeked outside, and then reverted her gaze back to the Literary.

"You're lucky they haven't arrived yet. I think I'll enlighten you on a few things in the meantime. Those ships you spotted out in the ocean earlier? Well, they weren't exactly trade ships; they were actually pirate vessels, which are now much closer to Neverland. Soon, they'll be anchoring on the edge of Neverwood Forest. Captain Hook will be quite happy to know he finally has the opportunity to fulfill his lifelong goal."

"Which is?"

"To kill a Literary," Gretel said simply.

Dodger's throat went dry. "Why?"

"You see, Dodger, there are many stories circulating in this world, just like there are in yours. One of the most famous legends describes how anyone who successfully kills a Literary will be granted omniscient powers and immortality.

"Why do you think your survival was so integral this whole time?" continued Gretel. "Humpty and those other idiots didn't want anyone to gain that type of power or else there'd be chaos. Your life held the balance of Storyworld."

It took several moments for this information to sink in. Dodger wished his heart would stop beating so fast before it leapt out of his throat.

"If that's true," he said slowly, "if anyone who kills a Literary becomes immortal, then why do Literaries always get brought along on these dangerous missions?"

"I thought you knew about this already," said Gretel, shaking her head. "Don't you get it? Literaries are brought into this world in times of desperate need. Nobody can control when or where they arrive. But once they're here, they're tasked with completing certain quests. You Literaries have something that's absent among our people: the power of the other world."

"Hasn't Hook ever gotten a Literary? Or what about you and Hansel? Why didn't you ever kill them?"

Gretel sighed. "Literaries only appear on this main continent. The pirates' homeland has never been graced with your kind, probably from the lack of magic. Neverland and its borders are flowing with magical resources, making it a prime spot for Literaries. Wonderland has had its share of visitors, but its magic has waned over the years. We've only seen two or three Literaries in my lifetime, and that was long before my brother and I were in league with Hook."

"Okay," said Dodger, nodding and fiddling with his piercing as he thought of more stalling questions. "Why didn't you try to kill me yet? You could be immortal and have all the power." This may have been a stupid question, but Dodger thought it was important to know.

"Captain Hook is the sole person to hold that power and I'll do everything in my reach to make sure it happens. My brother and I may be double agents, but we're loyal to our true leader. We're perfectly fine being at the right hand of the ruler of Storyworld."

Dodger dissected what she had just said. *If she's not going to kill me, why is she using the crossbow?* For a moment, Dodger considered calling her bluff. The agent smirked again.

"I know what you're thinking. I won't kill you, but I have no problem crippling you if need be. Actually, I might take care of your legs right now so that you won't be able to run."

The color rushed out of Dodger's face. Gretel lowered the crossbow's aim at Dodger's feet when the door to the room burst open. Humpty Dumpty stomped in, his face glowing with pure rage.

"I knew it!" roared the egg-man, unsheathing his sword and dagger. "You treacherous wench! How dare you double-cross us?"

Gretel swung the crossbow to the door and fired an arrow at Humpty. The egg-man dove out of the way and rolled to his feet. The agent dropped the crossbow and grabbed a sword hanging off the wall of weapons.

"Beware, Sir Humpty," said Gretel, twirling the blade in her hands with surprising nimbleness, "you're not the only sword-master in these lands."

Not taking his eyes off Gretel, Humpty shouted to Dodger. "Get to the main chamber and raise the alarm!"

Dodger did as he was told and ran for the door. Gretel motioned to stop him, but Humpty ran forward, meeting her sword with his own blades. As the Literary rushed out the door and down the stairs, he heard the clashing of weapons and the screams of the combatants echoing out of the room.

Horror gripped Dodger when he reached the bottom of the tower stairs. It was then he remembered that Rump was in his own tower with Hansel. Did the Stronghand have Rump held hostage? Dodger attempted to get his bearings, twirling his head this way and that, squinting through the darkened stone hallways.

Where's Rump's tower? Though he'd never been to the alchemist's room, he slightly recalled seeing the staircase to his room the first night he was in Storyworld. Instead of going down another stairwell that would lead to the main chamber, he figured he could cut across the upper level of the castle through a wide hallway.

Following a steep incline, Dodger arrived at the entrance to another spiraling stairwell leading up several floors. The Literary hopped up the stairs, hoping that this led to Rump's tower. The food in his stomach was churning and making him feel sick, and his pounding heart was hardly helping. As he reached the landing, he yanked the Hunter's Dagger from the sheath on his leg. The castle was even more dimly lit up here, and he didn't want any unfriendly surprises.

A door across the landing had apparently been torn off its hinges and tossed to the ground nearby. Flashes of blue light and deep laughter came out of the room. Dodger snuck up to the doorway and poked around the corner.

The room was in shambles. Bookcases were toppled over, broken glass bottles and test tubes littered the floor, and the bed was currently on fire, its black smoke wafting out of the wide window. Hansel was strolling around the room, chasing Rump and jeering at him. The alchemist hopped from one piece of furniture to the next, tossing blue balls of light at his opponent. Rump was in the middle of casting a spell when he spotted Dodger peeking in.

"Dodger! Go alert everyone!"

Hansel spun on the spot and smiled when he noticed the Literary. He stomped toward him with his hands outstretched. Rump unbuckled the mace from his belt and swung it right at Hansel's buttocks. The agent's chainmail suit protected the worst of the blow, but the painful look on his face indicated that he felt the tips of the spikes poke through the links. He howled in pain and resumed chasing the alchemist.

Blood now pounded in Dodger's ears, and there was a stabbing pain in his lungs as well as a heavy lead feeling in his stomach. But he never stopped running. He bowled down the stairs and across another hallway until he saw a door leading to the chamber. Not losing his momentum, he barreled through the door and spilled into the room.

"Everybody get out! Hook's coming! Hansel and Gretel are double-"

Dodger's heart dropped into the pit of his stomach. Tinkerbell, Pinocchio, and the rest of the Neverland guests were backed up to the wall, their weapons drawn. Across the chamber stood a troop of at least thirty armed men. Right away, Dodger knew who these men were: pirates.

They were scarier than anything Dodger had seen in Storyworld thus far. The Jabberwocky, the troll, and the bounty hunters were all frightening in their own sense, but the pirates were terrifying because of how humanly they appeared. They all shared the same pockmarked skin covered in scars and sores. A dozen had the cliché eye patches, but their uncovered eyes glared ominously, and it almost seemed like they didn't have eyelids. Their gangly frames were covered in blue and white torn rags hanging off them like oversized cloaks. A handful of pirates at the front of the group had wooden legs extending from the bottom of their knees and ending on the ground in clubbed feet.

All of them wore the same red shirt over their ragged outfits. Dodger recognized it as the same kind of shirt worn by the bounty hunters, branded with the same skull and crossbones logo Humpty had dubbed the Jolly Roger.

One pirate in the front sporting an eye-patch, a peg-leg, enormous gold hoop earrings, and a red bandana tied over his head had a little black winged creature sitting on his shoulder that resembled a miniature Jabberwocky.

"Glad ya' can join us, mate," said the pirate. "Drop the dagger and don'
be doin' anythin' sneaky-like."

Dodger's fingers twitched. Figuring that there was no way he could take
on a troop of pirates by himself, he took the Hunter's Dagger and placed it on the
ground in front of him. The pirate who had spoken to him whispered to the
creature on his shoulder. It gave a loud squawk and flew out the open doors behind
them. At the same time, the door that Dodger had just came through squeaked
open.

Hansel entered, dragging a bruised and bloodied Rump in by his leg. The
alchemist had lost his helmet and was squirming as he was dragged across the
floor. The Stronghand had Rump's belt of vials swung over his shoulder and the
mace clutched in his free hand.

Gretel entered the chamber after her brother, tugging something at the
end of a long rope. Her sleeve was torn and bloody, and her hair was a sweaty
mess. She gave another hard tug on the rope and the unconscious body of Humpty
came into view, wrapped in his hammock. His swords were gone, and his shell
appeared to be indented at the top of his head.

The winged creature returned to the chamber and landed on its master's
shoulder. From the entrance hallway of the castle came the sound of loud
footsteps. The pirates parted ways and cleared the threshold, allowing a giant of a
man to stroll in. His elaborate attire made him look cleaner and more presentable
than his cohorts. He wore a dark red coat with a white, baggy shirt underneath and
a pair of brown velvet pants that stopped at his ankles, followed by white socks

and polished black shoes. He kept a wooden pistol holstered on one side of his belt, and a thin saber sheathed on the other. His shoulder-length black hair was tucked under a black cap imprinted with a Jolly Roger on the front. Jagged teeth filled in the wide smile that sat under a crooked nose and blaring red eyes. The enormous rusty hook in place of his right hand was what gave his identity away.

"Hello, all!" said Captain Hook, bearing his teeth in an enormous smile. "Am I too late for the festivities?" The way he spoke was eloquent with the hint of a growl, and he seemed to carefully enunciate every syllable in his speech.

Nobody moved as Hook approached the main table and grabbed what was left of the roasted animal with his hand. The captain took a bite out of it and chewed the morsels loudly with his mouth open. As he spoke, bits of food flew out and dribbled down his face, instantly chipping away at his presentable demeanor and replacing it with a savage disposition.

"Why is it so quiet now? Did I ruin the mood, Ahab?"

"Aye, they're not much for our humor, Cap'n," said the pirate with the red bandana and the creature on his shoulder.

"'Tis a shame," replied Hook. His eyes wandered across the room and rested on Tinkerbell. "Hm, the princess has grown up quite a bit. With age truly comes beauty."

Tinkerbell went pale, but she maintained a forceful glare and held on tightly to the carving knife in her hand.

"And that would be the Literary?" Hook nodded at Dodger. "He's just a child!"

"He's as much a nuisance as any grown man could ever be," growled Hansel.

"I'm both surprised and disappointed in you two, Hansel and Gretel. It took you this long to capture him. Had I been in the area, I would have had him within hours of his arrival."

Gretel shook her head nervously. "There were complications, sir. We set off for the task the moment we received notice from Ahab's rodent."

"Her name is Polly!" said Ahab. Hook shushed him and motioned for the agent to continue her explanation.

"We set off from Wonderland," said Gretel, "and into Neverwood Forest whe-"

"After," interjected Hansel, "we spent a good deal of time telling Queen Alice where we were going and what we were up to. I think she's catching on to us."

"As I was saying," Gretel said over her brother in an annoyed tone, "we went through the forest and took a wrong turn. My moronic brother suggested that we stop at a cottage and ask for directions, and that cottage happened to belong to the Forever Witch."

The pirates all chuckled in unison, except for Hook, who had finished his snack and was now munching on a pineapple he had snatched from the table. He waved his hand at Gretel to go on.

"She imprisoned us in her cellar for the night. We found out she had taken Neverland's General Pinocchio as her prisoner as well, and that she was holding him in an adjacent cell, though we didn't get to speak with him. The Forever Witch's lover, Geppetto, came and took the puppet away. Still, we knew we must've been close to Neverland.

"The Literary and his hosts eventually rescued us. After that, we journeyed to Geppetto's cottage to retrieve the puppet. It was there that Hansel's lack of intelligence almost ruined the entire mission when he attempted to kill the Literary."

Dodger could tell that Gretel didn't mean to say this last sentence. She covered her mouth with her hand and cast a frightened look at her brother. All of the pirates immediately stopped laughing and fearfully gazed at their leader. Hook dropped the pineapple and glared at Hansel, his red eyes burning with rage.

"You," he whispered in a deadly tone, "tried to take away my destiny?"

"I-I just hate those damn Literaries!" pleaded Hansel. "You know how they are; always coming here and meddling in our affairs. I wasn't trying to take anything away from you! It was a mistake!"

Captain Hook approached Hansel and slashed his rusted hook across his chest, slicing through the chainmail. The blade cut the armor and also Hansel's black scale suit. A thin line of blood seeped out of the gash, making Hansel grimace and step back.

"You almost meddled in *my* affair," hissed Hook. "You're lucky that I don't kill you where you stand, Stronghand."

Hansel twitched. Hook spun around and retrieved the pineapple. He resumed eating it as if nothing had happened.

"Go on," said the captain.

Gretel's gaze shifted from her brother to the captain. "As-as I was saying, we returned to Neverland, ready to send the signal for you to come, until we were interrupted again. The Amryan named Jack Horner had come to Neverland to seek assistance from the Literary.

"He took us to the kingdom of the Lillis, where we were forced to play in their games. A skirmish broke out and, once again, we almost lost our lives, the Literary included."

Hansel nervously glanced at Hook, but the captain didn't pay attention to him. After finishing what was left of the pineapple, Hook wiped his hand on his shirt and leered at the prisoners against the wall.

"Show me this Jack Horner," demanded the pirate loudly.

There was more silence. Nobody standing against the wall responded.

"Who is Jack Horner?" said Hook even louder. When nobody answered again, Hansel pointed out the culprit. Hook paused for a moment, then drew the wooden pistol from his belt and shot Jack in the chest.

Jack crumpled to the ground, the front of his robes darkening from the blood appearing around the bullet hole. His sister screamed and went to cradle his head in her arms.

"No!" screamed Jill. She stared at the wound, horrified, and lightly touched her brother's cheek. Ugu knelt down as well to check the wound, but he did not look hopeful. Jack didn't say a word as the color rushed out of his face.

Dodger was frozen with fear and could only watch in terror as the life slowly slipped from the Amryan's face.

"Finish the tale already," said Hook, pocketing his pistol nonchalantly.

Hansel seemed to have been slightly disturbed by what had just happened, but did his best to carry on with his explanation. "We escaped from the Lillis and chose to rest in a tavern owned by an old friend of mine named Minos. I swiped a sleeping potion from the alchemist's belt and spiked their drinks, which knocked them out."

Rump, who was lying on the ground with his eyes closed, groaned and said, "I thought I tasted something familiar."

"Good plan," commented Hook, making Hansel cast a smug grin at his sister. "I *did* receive your message, by the way. Rather enjoyed the carpet. But why did neither of you come for the ride?"

"He's afraid of heights," Gretel injected, returning Hansel's grin with a smirk of her own, "and we wanted to stay here to keep an eye on the Literary. We found out that the boy had a little crush on me, so we thought to use that to our advantage.

"After we sent the carpet to you with our message, we came back to the tavern and discovered that Minos took the Literary and our other guests to Sleepy Hollow. Yet again, there was the issue of the Literary almost being killed."

There were murmurs passing through the pirates now. Hook looked inquisitively from Gretel to Hansel.

"That was not our fault at all!" said the Stronghand. "Gretel tends to misconstrue facts. We only asked Minos to watch the prisoners while we sent for you. Then we came back and he told us that he'd taken them to a friend's laboratory in Sleepy Hollow. We were unaware that his friend was a sadistic scientist."

Hook grunted and scowled. "I will take care of this Minos and the scientist after we're finished here. Enough interruptions; just finish the damn story!"

"Gretel and I ventured to Sleepy Hollow to find them before it was too late. Instead, we arrived in Oz and were lucky enough to encounter the Literary and his companions in the city."

"Is this when my bounty hunters found you?" inquired Hook. "I hadn't heard from you for days and I figured I would send them for insurance; one of the troops that came back reported that there was a little trouble in Oz."

"Well, Captain, to be quite frank, you could've picked a better team. Do you know how quickly that army was decimated?"

"If I recall correctly," said Pinocchio, "you helped us during that battle, Hansel. I'm sure you slaughtered a spring-heel or two."

"I had to gain their trust!" Hansel quickly explained to Hook, who had raised an eyebrow at him. "You have to understand that if I didn't fight, it would've been suspicious!"

"You should've hid in the tavern with me and the Amryan girl," said Gretel. Turning to Hook, she said, "The Neverlanders had no idea I was quite skilled with a sword and thought I was simply a helpless maiden traveling with my brother. It was quite the surprise for Sir Humpty a few minutes ago." Gretel nudged the egg-man's motionless body with her foot. "As for the rest of the story, Oz's Wizard-King provided us with transportation, assisting us in returning to Neverland. You all came at the perfect time."

Ahab chimed in. "The moment I saw those griffins flying to the castle, I told the Cap'n that we should move in. Figured we should strike before your lot went off on another adventure…"

"On a related note," added Gretel, "you should learn to sail a little more discreetly next time. The Literary spotted the ships a few hours ago and almost spoiled the plan."

Hook sighed loudly and shushed them both. He had finished his meal and was licking his fingers loudly. This was the only sound in the chamber aside from Jill, who continued to sob over her brother's corpse, desperately clinging onto his hand.

"Well, I think it's time we do this, then," said Hook. He unsheathed his saber and pointed at Dodger. "This will be a great honor for you, boy. It's not every day that someone gets to be sacrificed for such a worthy cause. You'll be the Literary who aided me in taking over this world. Sad to say, you won't be alive to see it."

The pirates all started up a loud, raucous cheer for their captain. Dodger found himself rooted to the spot, unable to move.

Dodger's Doorway

Hook took one step at the Literary, and the chamber doors flew open. In came John Tell and the Neverland Sentries, swords and bows at the ready. With a cry of "For Neverland!" they charged at the pirates. At the same time, the Royal Guard of Oz armed their weapons and shouted "For Oz!" and joined them in battle. A massive melee ensued. Dodger picked up the dagger and quickly looked for an escape. Hook was momentarily distracted by the ambush, but soon began pushing his way through the crowd toward the Literary.

John yelled, "Dodger! We'll take care of the pirates! Go into the forest and hide!"

The captain stabbed a pirate in the chest and sent his elbow into the temple of another enemy. Scarecrow and Maxis grabbed Dodger's arms and steered him out of the chamber, followed by their other allies. The group sprinted down the hallway and out the main gate, which had been ripped out of the stonework and was lying on the ground outside of the entrance. Countless dead sentries' bodies and slaughtered griffins were strewn about the area.

It was nighttime. A large moon was out, illuminating the area in an eerie pale glow much like in Sleepy Hollow. Dodger and his escorts escaped into the forest. They didn't stop moving until they felt like they were at a safe distance, and by the time they paused to catch their breaths, Dodger felt like vomiting again.

His mind was a mess right now from the mix of adrenaline, fear, shock, depression, and anger. The Literary pressed his palms into his eyes and cringed. There was nothing he could do to control the flood of emotions. It was overwhelming.

Dodger sighed and attempted to even out his breathing and his out-of-control heart rate. Jill, Maxis, Nick, Scarecrow, and Ugu stood in a semi-circle around him.

"Wait a minute," asked Dodger, his heart rate firing back up, "where's Tinkerbell? And Pinocchio? And everyone else?"

Nobody said anything. The Oz guardsmen simultaneously looked back at the demolished gates of the castle. Dodger leapt to his feet and tried to leave the forest, but Maxis blocked his way.

"Let me go! We have to go back and save them! They need us!"

"We can't do that!" stated Maxis. "You're a marked man and Hook is after your life. We need to keep you here, safe and protected."

Anger swelled in Dodger's heart. He started punching Maxis in the chest.

"No! Let me go! You can't do this! Are we supposed to just let the pirates take over? We have to do something!"

"We need to formulate a plan!" insisted Maxis.

"We *need* to go in there and fight!" Dodger didn't relent in his punching. "I thought you were supposed to be the Courageous Lion! What, are you too scared to fight?"

This was the wrong thing to say. Maxis grabbed both of Dodger's arms and pinned them to his sides. The lion-man had a maniacal gleam in his stare that frightened Dodger more than Hook's red eyes.

"Watch your words, Literary," said Maxis. "I am not scared; I'm just sensible. Those pirates will slaughter us the moment we step foot back in the throne room."

Dodger had found his voice through the lion-man's petrifying glare. "Why do you think that? Why can't we beat the pirates? I'm a Literary. Maybe this was something I was destined to do?"

"Maxis is right," Nick said in his metallic voice. "We're no match for the pirates. There are only six of us. We're severely outnumbered. Without a plan, we stand no chance."

"There were only a few of us fighting that army of bounty hunters in Oz," reasoned Dodger.

Maxis let go of the Literary. "You don't understand, Dodger. Your emotions are clouding your logic. Pirates aren't as moronic or as careless as bounty hunters. They're brutal and ferocious fighters. Like Nick said, we have no chance of defeating them, especially with Captain Hook in command. He can hold his own against five soldiers alone without breaking a sweat."

Dodger sat back down and put his head in his hands. The adrenaline rush had left him feeling dizzy. On top of all that was happening now, his mind was still reeling with hundreds of thoughts, including his feelings about Gretel.

We found out that the boy had a little crush on me, so we thought to use that to our advantage.

These words kept running through his head over and over again. How could Dodger have been so stupid to fall for someone so quickly?

The more Dodger thought about it, the worse he began to feel. The worst part of it all was that this could have been avoided after the incident at Geppetto's home. If Dodger had just let Humpty banish Hansel and Gretel from the group, they wouldn't be in this situation now, but Dodger had to be stubborn and insist that the agents stay, all so he could spend more time with Gretel. It made the Literary feel sick to his stomach.

The group sat in the forest for a long time. To Dodger, it seemed like hours, especially as he watched the moon make its way across the sky. At one point, Scarecrow suggested they go to a nearby town for reinforcements. Right after he said this, they heard a noise coming from the distant castle gate. A figure came staggering into the forest. The Oz guardsmen readied their weapons and watched this person limp forward while groaning loudly.

Dodger gasped. It was John Tell. He recognized the man's face even from this distance. The Literary hurried forward in spite of the hisses from the others to stay away from the castle. Once he got close to John, he gasped again.

The captain's armor was gone and his clothing was torn and covered in splotches of blood. There was grime and blood on the right side of his face, and part of his ear looked like it had been sliced off. He was carrying a small, ovular, metal platter. When John reached the edge of the forest, he collapsed into Ugu's arms.

"Fight" was all he could mutter. With one final cough, his body went limp.

In the pit of his heart, Dodger felt the sadness and guilt grow larger. Ugu gently laid the captain on the ground and muttered a few words while waving his hand over the body. The Oz guardsmen and Jill repeated this silent prayer.

"What's that in his hands?" asked Scarecrow.

For a brief moment, Dodger's sadness was overtaken by curiosity as he focused on the object John was holding. Gently, he pulled it out of his grasp and held it up. It was an ovular mirror with a frame made of black iron. The glass in the center was impeccably clean and polished, giving off a slight sparkle from the overhead moonlight. The words "Mirror of Cagimarin" were etched into the bottom of the frame. Dodger peered into his reflection and was aghast when he saw his own appearance for the first time in days.

His five o'clock shadow had grown into thin stubble covering most of his face and creeping down the top of his neck. The two eyes looking back at him were bloodshot and sunken in. The piercing in his lip was still intact, but the area around it was slightly bruised, possibly from when a spring-heel punched him in Oz. Dodger angrily yanked it out and tossed it to the ground. A tiny bloody hole was left in his bottom lip.

"I would have taken that if you were going to toss it away!" said a voice.

Dodger nearly dropped the mirror. His reflection melted away, and replacing it was a moving image of Captain Hook and his legion of pirates. Everyone in the mirror laughed in unison.

"I'm glad you got our message, boy," said the televised image of Hook. "We were afraid the sentry wouldn't reach you. There was actually a gamble placed on whether he would even make it past the gates. I personally thought he would keel over at the entranceway."

The pirates all roared with laughter again. Dodger shook with anger and Maxis growled nearby. The image in the mirror zoomed out to reveal Rump, Pinocchio, and Tinkerbell kneeling with a line of armed pirates standing behind them with swords above their heads. Humpty was still unconscious in his hammock. In the background were a couple of bodies of sentries and pirates scattered on the floor. The top of Pumpkinhead's cranium was slightly out of frame with a chunk missing off the side.

"I give you credit for slipping through my fingers," continued Hook, "but I have to say that I'm growing tired of all this. Therefore, I shall offer you a proposal."

"Should I just come in and let you kill me?" said Dodger with aggressive sarcasm.

"Easy with that tone, young man. You have two options. First option, you can stay and hide in the forest. By sunrise, if you aren't here, I will lead a team of a hundred men into the Neverwood and scour the entire area until you're apprehended. When we find you, and I can promise you that we will, I'll make you feel pain like you've never experienced in your life. The same punishment goes for everyone else in there with you along with the Neverlanders who are currently our prisoners. Upon cleansing this castle, we'll move onto the rest of the kingdom and ensure that every living thing within these walls is dead."

Dodger shuddered yet tried to hold himself together in front of the mirror. "And what's the other option?"

"You come back into the castle before sunrise. Instead of killing you, I'll merely have you transported home to the world of the Literaries. If I can't kill you, I would rather nobody else has the opportunity either. Mercy isn't a generous offering by me so I recommend you take this option."

"I don't trust y-" Dodger paused. "Hold on. How're you gonna teleport me back to my world? You know how to?"

Captain Hook raised his eyebrows. Behind him, Humpty stirred and slowly rolled over. Rump didn't move a muscle and kept his head down. Dodger's voice shook from his newly directed anger.

"You mean, I could've gone home this whole time, and you didn't tell me?"

Humpty and Rump remained silent for a long time. Dodger repeated his question louder.

"We needed your help, Dodger," wheezed Rump, keeping his head down. Hook stared between the alchemist and the Literary with mild amusement.

"I *did* help you!" shouted Dodger. "I helped you find Pinocchio, just like you said! I put my life on the line for you guys! Do you know how many times I almost died? What else did you need me to do?"

"We were trying to find King Gabriel."

Dodger paused. "You told me he was dead."

"No, we said he was lost."

"Well, what's that supposed to mean?"

"After the pirates' siege of Neverland," responded Pinocchio this time, "the king went into exile, unable to bear the death of Peter Pan. Nobody knows where he went. One thing was for certain, though: the kingdom was falling apart without him. That is why I went searching for him years ago."

"Peter Pan?" said Hook. "That was the young red-haired lad, right? Oh, he was a fool. I was so close to nearly slaying a Literary until Pan interfered. Stupid, stupid boy."

Pinocchio twitched in his chains, scowling fiercely at the pirate captain. Dodger was angry as well, but not because of the Peter Pan comment; he was angry that Rump and Humpty had lied to him.

"I find it funny that you mention your king because we have a special guest with us tonight," announced Hook.

The mirror flipped around to view the entrance to the throne chamber. Three pirates entered, and they were pulling on a long chain attached to a fourth person's shackled wrists. The prisoner wore a tattered brown cloak and thin sandals, and had dirty, tangled, black hair that was so long that it reached past his shoulders. One of his eyes peeked out from the mange of hair.

"King Gabriel!" said Humpty, Rump, and Pinocchio off-screen.

"Father!" cried out Tinkerbell's voice.

Hook smiled. "Yes, yes. We found him drifting in a boat out in the middle of the sea many years ago. It was a pleasant surprise when we discovered him to be the very King of Neverland himself. Instead of slaying him on the spot for our embarrassing defeat during the siege, we kept him as our prisoner, knowing he could serve us well in the future. It looks like my prediction was right.

"But as I was saying, you have until sunrise to surrender, Literary. Once you arrive, I'll order the alchemist to conjure a portal into your world, thus allowing you to go home. Also, I think I should provide a little incentive to make sure you arrive sooner rather than later."

Hook drew his pistol and aimed it at the back of Gabriel's head. The mirror zoomed into the king's face as he met Dodger's gaze. A thin tear fell from his eye right as Hook pulled the trigger.

Dodger turned away, but he couldn't block out the sound of the gunshot. Following this was the sound of a heavy object thudding to the floor and several deep shouts of "No!" Amidst the screams came Tinkerbell's sobbing.

Hook chuckled. "You had better hurry up. Do not keep me waiting too long or the next bullet goes into the princess's head!"

The image in the mirror clouded over and disappeared, reverting to its reflective surface once more. Dodger angrily tossed the mirror away. It struck a rock, cracking the glass right down the middle.

There was too much for Dodger to digest right now, and it brought back the familiar lightheaded feeling. He leaned his hand against a nearby tree and tried to collect his thoughts.

"What do we do now?" asked Jill.

"It's obvious, is it not?" stated Ugu. "We need to organize an assault on the castle!"

"Are you seriously suggesting we fight the pirates?" replied Nick.

"We have to infiltrate the castle and rescue the prisoners. You heard what Hook said. We lost Pumpkinhead, and the Neverlanders just watched their king perish. How much more blood must be spilled?"

"Please reconsider your thoughts, Ugu. You mustn't let your emotions take over like they did for the Literary," said Maxis.

"I'll turn myself in. That's what he wants, isn't it?" suggested Dodger. The guardsmen stared at him like he was insane.

"You cannot give up that easily, Dodger!" exclaimed Scarecrow. "After the battle with the bounty hunters, the death of Horner and Pumpkinhead? Everything we fought for will have been in vain! How can you even think of surrendering?"

"I shouldn't even be here! I'm not a soldier or whatever you people expect me to be. I don't know what Humpty or the princess or anyone wanted me to do. Did you know they actually asked me to join the army? I'm just a kid! I don't belong here. I'll go in and tell Hook to send me home. Then maybe he'll let everyone else g-"

"This is Captain Hook we're discussing, Dodger," said Maxis. "Do you understand what you're saying? You want to negotiate with one of the most vile and despicable characters in existence? Do you think he will really let you go home? I can promise you that he will slay you the moment you enter his sight."

"What else can we do? There's no other way!" Dodger fired back. "And as for helping Rump and Humpty, they lied to me! They nearly got me killed by bringing me into this world, then lied to my face! They told me they couldn't send me back, so they kept me here to get attacked by trolls and bounty hunters and giants."

"Send you back?" said Maxis. "Send you back to what? You would rather go back to the world of the Literaries where you were abused by your peers and neglected by your parents? If I didn't know better, I would say that you're better suited for this world. Humpty and Rumpelstiltskin may have actually improved your life. Think of all you've learned and experienced here."

Dodger opened his mouth to argue, but stopped before he could get the words out. What Maxis said made sense, though he didn't want to admit it.

The Literary pushed himself off the tree. A second later, an arrow had implanted itself right where his hand had been. The forest suddenly seemed to come to life as dozens of shapes materialized out of the brush. At least thirty men dressed in green and brown formed a circle around Dodger's group. Robin Hood was the last to appear, carrying a bow in his hand and smirking. The Royal Guard of Oz readied their weapons.

"We meet again, young man," said Robin. "This time, I see, you don't have anyone from Neverland by your side. Also, I vastly outnumber you, meaning I'm free to do as I please!" Robin shouldered his bow and approached Dodger. "Hmm, did you pawn that jewelry from your lips? I was hoping I could've taken it. No matter. I'll jus-"

Dodger put all of his strength into a punch that knocked Robin off his feet and onto his back. His cronies started forward, loading their bows and unsheathing their swords, but the Literary stooped over Robin with his dagger out. Jill and the Oz soldiers circled them, protecting Dodger from the other Merry Men.

"Now's really not the time!" said Dodger, his hand clenched on Robin's collar. "What is your problem? Do you seriously not have anything better to do than harass people in the forest?"

The Merry Men closed in, but their leader held up his hand to stop them. Robin stared at the dagger point and sneered. "Go ahead. Do it, if you have the nerve."

Dodger pursed his lips and tightened his grip on the dagger handle, ready to drive it into Robin's chest. This was the same man who had threatened him twice already. In Dodger's opinion, the thief was hardly better than Hook.

"Well?" asked Robin. "Why won't you do it? Is it because you're afraid?"

"Let him go, boy!" warned the huge Merry Man named Little John. "You do not want to harm him."

Dodger turned to Little John in disbelief. "Are you serious? How do you know I don't want to? He just tried to take off my hand. A few days ago, your friend almost killed Humpty! How do you know I won't shove this dagger into him?"

"Because if you truly wanted to, you would have done it by now!" snapped Robin.

He was right. Dodger couldn't find it in himself to do it. He cursed loudly and threw Robin down into the dirt.

Robin scowled. He casually dusted himself off as he rose to his feet. "For the record, I'll have you know we've never murdered anyone in this forest. We may be robbers, but we're not killers; though, you saw how Humpty slayed my cousin, Will. And the alchemist's botched magic killed our companion, Tuck, when he attempted to teleport him. It was unjust!"

"You started it. And you almost tore my face apart for my lip ring, so how about we call it even?" said Dodger.

Robin shrugged. "Fair enough. We've made mistakes. Will wasn't supposed to attack Sir Humpty. But ultimately, none of us would kill anyone. You must understand this. We're not evil; just misunderstood – and hungry."

"I don't have time for this," said the Literary. "The last thing we need right now is you and your friends causing problems. In case you haven't noticed, we're in the middle of a little war right now."

"What war?" asked Robin.

"Captain Hook and his pirates took over the castle."

Robin looked at his Merry Men, and then back to Dodger. "He's back? We thought he was gone for good."

"No. He's got Humpty, Rump, Pinocchio, and Tinkerbell as his prisoners, and he just killed the king."

Robin's eyes widened. "King Gabriel? He went into exile after the siege and nobody has heard from him in ages."

Dodger explained the story to the thief. The Oz guardsmen remained in their protective circle around the Literary, but it wasn't necessary. The Merry Men had lowered their weapons and were listening intently to Dodger.

"That's a shame," said Robin sadly. "King Gabriel was a fair ruler. He hired my band long ago, when we were rogues out in Himshire. He saved us from a life of crime and made us sentries. It was an honor to fight alongside him during the last war with the pirates, but after he went into exile, we lost a bit of our morale. We got carried away with the drinking and our shenanigans. Hence why Humpty banished us."

Dodger was only half listening. He was too busy picturing the Neverlanders chained against the wall. He then imagined a horde of pirates chasing him through the forest.

What do we do?

"You were in Neverland during the last war with the pirates?" Nick asked Robin. "How did you defeat them?"

"Wonderland sent reinforcements," responded Dodger, recalling what Rump had told him. "I doubt we could make it there in time to get troops. Everyone will be dead by sunrise. We need an army right now to fight the pirates. That's the only shot we have."

After a long pause, Robin said, "What about Neverland's army?"

Dodger slowly turned to face the thief. "No, Rump said there was no army left after the pirates' siege. He said people didn't want to fight anymore."

Robin chuckled. "You're not the brightest Literary to stumble into our world. Do you really think Neverland would be standing if it didn't have an army at its disposal?" Dodger's angry glare made Robin stop laughing and he continued with his statement. "What I'm saying is that, after the siege, there was a project to create a new army of automatons similar to Queen Alice's card soldiers.

"This army was modeled after General Pinocchio. In the very depths of Neverland Castle is a legion of at least one hundred wooden soldiers, all ready for battle. Where else do you think the Neverland Military Arm resides?"

Dodger felt a tiny sliver of hope. "Really? Then what's stopping them from coming out and helping us right now?"

"From what I remember," said Robin, rubbing his chin, "they were locked in one of the dungeons. Yes, yes, they were locked away and only Pinocchio had the ability to command them. I believe his war hammer granted him the power of control."

"That's it!" Dodger could hardly contain the excitement in his voice. "This can work. We have to go in, get the hammer, and let the army out so they can fight the pirates!"

"Do you know how difficult that sounds?" asked Scarecrow. "First of all, how do you expect us to get to the dungeons? We would need to get past a small army of pirates. They'd cut us to ribbons in minutes. Second, how are we supposed to know which dungeon houses the army? I don't want us to get lost in the depths of Neverland Castle and then be cornered by a horde of pirates. Unless we have someone who can find the dungeon and navigate the castle, we stand no chance."

Dodger's spirits sank. He knew his way to the main chamber and the upper towers of the castle, but he'd never been to the lower levels and would surely get lost. Scarecrow was right. It sounded more reckless to try to free the army than it did to face the pirates. The Literary was about to sit back down, crestfallen, when Robin spoke.

"I know the way."

"... *they were locked away and only Pinocchio had the ability to command them. I believe his war hammer granted him the power of control.*"

Captain Hook grinned. Although the Literary had broken the mirror, it still transmitted a faint image and sound back to the pirates. The picture kept fading in and out, but Hook could still hear certain parts of the conversation. After Robin mentioned the war hammer and the wooden army, Hook turned to Hansel and nodded.

"*We have to go in, get the hammer, and let the army out so they can fight the pirates!*" was the last thing to come through the mirror before the glass clouded over and went back to its reflective state.

"They want a battle?" Hook said to himself. "Then we shall give them a battle."

Chapter 14

A Helping Hand

The moon had reached its highest point in the sky by the time Dodger exited the forest. Slowly, deliberately, he made his way to the castle. Ahab's pet, Polly, had perched herself on top of the gate. When the Literary stepped out of the shadows of Neverwood Forest, she gave a loud cry and flew into the castle.

Dodger shook violently. The plan was about to be set in motion and he was starting to have second thoughts about its success. In his mind, he kept going over a series of different scenarios and how he would have to work around any flaws.

At the end of the hallway, Dodger could see the doors propped open leading to the chamber. His pace quickened down the long threshold, and he paused before entering the main chamber.

Upon stepping through the door, the first thing he saw was a group of ten pirates gathered at the opposite wall. They were standing in front of the imprisoned Tinkerbell, Pinocchio, Rump, and Humpty, who were all chained by their wrists and ankles. All of the Neverlanders were disheveled and covered in bruises and scratches, except for Pinocchio; he had deep notches carved around his wooden body.

Hook sat in one of the royal thrones next to Gretel, with an armed pirate on either side. They didn't immediately notice the Literary when he entered.

"I'm here," Dodger called out. Every head in the room turned to him.

"No, Dodger!" cried Humpty.

Hook grinned, raised his pistol, and shot Dodger in the chest. The Literary froze and collapsed onto his back. Captain Hook's dark laughter echoed around the room.

"Dodger!" screamed Rump.

The pirates cheered for their leader as he rose from the throne and lifted his arms in triumph. Gretel marveled at him with twinkling eyes.

"Behold!" boomed Hook. "I am the first person to ever kill a Literary! You are all in the presence of an immortal man!"

The pirates bowed to their master. Hook waved to them and smiled. He sauntered up to Dodger's body.

"Stupid, stupid boy," he muttered. "It looks like your plan didn't work out as you intended."

It wasn't until he was standing right over the Literary's corpse that Hook noticed something was amiss.

There was no blood from the bullet hole.

Dodger's eyes snapped open and his leg shot up between Hook's legs. The captain howled loudly and doubled over, grabbing at his groin. Dodger stood and pulled an object out from under his shirt: the magic mirror, which now had a spider-web of cracks sprawling from where the bullet was lodged.

Dodger wound the mirror back and swung it as hard as he could, striking Hook in the face with the iron frame. The mirror shattered to pieces, and its iron frame bent into an oblong shape as the captain keeled over.

The pirates drew their swords, roaring like animals. Dodger took out his dagger and tapped it loudly on the ground. Out of the darkness of the hallway, the Royal Guard of Oz charged in with their weapons at the ready. Even Jill stood beside them with a short sword in either hand.

Ahab's pet let out a series of piercing chirps. Twenty more pirates spilled into the chamber from various doorways. Dodger backed up and fell in line with his allies.

"G-get them!" said the writhing Hook.

With another series of roars, a squad of pirates rushed across the chamber. Ugu stepped forward and blasted an orb of energy up at the ceiling, hitting the chain of the enormous chandelier. The links snapped, and the entire fixture fell, landing on the attackers.

A second wave of pirates yelled even louder and rushed around the wreckage to attack. Nick dropped down into a sitting position with his knees drawn up to his torso and his arms buckled over them. Maxis picked him up over his head and tossed him at the enemies. The ball of heavy tin whistled through the air and knocked over numerous pirates. Nick popped out of his crouched position, unsheathed his axe, and started attacking anyone in his reach. Dodger and the others charged forward to meet the next band of charging enemies.

All the commotion must have sounded throughout the castle, for additional pirates swarmed into the chamber. Ahab helped Hook to his feet and attempted to drag him away from the battle, but the captain shoved him off. His raging eyes scanned the clashing bodies for his target.

One pirate dove for Dodger and was swatted away with a swing from Scarecrow's sword. Maxis grabbed another pirate sneaking up on the Literary and slammed him headfirst into the ground. More pirates flooded in by the second. Dodger yelled over his shoulder, "NOW!" and Robin and his Merry Men entered the room.

A volley of arrows zipped into the pirate army. The rest of Robin's band unsheathed their swords and small axes and charged. The two opposing armies clashed in the center of the chamber where they engaged in a hectic skirmish.

"Tell the resta' the ships to unload!" Ahab said to Polly over the melee. The creature squawked and started flying for the window. In one smooth motion, Robin pulled an arrow out of a pirate's corpse, loaded it into his bow, and let it fly. Polly fell out of the air with the arrow through her body.

"No!" cried Ahab.

"Go signal the ships yourself!" ordered Hook.

Ahab glared at Robin before taking off in the opposite direction, exiting through an open door. Robin attempted to hit him with another arrow, but a pirate swung his sword wildly at the archer's head, causing him to miss. Dodger leapt forward and dispatched the pirate with a stab to the side. Black blood covered the dagger's blade.

"We need to stop Ahab from signaling for reinforcements," said Robin, firing another arrow into the fray.

"I'm on it," said Dodger.

Robin grabbed the Literary's arm. "No, you have to release the army. In all honesty, the dungeons may be the safest place for you now. I'll take care of Ahab."

"What? No! You're supposed to help me find the army!"

Robin had already taken off after Ahab. Dodger cursed out of frustration. Prior to the assault on the castle, Robin had drawn out a diagram of where exactly the dungeons were located, giving Dodger a faint idea of where to go, yet he felt more comfortable if the archer was accompanying him.

Hook had recovered from Dodger's hit and was now participating in the battle, his body towering over his cohorts. It was a frightening sight. Dodger witnessed the pirate captain swatting soldiers left and right with nothing hindering his attacks. Hansel was nowhere to be seen, and Gretel had escaped from the area right after the first charge. Dodger thought he glimpsed her fighting past the Merry Men to get to the staircase heading up to Humpty's tower, but he didn't pursue her. There were more important things at stake.

Maxis and Dodger cleared a path to the opposite wall, dispatching of any pirates in their way. The Neverland prisoners were all worse for the wear. Pinocchio and Tinkerbell were unconscious. The lion-man grabbed the ends of the chains holding the princess and tugged at them with all his might.

"Who has the keys to the shackles?" he asked in between grunts.

Rump groaned. "I believe it was that fellow, Ahab."

"Terrific," muttered Maxis. He gave another unsuccessful yank at the chains. No results. A pirate swooped in, ready to impale him with his saber. The lion-man backhanded him across the room. "I'm in no hurry," he muttered, fingering the chain and inspecting it closely.

While Maxis fiddled with the restraints, Dodger looked for Pinocchio's hammer, but it was nowhere to be seen. He wondered if maybe one of the pirates must have taken it. There was no time to waste. He decided to just head to the dungeon so that he could at least locate the army.

Dodger fought through more enemies, making his way to the door that supposedly led to the dungeons; the same door they entered to get to the private lake earlier. At all times, one of the Oz soldiers stood by his side. Every pirate was out for the Literary, except Hook, who seemed to have found more enjoyment picking off the Merry Men.

Two pirates flanked the Literary and almost subdued him, but Jill and Scarecrow came to the rescue. Another pirate jumped into the air and was blasted away by Ugu's magic.

"Go now! We'll hold them off," said the Maker.

Kicking a pirate's body aside, Dodger slid through the crack in the door. Ahead, he spotted the stairway leading to Pinocchio and Humpty's room. Instead of going upwards, he went down the stairs.

At the very bottom of the stairwell, Dodger followed a narrow hallway lined with more torches, albeit they were much dimmer than the lights up on the higher levels of the castle. The walls were wet and slimy, a combination of misshapen stones and mud. It looked like a sewer, and the foul smell only enhanced the atmosphere.

Dodger's Doorway

Dodger crept down the deep passageway, his breathing becoming shallower as the path sloped into the ground. A low humming noise pulsated from the walls and made the Literary feel nervous.

The tunnel eventually came to an end at a large doorway, wide enough for ten people to file through side-by-side. Two tall wooden doors must have once stood there, but all that was left were splintered remains. Dodger tiptoed to the edge of the doorway and peered around the corner to look inside.

There must have been a hundred wooden replicas of Pinocchio standing in this room, all lined up in rows of ten. They were identical to their general except they didn't wear shirts; instead, they had the Neverland crest carved right into their chests, and there were long swords tucked into their hands. Dodger marveled at the wooden army until he noticed something moving within their ranks. A closer look revealed that it was Hansel, and in his hand was Pinocchio's war hammer.

The agent moved among the soldiers, holding Pinocchio's war hammer up and yelling. "Awaken! I command you to activate!" No response came from the soldiers. Hansel repeated variations of his command several times, once tapping a soldier on the head with the hammer. No movement at all.

Dodger entered the room silently and remained tucked away in the shadows. *So the hammer doesn't active them?* he thought.

Hansel huffed and moved on to the next row of soldiers. "Why won't you listen to my orders? You should be subjected to my will!"

"Maybe you're doing it wrong," said Dodger, stepping out of his hiding spot.

Hansel emerged from the depths of the wooden army. "You? You're supposed to be dead!"

"Hook's plan didn't work out. I think he'd appreciate it if you hurried up on getting that army moving. Sounds like he could use the help upstairs."

Hansel stared up at the ceiling. The faint sounds of battle could be heard above. The agent smirked at the Literary.

"I may not be allowed to kill you, boy, but I'll take great pleasure in breaking every bone in your body. Captain Hook won't care about an injured Literary as long as he's the one who gets to finish you off." He tossed the war hammer aside and advanced on the Literary while cracking his knuckles.

Dodger's ducked under Hansel's punch at the last second and jumped out of the way. The Stronghand's fist soared into a stone column, leaving an enormous crater. Dodger tightened his grip on the dagger, his heart racing once again. Hansel spun around and launched a kick that would have caught Dodger under the ribs had he not rolled over. The Literary sprung to his feet and punched Hansel in the face as hard as he could.

It felt like punching a brick wall. The hit didn't faze the agent the slightest bit. He laughed, picked Dodger up, and tossed him into the wooden army, knocking over a section of soldiers.

"You dare challenge me?" said Hansel. "I'm a Stronghand! You've seen me hold up bridges and take down giants. What chance do you have against me?"

"Yeah, you might be strong," Dodger said through his grimace, "but you're still a coward."

Hansel's smirk disappeared. "Did you just accuse me of being a coward?"

For a moment, Dodger wanted to kick himself for the stupid remark, but then he smiled. "Yeah, a big coward. You've been picking fights with me since we rescued you from the Forever Witch. You think picking on someone smaller and weaker than you makes you some big tough guy?"

Hansel grinned. "I picked on you because it was fun to see you squirm, you stupid child; much like my sister found it fun to play with your heart, just to see it get crushed in the end. Whenever we spoke and you weren't around, she told me how she almost pitied you and how pathetic you were. I've heard everything you told her. Such a sad life you lead."

"This isn't about Gretel and me," said Dodger defiantly, avoiding the stinging truth in Hansel's words. "This is about you. You're afraid to take on anyone who has even the smallest chance to kick your ass. All you are is a big bully. We all saw you back down whenever Humpty or Pinocchio talked to you. That's why you work for Hook. It's not out of loyalty; it's out of fear! You're just a big scared pansy!"

Hansel may not have understood what Dodger's insult meant, but it was apparent that he didn't appreciate being insulted. The agent charged with his arms outstretched and leapt at the Literary.

Dodger closed his eyes and covered his head, expecting the Stronghand to crush him. It never came. All he heard was the sound of a grunt and a gasp. The Literary opened his eyes and was astounded to see Hansel kneeling in front of him with a long blade impaling his chest. He had fallen onto the sword of one of the downed wooden soldiers, the blade piercing the gap that Hook had left in his armor. The Stronghand touched his fingers to his chest and gaped at his blood-covered hand before falling to the ground.

Dodger needed a moment to regain his senses, but he didn't even have a chance to blink before Hansel's body started to glow and tremble. For a moment, it looked like the agent was about to explode. Dodger watched in astonishment as the body turned a shade of gray, and then dissolved into a large pile of ash.

It took a moment for Dodger to collect himself. He wasn't even going to begin to ask why Hansel's body turned to ash. He was too busy trying to get over the fact that not even a day ago, he and Hansel were almost friends, fighting bounty hunters side-by-side in Oz and sharing a drink at the Fallen Timber Inn. But then he remembered how much pain and humiliation the agent had caused him, jeopardizing his life on multiple occasions.

Good riddance, Dodger thought, sneering at the pile of ash with a sense of bitter satisfaction.

He gazed at the wooden soldiers, who all remained immobile and silent. There was no other sign of life in the room except for the Literary. Dodger picked up Pinocchio's hammer and examined it closely. *Why didn't this work?* he pondered. He suddenly remembered the battle going on upstairs and hurried out of the dungeon.

Sprinting up the stairs, Dodger broke into the main chamber, where he found the ground littered with the bodies of pirates and Merry Men. Nick and Scarecrow were fighting the last of the pirates left in the room, and Ugu and Jill were sitting by the wall with the prisoners. Tinkerbell, Humpty, and Rump had come to, but they all looked extremely weak. Jill shook Pinocchio's shoulders, desperately calling out to the general to wake up. He remained completely still with his mouth hanging open and one of his eyelids drooping.

Hook and Maxis were locked in combat, the lion-man throwing his fists in a series of wild arcs. The pirate captain bounced from one foot to the other, dodging each attack. Every time Maxis missed a punch, his opponent would poke him with his sword or gash him with his hook.

"Come on, kitty! You'll have to be much faster than that if you want to reach me!"

Maxis panted, his furry face drenched with sweat, but he refused to lower his fists. The taunt from Hook only seemed to invigorate him, and the lion-man resumed his attack, unleashing a barrage of punches at his enemy. Hook didn't let down his guard. He continued blocking and dodging the attacks until Maxis was thrown off balance by a heavy right swing. The pirate captain caught his wrist in the curve of his hook and, with his free hand, flipped the sword around and stabbed it into the lion-man's chest.

"Maxis!" cried out Scarecrow.

Hook yanked the blade from his chest. The lion-man dropped to his knees and collapsed to the floor. Dodger sat stunned, unable to comprehend what just happened. Anger soon replaced this shock, and he felt the sudden urge to draw the Hunter's Dagger and charge at Hook.

"He's ours!" Scarecrow and Nick slayed the last of the pirate minions and attacked Hook. Ugu abandoned the prisoners to join in the fight as well.

Suddenly, Robin burst into the chamber holding a ring of keys in one hand and his bow in the other. Splotches of blood covered his tunic, and his nose looked broken.

"Sorry for the dawdling," said Robin, ignoring Humpty's questioning glare and unlocking everyone from their shackles. "There's good news and bad news. The good news is, even though Ahab put up a bit of a fight, he's dead."

"And the bad?" asked Rump.

"Well, I wasn't able to stop him in time from sending a signal to the other pirates. I saw their ships on the other side of the Neverwood and it looks like they're on their way."

Dodger's heart sank. "This isn't good. I found the army downstairs, but they won't move. They're like statues, and the hammer didn't do anything. I thought you said it controlled them!"

"Of course the hammer doesn't command the army," commented Rump weakly. "To awaken the Neverland Military Arm, you'll have to awaken their general."

Dodger tossed the hammer away and grabbed Pinocchio's shoulders. "Wake up! We need you!"

It was no use. Peeking over his shoulder, Dodger could see Hook battling the Oz soldiers. They were putting up more of a challenge than Maxis did, but the pirate captain was hardly breaking a sweat. His broad, heavy stature didn't deter his movements in the slightest. Like Humpty, he was agile and skilled in battle. Scarecrow and Nick would try to swing their blades from either side, and Hook would block both attacks, pivot, then swipe at their legs or arms. Ugu attempted several times to blast him with his magic, but the green orbs of energy made no impact on the pirate captain aside from burning small holes in his shirt.

"This is quite fun!" exclaimed Hook amidst the fighting. He punched Ugu in the face and kicked out one of Scarecrow's legs before knocking Nick onto his back.

"Robin, can you hit him with an arrow?" asked Dodger.

"My accuracy may be excellent, but I don't want to risk hitting one of our own," admitted the archer. "They're all moving too fast."

Again, Dodger's heart sank. How were they going to overcome these odds? Their forces were dwindling, the army was unresponsive, and even now, Dodger could hear the other bloodthirsty pirates coming their way.

Scarecrow was pitched into the royal thrones, only to get up and charge back at Hook. In that instant, Dodger spotted something that made his heart skip a beat. Behind Tinkerbell's throne was the Hunter's Rifle. A tiny speck of hope awakened in the Literary's soul.

"Okay, I have an idea. Humpty, I want you and Rump to take Princess Tinkerbell out through the back of the castle and as far away from here as possible."

"No," muttered Humpty. "We need to defend the castle."

"No," countered Dodger. "You need to get out of here. You're not fit to fight. We'll handle this. Just protect the princess!

Humpty and Rump glanced at each other. Rump gave an affirming nod and the two Neverlanders did as they were told. Tinkerbell was in a weakened, but she was strong enough to follow her subjects out of the castle.

"Robin, follow my lead," whispered Dodger. He waited until Hook's back was turned before he crept to the throne and grabbed the rifle. Fortunately, two bullets had been loaded into it, leaving it ready to be fired. There was little room for error so he had to make each shot count.

Dodger aimed the heavy gun at Hook's head and shouted, "Hey, Hook!"

The captain deflected another series of attacks from the Oz soldiers and spun around to face the armed Literary.

"And what do you intend to do with that, boy?" remarked the pirate captain.

"I'm gonna shoot you. How does that sound?" Dodger ignored the shaking in his legs and maintained a calm tone to his voice.

Hook backhanded a charging Scarecrow. "Do you think I'm frightened of you? I am not a normal man. I can withstand a cannon blast to the chest. I can swim through rivers of fire. I ca-"

"How would you fare with an arrow to the skull?" asked Robin, firing an arrow. It whistled across the chamber and impaled Hook's temple with a dull *thud*.

Dodger cheered and Robin grinned. Their celebrations were cut short, though, as Hook swiftly plucked the arrow from his head, snapped it in his fingers, and threw it aside.

"It will take a lot more than that to kill me, fools," Hook said. He took a step forward, causing Dodger to panic and squeeze the trigger. The rifle fired a bullet into the pirate captain's chest. It did nothing to stop his approach. Firing the gun again, a bullet struck Hook in his cheek, right underneath his eye. This also hardly made a difference as the captain kept advancing.

"You're already immortal?" asked Dodger, panicking.

Hook plucked the bullet from his face and flicked it away. "Close to it. The only way to achieve absolute immortality is to kill a Literary, which I intend to do right now!"

Dodger desperately swung the rifle at Hook. The pirate captain merely swatted it with his hook, cracking it in half. Dodger stabbed at him with the dagger. This attack was also repelled as the captain caught the blade in his free hand and tossed it aside. Hook kicked Dodger in the chest so hard that he was knocked to the ground several feet away.

The blow knocked the air out of Dodger's lungs. Gasping for air and struggling to his knees, he watched the pirate captain stand above him with his hook raised, ready to deal the killing blow. In those final moments, a series of images flashed in front of Dodger's eyes: his father yelling at him in the kitchen, Ryan Martin shoving him at school, his first meeting with Humpty and Rump, his fight with the spring-heels, Gretel kissing him, and him defeating Hansel to steal back the hammer.

A surge of positive energy suddenly shot through Dodger's body. Out of the corner of his eye, he spotted Pinocchio's war hammer lying next to the corpse of one of the Merry Men. The pirate captain swung his hook down, missing the Literary by inches as he thrust himself backwards out of harm's way. Dodger reached for the hammer and slipped the metal handle into his grasp.

Hook cursed and cocked his arm back for another swipe. He swung again, and Dodger retaliated by swinging the hammer in the opposite direction, making full contact with the hook. The force from Pinocchio's hammer was so powerful that it broke the hook right off the pirate's arm. The captain screamed and fell to his knees, grabbing the stump at the end of his wrist.

"You… you will regret that, boy!"

Hook reached out with his remaining hand. Scarecrow appeared behind him and severed his arm with a downward swipe of his sword. Another scream came from Hook as he fell onto his back. Nick leapt at them and threw his axe down, cutting off one of Hook's legs. The pirate captain howled in agony. Dodger picked up the Hunter's Dagger.

"You can't kill me," said Hook.

Dodger took his dagger and, with a final yell, stabbed Hook in the heart. The pirate captain coughed and sputtered before falling completely limp. While his red eyes remained open after his death, the fiery rage that consumed them had been extinguished.

The chamber was quiet. A slight sense of nausea came over Dodger, like when Geppetto was killed. He shared a brief look of relief with his companions amidst their heavy breathing, happy that it was over. All of a sudden, they heard the sounds of shouting and stomping right outside the castle. The pirate reinforcements had arrived.

"What do we do?" asked Scarecrow.

Dodger took several breaths. "We'll fight."

"They outnumber us vastly! We can't beat them, especially without Maxis or the Neverlanders."

"We didn't stand a chance versus Hook either," reasoned Dodger, the optimism growing in him with each second. "I think we can handle the pirates."

"Don't be a fool, Dodger," said a voice. It was Pinocchio, who had come to stand beside the Literary, holding his hammer over his shoulder. "Your positive outlook is grand, though it's no replacement for weaponry and warriors. I think we should go down to the dungeons and let my soldiers loose so they can have some fun."

"The doors are already open," said Dodger with a grin.

Pinocchio's eyes clouded over in a bright white fog. Dodger heard the faint sounds of hundreds of wooden feet stomping on stone coming from the bottom of the castle. When Pinocchio's eyes reverted to their normal state, he raised his war hammer, ready to battle. Dodger took up a fighting stance alongside him. Ugu, Scarecrow, Nick, Jill, and even Robin joined their ranks. They formed a solid line in front of the thrones, facing the entrance to the chamber. It wasn't long before a horde of pirates barreled through the chamber door and spilled in.

Robin's arrows and Ugu's magical blasts stopped the first couple of attackers. The rest charged at Dodger and his fellows, but they had barely reached the middle of the room when the back door to the chamber flew open and released the wooden army. The soldiers met the opposing pirates in the center of the room where a full-scale battle ensued.

This battle lasted for hours, even though it was vastly one-sided in Neverland's favor. The wooden soldiers were outstanding fighters, a regiment of relentless warriors requiring no food or rest, and who could withstand the most vicious attacks without being deterred. Dodger saw one of them have its arm broken off and still manage to hold its ground against three opponents.

In the middle of the battle, Humpty and Rump returned, informing Dodger that they had taken Tinkerbell to a safe place in one of the towns. They armed themselves and dove into the skirmish. Dodger was ordered to stay at the back of the chamber with Pinocchio hovering close by at all times, picking off any pirates attempting to flank him. With Hook dead, it was an all-out manhunt for the Literary, but Dodger refused to leave. He had made it this far with his companions; he was going to stick with them until the fight was over.

At one point in the battle, a troop of pirates gathered the limbs and torso of Captain Hook and escaped from the castle. Dodger appeared to be the only one who noticed it out of the corner of his eye, but he was too caught up in the fighting to be concerned.

Dodger's Doorway

By sunrise, the last pirate had fallen under Pinocchio's hammer. As his corpse crumpled, the Neverland defenders all took a moment to stare at each other. There was a beat, followed by loud cheering that filled the chamber as they reveled in their victory.

Shortly afterwards, Humpty ventured out to retrieve Princess Tinkerbell while Pinocchio ordered the wooden army to retreat to the dungeon. According to the general, only four of the soldiers had been destroyed in the battle and a dozen merely lost a limb or two. The others suffered no more than slashes and nicks to their easily reparable wooden bodies.

Arriving with the princess, Humpty reported that he didn't see any sign of the pirates along the shorelines. Just to be sure, Robin went up to the castle towers and scanned the ocean horizon, returning to declare that he didn't see any ships in the distance either. The pirates were gone for good.

It took the entire day for the pirates' bodies to be cleaned out of the chamber. Humpty and Pinocchio rode into the towns to notify the kingdom's residents of what had just transpired, though it appeared that the battle did not reach beyond Neverland Castle. According to Humpty's findings, hardly anyone had even noticed what was going on.

"We were lucky that the pirates didn't make their way further into the kingdom," declared the egg-man. "But we can't lower our guard. Now is the time to be wary and vigilant, for who knows what evil could enter these halls again?"

Dodger's Doorway

The bodies of the dead Merry Men were carried away to Neverland Castle's exclusive cemetery to be properly buried with distinguished honors. Robin remained melancholic throughout the day, mourning the loss of his friends, but the Neverlanders showed their support and reminded him that he and his Merry Men were heroes who saved the kingdom.

Joining them in the cemetery were the dead sentries, the fallen wooden soldiers, and King Gabriel, who was buried with pieces of his broken rifle. The bodies of Jack Horner, Maxis the Lion, Pumpkinhead, the griffins, were transported to their respective kingdoms so they could receive their own honorable burials in their homelands. Even John Tell was sent back to Himshire to be laid to rest in his true home. Pinocchio promised to have memorials dedicated to each of them on Neverland's property for their services.

An enormous banquet dinner was held that night, consisting of a toast to the fallen heroes. Afterwards, Tinkerbell ordered everyone to assemble in front of her throne. Dodger knelt next to Jill and the Royal Guard of Oz.

"You have all shown tremendous bravery," said the princess. "You fought to defend Neverland like it was your own home. As Princess of Neverland, I welcome you all to forever be a part of this kingdom, no matter where you reside."

Tinkerbell approached Robin and placed her hand on his shoulder. "Arise, and welcome back, Sir Robin Lox."

"Arise, Sir Scarecrow." Scarecrow nodded and stood.

"Arise, Sir Nick Chopper." The tin-man rose to his feet.

"Arise, Sir Ugu the Maker." Ugu stood, beaming.

"Arise, Lady Jill Horner." Jill gave a weak smile as she rose.

"And arise, Sir Dodger, Literary Sol-"

"Actually," said Dodger, "could you call me Mark? Mark Bishop. I know it's weird, but it's just what I'd prefer."

The princess nodded and smiled. "Arise then, Sir Mark Bishop, Literary Soldier of Philadelphia."

Dodger climbed to his feet, smiling at his friends. He noticed Humpty was distracted and sadly staring at Tinkerbell.

"Princess," said the Literary, "I think Humpty has something he wants to say to you."

Humpty glared at Dodger. Dodger shrugged and waved his hand, inviting him to speak.

"Yes, Sir Humpty?" said the princess, smiling gently.

Humpty's shell flushed. "Um, well, yes. I think there are some words to be said. Hm, just give me a moment or two."

Humpty was interrupted by a loud thump in the back of the chamber. Everyone's attention turned to the doors. Out stumbled Gretel, appearing so haggard and disheveled that Dodger almost didn't recognize her. The agent held a serrated dagger in her hand and cackled madly.

"Gretel?" whispered Dodger. "What happened...?"

"Captain Hook will be proud of me," she said in an unusually high-pitched tone. In a flash, she started charging forward with her blade held high, causing Dodger to instinctively grabbed his dagger. But the agent wasn't running at him. She appeared to be going for Tinkerbell.

"Watch out, Princess!" shouted Dodger.

In one swift motion, Humpty leapt in front of Tinkerbell, unsheathed his sword, and stabbed Gretel through the stomach. The agent stopped instantly, like she had run into a brick wall. Her smile disappeared, and she crumpled to the floor.

Dodger's jaw dropped. "What the hell just happened?"

Gretel's body glowed and shuddered, and just like with Hansel's corpse, it slowly turned into a pile of ash.

The whole chamber was in shock, except for Humpty, who casually re-sheathed his blade. "Just an inconvenience." The egg-man turned to Tinkerbell. "Princess, will you do me the hon-"

Tinkerbell interrupted him mid-sentence to kneel and give him a kiss. The shock from Gretel's attempted ambush wore off for everyone, and they all cheered and clapped for the couple. Dodger seemed to be the only one stunned by what had just occurred, and his mouth was still hanging open. Rump nudged him and whispered something about being rude, so the Literary decided to clap along as well, though he continued staring at Humpty in disbelief.

A yellow light suddenly encased Humpty's shell, making Tinkerbell leap backwards. The egg-man's bright silhouette started to quiver and shake violently.

Everyone in the chamber stepped away. The light stretched and twisted, becoming taller and thinner, still covering Humpty's body. Finally, the light turned into a bright white flash, temporarily blinding Dodger and his companions.

When their eyesight returned, they were all astounded to see what stood before them. Humpty had transformed into a human. He was now double his original height and even skinnier than Dodger, with bonier arms. His complexion had darkened from solid eggshell white to a light tan. His eyes had become a light hazel, matching his brown, choppy hair, although they retained their slightly larger-than-average size.

"I definitely didn't expect that to happen," said a baffled Dodger, looking away; Humpty did not have any pants on, but he didn't seem to notice, as he was too busy admiring his new body.

Rump took off his tunic and gave it to Humpty to use as a cover. "We may need to get you a new wardrobe, my friend."

"I cannot believe this!" said Humpty, tying the tunic around his waist. "I am human!" He donned a solemn expression and turned to Tinkerbell. "My Princess, I have pined for you for ages, but my former body and egg-ish complexion prevented me from admitting my feelings. Would you do me the honor of marrying me?"

Tinkerbell smiled. "Sir Humpty, your body never mattered to me. You have long been by my side as a trusted friend and loyal advisor. I would have said yes to you a long time ago, even if you had remained an egg. It would be an honor if you became my husband, and my king."

The two shared a passionate kiss. The chamber exploded with applause, Dodger clapping the loudest.

"We would not be here if it were not for you, Dodger," said Humpty.

Rump agreed. "That is true. You've proven yourself a hero, just like we knew you would."

"I'm proud to say I fought alongside you," said Pinocchio, bowing. "I am even prouder to call you my friend."

"We are all proud of you," said Tinkerbell. "You are so different from the Literaries we have encountered in the past. Not only were you the youngest, but according to Pinocchio, Humpty, and Rump, you have also shown the most courage. Your bravery saved this kingdom. Therefore, I once again extend my invitation for you to stay here in Storyworld. Seeing as how Humpty will become my new king, we will need a new second-in-command for the Neverland Military Arm."

"I appreciate it, Princess," said Dodger with a smile, "but I think it's too risky to keep me here. More psychos like Hook will come if they know you've got a Literary. I don't want to put Neverland in any more danger. Plus, I have things to handle in my own world."

"Very well, very well. I respect your decision. If you ever find yourself in Storyworld in the future, you are more than welcome to stay in Neverland. You will always have a home here."

"Thanks. If I can actually make a suggestion, I think Robin would make a pretty good soldier. He's worked for you before and he knows the ins-and-outs of

Neverwood Forest. And if it wasn't for him, we wouldn't have been able to save the castle."

Tinkerbell raised an eyebrow at Robin. The former thief smiled and shrugged. Dodger glanced at Humpty, expecting him to protest, but he seemed to be neutral to the idea.

"Well, his reputation as a bandit in the Neverwood isn't favorable, but he *did* save us," said Humpty.

Tinkerbell nodded. "Yes, that is true. But maybe we shall leave the decision up to Pinocchio."

Robin's grin disappeared. Pinocchio slowly turned to the archer with his eyebrows quivering, one hand on his hip and the other scratching his chin inquisitively.

"You can all remain as part of the royal court," said Tinkerbell, addressing the soldiers from Oz and Jill.

"Thank you, Princess," said Scarecrow, bowing. "We appreciate the offering, though we will have to decline, for we are needed in our homeland."

"The same goes for me, Princess," said Jill.

"Speaking of which, we should depart as soon as possible. It is a long journey back to Oz."

"Ah! I almost forgot!" Robin reached into his pocket, producing a playing card-sized piece of cloth.

"The magic carpet!" exclaimed Dodger. "You guys can take that home!"

"Er, it seems a tad small," replied Scarecrow.

"Don't let appearances fool you," said Robin. "There is more to this object than meets the eye, as I found out a little bit ago."

"Trust me, it'll work," affirmed Dodger. "When you get outside the castle, put it on the ground and watch what happens."

Scarecrow took the carpet. "Thank you?" he said unsurely.

"Are you ready, Dodger?" asked Rump, holding a vial of black liquid.

Dodger nodded. Rump drank from the vial and extended his hand, pointing at the Literary. A twirl of black smoke erupted from his fingertips and wrapped around Dodger. The room started spinning rapidly, causing him to feel faint. Colors swirled together, blending into random mixtures and turning everything into a large blur. Dizziness overcame Dodger and he soon passed out.

Chapter 15

Back Home

The shrill chime of the alarm clock rang throughout the room. Dodger's eyes flashed open. It was morning, and he was lying on the floor outside his closet. He scrambled to his feet, ignoring the dizziness and the rapid thumping of his heart.

Was it all a dream?

It seemed so real. There was no way it could have just been a dream. Dodger checked his mirror to see nothing different or unusual about his appearance. His face was cleanly shaven, his hair was washed, albeit slightly messy from sleeping on the floor, and his eyes looked refreshed. Everything was exactly the same as the night before.

Dodger's heart sank as the truth struck him. It *was* a dream. Everything he'd gone through in the past few days was all in his mind. Devastated, he plopped onto his bed, ready to bury his face into the pillow, when he did a double take at the mirror.

His lip ring was missing!

Excitement took over Dodger. He ran his fingers over the front of his lip and felt the hole where the piercing used to be. His heart now skipping, he decided to check under his pant leg where he found the Hunter's Dagger still encased in its sheath and strapped to his shin. How could he have missed it?

It really happened! It was all real! Dodger thought happily.

Loud yelling erupted from the kitchen downstairs. It was the first fight of the day for Dodger's parents. Dodger couldn't help but crack a wide grin.

"This is going to be great," he said quietly. He took the sheath off his leg and threw it into the top drawer of his nightstand. Grabbing his backpack, he left his room to go downstairs.

"Well, look who it is," said Mr. Bishop as Dodger entered the kitchen. "You look pretty happy. Did you get a new high score in your video game?"

Dodger smirked and reached into the pantry to grab a cereal bar. He didn't say a word to his father.

"Whoa, got rid of the lip ring, eh?" said Mr. Bishop. "I guess they're not the 'cool, hip' thing anymore, right?"

Still ignoring him, Dodger walked to the door. Mr. Bishop looked taken aback.

"Hey! Mark! I'm talking to you! Don't walk away from me like that!"

"Or what?" replied Dodger.

Mr. and Mrs. Bishop froze, raising their eyebrows in unison. They stared at their son like he had three heads. Mr. Bishop approached Dodger so that they were face-to-face.

"Are you giving me attitude?"

"No, I'm just talking to you the same way you talk to me, Dad," said Dodger, turning away. Before he could reach the door, his father grabbed his arm. Without hesitation, he jerked out of Mr. Bishop's grasp. His father tried to grab him again and say something, but Dodger shoved him back into the kitchen table and pointed a finger in his face. Dodger was furious and wouldn't be surprised if his eyes became as red as Captain Hook's.

"Stop! Don't say anything!" said Dodger in a quivering voice.

His father was in shock, opening and closing his mouth wordlessly. Mrs. Bishop started forward, but Dodger rounded on her as well.

"You, too! Both of you can just shut up! I'm sick and tired of hearing you two! I never did anything to deserve what you guys put me through for the past eighteen years. I don't get what's wrong with you! Why can't you be normal, supportive parents? You're like these two miserable people who have to constantly fight and take your bad moods out on each other and on me. I'm done with it. I'm moving out on my birthday, and until then, I don't want you talking to me, and I better not hear any fighting anymore either!"

Dodger took several deep breaths. It was an enormous relief to get all those words out. All color had drained from his parents' faces, and they stared at him in complete shock. Taking a bite out of his breakfast, Dodger shrugged and gave a mocking wave to his parents.

"I'm going to school. Good day."

Mr. and Mrs. Bishop were still speechless as their son walked out the door.

Dodger strode to school with his head held high. It was different from any other day. This time, he didn't let the sight of the school sign diminish his spirits like it used to; in fact, he harbored a strange euphoria as he read "Northside High School" this morning. Things were going to change today.

Ryan Martin and his friends were smoking on the Gauntlet, which Dodger was actually happy to see. He slowly climbed the steps.

"Watch out, cause there's a new tough guy in town named Mark Bishop," said Ryan sarcastically.

"What's up, man?" said Dodger, smiling.

"Ohhh! You're pretty happy today. Did you miss out on your daddy's morning yelling?"

"Nah, I'm in a good mood because I don't have to take any more of your crap. Have a good one." Dodger went on his way.

Ryan and his gang gave a collective "Ohhh!" and tossed away their cigarettes. They formed a circle around Dodger, surrounding him and cutting off his escape so he had no chance of running like he did during the last confrontation. Ryan's cronies also peeked around to make sure there were no witnesses in sight.

"Feeling a little brave?" Ryan said with a shove.

Dodger was forced back a step, but held his composure. "You might wanna walk away."

Ryan looked taken aback. "What're you gonna do about it?"

Dodger sighed and put his backpack down. He took the cereal bar wrapper in his hand, crumpled it into a ball, and flicked it at Ryan's face.

Ryan flinched. He cocked his fist back, but before he could swing, Dodger punched him as hard as he could in the stomach, knocking the wind out of him. The bully doubled over, gasping for air. Dodger decided against punching him again and instead pushed him to the ground, where he sputtered to catch his breath.

"Anybody else?" asked Dodger.

Nobody made a move. Two of Ryan's friends looked at each other, but ultimately they refused to step forward. It was then that Dodger understood that these guys were no different than Hansel; they were just bullies who were afraid of anyone who stood up to them. Ryan finally stood, still clutching his stomach and wheezing heavily.

"All of you are gonna back off now, right?" verified Dodger. "Unless you wanna keep going. It's fine with me either way."

There was no immediate response. The school bell rang, notifying the students to go to class. Ryan glared at Dodger, but said nothing. He and his gang walked away without another word. Dodger grinned and followed them in.

As he went to class, Dodger kept running his tongue along the inside of his lip. He would have to get used to no longer fidgeting with his piercing whenever he was nervous or scared. It was like he was starting a new chapter in his life, a chapter where he wasn't the weak child who was afraid to stand up for himself.

Another thought that crossed his mind was about his adventures in Storyworld. Dodger was going to miss his friends in Neverland and beyond. It was strange how he had met these famous characters from fairy tales and folklore and learned about their true backstories. Previous Literaries had written vague and inaccurate accounts of the Storyworld inhabitants, and Dodger believed nobody did them justice. He decided that Humpty Dumpty, Rumpelstiltskin, Pinocchio, and his other companions deserved the proper recognition.

With that in mind, Dodger walked into English class and sat down. Like every morning, Mr. Jenkins was at his computer, absorbed in his work and seemingly oblivious to the students entering his classroom. Dodger noticed that a long screen had been drawn down at the front of the room, blocking the chalkboard.

"Good morning, Mark. How are you today?" asked Mr. Jenkins, his eyes glued to the computer screen.

"Phenomenal," replied Dodger with a smile. His teacher turned to him with a look of curiosity.

"Is that so? Go on."

"Let's just say I had an interesting night."

"Hm, well, I hope it wasn't more interesting than today's lesson."

The two-minute warning bell rang. Mr. Jenkins left the computer and tugged the projector screen, allowing it to roll back up into its canvas. Students began rushing into the classroom and taking their seats while Dodger read what was written on the chalkboard.

The greatest friends sometimes come from the strangest of places.

What does this quote mean to you?

Dodger paused. Before the final bell rang, he took out a blank notebook from his backpack, turned to the first page, and began to write:

Dodger was sitting in his room, playing video games, just like every other night. But his real name wasn't Dodger. It was Mark Bishop.

The End